The Last Note

A Miami Music Mystery

by

Zaida Alfaro

This book is fiction. All characters, events, and organizations portrayed in this novel are the product of the author's imagination or are used fictitiously. Any resemblance to actual persons—living or dead—is entirely coincidental.

For information, email Cozy Cat Press, cozycatpress@aol.com or visit our website at: www.cozycatpress.com

ISBN: 978-1-946063-48-9
Printed in the United States of America
Cover design by Paula Ellenberger
www.paulaellenberger.com

10 9 8 7 6 5 4 3 2 1

To Mom and Dad.
Thank you for always believing in your little girl.

I would like to express my gratitude to the many people who saw me through this book; to all those who provided support, read the book at its roughest stage, offered comments, opinions, and critiques. But I especially want to thank my copy editor and pen pal, Glenn McCormick, for taking a chance in professionally editing my first book. Who knew that a gig at the Dive Bar would turn you into an editor?

I'm genuinely grateful for my best friend and soul mate. Thank you for being supportive of every crazy thing I set out to do. You are my never-ending love song.
I want to thank my big sister. If it wasn't for you, Alexia would have not transpired. I'm grateful to my friend, Triple D, from the Miami-Dade Police Department, Homicide Division, for answering my endless questions on crime scene investigations, police terminology, definitions and most importantly, how to properly kill off a character.

I would like to thank Cozy Cat Press for publishing my first book. Thank you for giving my dream a chance.

And lastly, I want to thank my family, dearest friends, and fans. Being surrounded by so much love encourages me and inspires me to start on my next novel

!

PROLOGUE

"Please, someone let me in!" Vy screamed while banging on the individual apartment doors. She briefly looked back, to only see the hooded, faceless person getting closer to her. It didn't matter how quickly she ran, the person was only a step away from grabbing a hold of her.

"Please help me," Vy cried as she reached the final apartment door of the hallway. She banged once more on the door. She had nowhere else to go. She stared at the beige, cement wall. She turned around, and the faceless figure was only a few steps away from her. She looked at the door, and this time she tried the doorknob. The door was unlocked, and she tumbled inside. Vy quickly crawled to the door, reached for the knob, and locked it.

There was now a fierce banging on the other side of the door. The person was trying to unlock the door by continuously turning the doorknob.

"Why me?" Vy yelled, and at that instant, the banging on the door halted, the doorknob was still, and she heard a cynical laugh.

Vy remained on the floor of the apartment. She quietly placed her ear on the crevice of the door, closed her eyes, and focused on any sounds coming from the other side. She then heard a muffled sound precisely where her ear had been placed, "Don't you get it? It's your time."

Vy stumbled backwards. The apartment was in total darkness. “Hello? Is anyone there?” she whispered. She assumed that no one was home.

“Come, come, dear. Why don’t you rest?” The woman’s voice was calm.

Vy couldn’t see the woman. “I’m in danger; I need to use your cell phone.”

“Sit on the couch, dear. It will all be okay.” An elderly woman stepped out from what seemed to be the living room. There was only a nightlight glowing from her direction. Vy didn’t know why, but she went to the couch, and slowly sat down.

“Please, I need a phone,” Vy pleaded. The woman simply pointed to a door. Vy quickly ran to the door, and stumbled through it.

Vy was sweating profusely. It felt as though her shoes were super glued to the cheap linoleum flooring of the stage. The probe lights were blinding. Vy could see silhouettes of the audience, but she couldn’t hear one single sound coming from the audience.

“Hello? Is this working?” Vy tapped on the wireless microphone, but there was no sound projecting from it. Then from a distance, she heard a man laughing. It was an evil laugh.

“I’m sorry, I’m not sure why my microphone isn’t working,” Vy yelled out to the audience. There was no reaction. It was as though the words did not make it out to the crowd. Again, the man’s cynical laugh made its way to Vy’s ears. “Start the song,” he finally yelled to Vy.

Vy felt hot tears streaming down her face. She closed her eyes and hoped for the best. She slowly opened her mouth, and began singing, but her voice gave out.

“Now,” said the man.

Vy's heart was pounding so quickly, she thought she was going to pass out. From a distance, she heard a woman speaking. If Vy focused enough on her voice, she could decipher what this woman was saying. But the faceless man overpowered the woman's voice. "You consider yourself good enough for this stage?" Vy disregarded his comment, and continued focusing on the woman's voice.

"Focus. What is she saying?" Vy said to herself. She closed her eyes tightly, trying to concentrate on the words, which finally made their way to Vy's ears.

"Get ready for morning showers, and a high of ninety degrees," said the weatherman on the radio.

Vy's alarm clock had gone off, and she slowly awoke from her stressful nightmare. She sluggishly opened her eyes, reached for her alarm clock, and turned it off. She stared at the ceiling, and in one breath let out a musical note. "Thank goodness, I still have a voice."

TESTING 1

"Come on, buddy; the light is green." Not wanting to conform to Miami's society, Vy refrained from honking her horn at the red Corolla. Even though it was only eight in the morning, Vy had been stuck in traffic for forty minutes. Because she was claustrophobic, she refused to take public transportation, but the upside of driving was listening to Larry and David's Morning Show.

"Who do you think is the greatest guitarist of all time, Larry?"

"Obviously, Stevie Ray Vaughn," Vy answered the radio as if both Larry and David could hear her. She focused on the morning show to survive the excruciating drive to her favorite gas station, which offered an array of flavored coffees for each day of the week. She finally pulled up to the gas station, and made her way inside to her personal heaven.

"Good morning, Diana," Vy said.

"Hi, my Coco Chanel," Diana replied.

The daily discourse with the gas station attendant Diana was part of Vy's morning routine. She always had a smile on her face and was kind to Vy. Vy poured herself a twenty-four-ounce hazelnut flavored coffee, added three hazelnut flavored creamers, and three packets of sugar. She took in the aroma, savored it, and placed a lid on the cup. She walked over to Diana and handed her the coffee frequency card. She gave Vy an extra hole punch on the card, and greeted her with a smile.

"Are you singing tonight?" Diana asked.

"Yes, I am," Vy replied. "I can't wait until this day is over. I'm ready for my Friday to begin."

"Like I always tell you, be careful," Diana warned, "There are a lot of crazy people out there."

"Thanks, Diana," Vy said. "Have a great weekend."

Vy finally arrived at the Happy Corporate America Building, which she fondly referred to as work. But it wasn't a simple task. She had to drive up and park on the seventh level of a seven-story parking garage, only to get into an elevator to go down the same seven floors. Once in the main building, she would walk to another elevator, to make her way up to the twenty-ninth floor.

Being claustrophobic, the back-to-back elevator rides caused her great anxiety, but twenty-nine floors was too great a climb. Patiently waiting for the elevator to arrive, she opened her e-reader and proceeded to read the page where she left off on the previous night.

The bell sound indicated that an elevator had finally reached the lobby. The group of people waiting for the elevator, rushed into what Vy called a shoebox. They resembled a herd of stampeding animals. Not wanting to pass out amongst strangers, Vy watched the elevator doors slowly close, and patiently waited for the next one to come. One minute later, another elevator arrived, and there was less of a crowd this time. She got on and stood in the far back right corner. She observed the different faces surrounding her and speculated what double lives they might be leading. Since she was a singer in a band, perhaps the man next to her acted as a circus clown on the weekends. She smiled to herself at that thought.

Vy worked as a legal assistant in a very prestigious law firm. Today, she passed her time by eagerly pecking away at the keyboard, redlining a settlement agreement, drafting a motion, and finalizing a retainer agreement. Although she'd graduated with a bachelor's degree in English, she quickly found a better paying job in the field of law. At the end of the day she looked at her cat-shaped watch, and saw that it was precisely five o'clock. Vy pressed control-alt-delete on her keyboard, pressed enter, and logged off her computer. She grabbed her keys and purse, stepped into that shoebox with the rest of the herd, and repeated the oppressive ritual. She gladly drove down the seven-story parking garage, and exited into rush hour traffic.

A horn blared. "What do you want me to do, take the red-light, you idiot?" Vy yelled into her rearview mirror. She saw the driver, an elderly man, casually give her the middle finger. Because she was raised to respect her elders, she abstained from returning the gesture and simply responded to herself, "Same to you, bud."

Miami had many impatient drivers, especially during the Friday evening's rush hour traffic. Although she was sympathetic to people wanting to arrive at their destination sooner rather than later, moving her car a half an inch closer to the vehicle in front of her was not going to make a difference.

To drown out the resonance of the annoying car horns, Vy turned on the radio and blasted a Willie Nelson tune about being on the road again. She tapped her thumbs on the steering wheel, echoing the guitar riffs of the song. She looked at the clock on the dash board, "Crap, it's already five thirty," she said out loud. She only had three hours to glamorize herself for the show that she referred to as "a gig" tonight at the Steel Horse Bar.

By six o'clock, Vy finally arrived at her two-bedroom apartment. It was a quaint apartment complex, the best she could do as a struggling musician. One reason she was struggling was because she refused to sleep with the executives in the music industry. Aside from her mediocre paycheck, she supplemented her income by gigging on the weekends at sports bars, with the occasional wedding, and private parties on the side. The extra income gave her the leverage to continue to chase her dream of being a professional entertainer.

"I'm home," Vy sang as she walked into her apartment. Her cat Marilyn, named after the infamous Marilyn Monroe, welcomed her home. Marilyn let out a soft purr and rubbed herself against Vy's right leg.

Vy had found Marilyn after one of her late-night gigs. It was three a.m., and as she was loading her gear into her car, she heard a meowing sound coming from across the street. She ran towards that direction into a parking lot, and found a Calico breed kitten tucked beneath the wheel well of a truck. Vy took her home with the intention of taking her to an animal shelter that didn't euthanize animals. But four years later, Marilyn was still sitting on her bed, watching Vy with her intense, big brown eyes, go from the closet to the mirror and back.

"I know you want the soft food. Let me get ready first, and then I'll feed you your special feast."

Out of the three hours she had to get ready, she took about half the time choosing her outfit. Aside from the vocals, the proper outfit was the key to becoming an unforgettable lead singer. Vy had to come across as sexy, but not loose; available, but possibly taken. There was a special technique and method to her madness.

When she had successfully chosen her outfit for tonight, she asked Marilyn, "Alright, what do you think?" Marilyn slowly blinked, then closed her eyes, and drifted away. "That's what I thought," Vy said. She was wearing tight fitting light blue jeans, with a horizontal rip on the right knee, and a somewhat tight t-shirt, slightly exposing her mid-riff that read, *Daddy's Little Monster.*

Although Vy was a Cuban American, she didn't look like a traditional Latina. The four-inch heels added to her five-foot seven height. Her fair-skin and hazel eyes accentuated her short, red, Victoria Beckham styled hair, which went against the notion that all Latin women must have waist-long, black hair.

Vy looked at herself in the mirror and thought to herself, "Who wouldn't want to be in a rock band?" Being in a band allowed her to meet interesting people, hear a lot of gossip, and get free drinks. She looked at her watch, "Let's party like its nineteen-ninety-nine," Vy sang to Marilyn, who slept through it all.

She went into the kitchen and prepared her hot tea, and poured it into her thirty-two-ounce mug. She peeled opened Marilyn's can of soft cat food, and emptied it into her Marilyn Monroe food plate. Marilyn swiftly made her way to the kitchen. She maneuvered herself between Vy's legs, and inhaled the cat food before Vy could even walk away. "You're welcome." She blew a kiss to Marilyn and headed out the door.

Walking down the stairs in four-inch heels was quite a challenge, but beauty was sometimes painful. Avoiding the speed bumps and the deformities of the parking lot's asphalt, Vy reached her 1996 red Mustang, that she called Sam. She'd named her car after Patrick Swayze's character from the movie *Ghost.* She always fantasized about meeting a man like Sam, sans the scene where he dies in an alley.

Before getting into the car, Vy took a moment to take in the evening air. The summers in Miami were hot and humid, but around eight in the evening, the temperature was almost perfect. It was hot enough to send a tingle throughout Vy's body, but it wasn't hot enough that she was sweating profusely. The night sky was pristine and beautiful. The glistening of the moon was telling her secrets of what its eyes had seen through the ages. Vy instantly turned that into a song.

Tonight, Vy decided to drive with the windows down. Well, her one window. The passenger window was broken. She didn't have the time to fix it due to her rock star schedule and lousy salary, but she managed. She turned up the radio to hear her favorite Matchbox Twenty song "Real World," and pumped herself up for the night ahead.

TESTING 2

After a twenty-minute drive, Vy arrived at the Steel Horse Bar, her home for the next four hours. The bar was in a neighborhood shopping center. It shared its space with a grocery store and a restaurant called, Eat 'Em Up. She drove in through the back alley of the shopping center, where the back entrance of the bar was located. The back entrance and the alley parking, was for the bands, cook, bouncer, waitresses, bar backs, and the owner.

Vy parallel parked, took a deep breath, looked at herself in the rearview mirror and whispered, "Let's rock on."

Every time Vy arrived at a gig; she had to call her lead guitarist Carlos. He said that he didn't trust the area. He didn't know what creeps were lurking behind the bushes or garbage cans, and he wanted to be the first one to see what Vy was wearing.

She called Carlos upon her arrival, "What's up, handsome? I just pulled up."

"Okay, I'll be right out," Carlos said, shouting over the noise pollution inside the bar.

From her rearview mirror, Vy saw Carlos push the metal door opened. He approached her car, leaned in the car window, and said with his sexy voice, "Your Prince Charming is here."

Vy carefully stepped out of the car, making sure not to step into a puddle of water, or that's what she liked to imagine it was, so she wouldn't gross herself out. Carlos shut the door for her. He was also Cuban-

American, but he was raised in North Carolina. His Spanish-speaking skills were worse than Vy's. At least she could carry on a conversion in Spanglish, speaking both English and Spanish in the same sentence.

He was about five-nine, brown hair with hints of grey, and a perfect smile framed by a goatee. Carlos was a very energetic man, which resurrected Vy on the nights she felt less than vivacious.

"What's up, buddy?" Vy inquired.

"What's up, sugar?" Carlos asked. "It's great to see you."

"Do you call me sugar cause I'm so gosh darn sweet?" Vy asked, in a southern accent as she hugged him.

"But of course," he replied.

"How's it looking in there tonight?" Vy asked.

"It's awesome. The regulars are here, and there are a lot of new faces. But there's one dude in there that looks like a lady!"

Carlos stepped back and observed Vy. "By the way, I love the outfit!"

Vy popped opened her trunk and took out her microphone stand and a plastic bucket, which contained her tambourine, cowbell, and her e-mail sign-up notebook.

"Here, let me get that for you," Carlos said, grabbing a hold of Vy's bucket, and following her inside.

Vy walked into the Steel Horse Bar holding the microphone stand in one hand, with her purse dangling from her wrist. The cloud of cigarette smoke welcomed her inside. When Vy first started singing at the bar, the first five minutes of being inside it was atrocious. Her eyes became red in a split second, and the smell of her perfume was quickly dominated by the odor of cigarette smoke. But after a few years of gigging at the bar, her body, hair, and clothes had all become accustomed to it.

As she walked towards the stage, many people smiled in her direction.

"You singing tonight?" a voice at the bar slurred. Larry, a regular, was a kind soul with a genuine smile. His wife died two years ago, so here he was at sixty-three, trying to find his soul mate, again.

"Yes, I am, Larry. Are you drinking tonight?"

"I already started sweetheart. I'm fixin' on getting myself a hot little number tonight. Make it happen, girl." Larry said with a sly grin.

"Don't worry, I'll sing a slow one just for you," Vy said.

Vy made it to the stage, walked up the side steps, and started to set up her microphone stand.

Adrianna, the drummer and the computer guru of the band, was in the center of the stage setting up her drum kit. She then proceeded to set up her laptop to control the band's sound.

"I have uploaded a new app that allows me to synchronize the bass guitar and lead guitar with just one click of the spacebar."

"That sounds cool. Now you can avoid dropping the drumsticks." Vy stuck out her tongue, and then smiled at Adrianna, who had an uncanny resemblance to Velma from Scooby Doo. The only differences were that Adrianna had shoulder length, curly hair, and wore contacts. Adrianna and Vy had started out as friends, and later formed the band.

"I'm excited about the gig," Vy said. "I need to release some frustrations out into the crowd."

"I know what you mean," Adrianna said with a smile.

Vy tucked her purse behind Carlos' guitar stand and jumped off the stage onto the wooden dance floor. Rob, the bass player, who was to Adrianna's left, continued to set up his gear. Vy walked over to his side, "Hey, Rob, what's going on?"

Rob was losing his hair, so he compensated by shaving it off. He turned around and leaned down. She gave him a kiss on the cheek and a quick hug. He automatically grabbed the white hand towel that he had on his shoulder, and wiped his forehead. "Man, those strobe lights are killer, eh?" asking in his Canadian accent.

"Where's your fedora hat?" Vy inquired.

"In my bag. I'll put it on when the gig starts."

"Everything cool?" Vy asked.

"Everything's fine," Rob said. "Tough week at work, but aside from that, it's been good. Are you ready to rock your face off?"

"You know it," Vy said. Rob proceeded to check the cables, change the batteries to the ear monitors, and make sure everything was intact with his bass guitar.

"What will it be, honey?" Kendra, the band's waitress, sweetly asked Vy.

She and the other waitresses were dressed as sexy sports referees. They were obligated to wear a black and white, horizontal stripped top showing major cleavage, with either tight, black pants or shorts. Because they crazily ran around making sure everyone was getting what they needed, they wore white sneakers.

"I'd like an Apple Martini tonight."

"You got it, honey. I'll be right back."

As Vy watched Kendra walk to the center bar, she noticed a Brad Pitt look-alike staring in her direction. He had no expression on his face and his eyes seemed empty. Vy hadn't remembered seeing him at the bar before. A few minutes later, Kendra reappeared with Vy's cocktail. "Hey, K, who's that guy standing by the bar?" Vy asked.

Kendra turned around, then looked at Vy again, "Who, sweetie?"

"Right over there." Vy pointed to where he was standing, but he was no longer there. "No one I guess. Sorry, I must be tired."

"That only means that you're ready for a shot, girl," Kendra stated. "I'm bringing you a watermelon jolly rancher ASAP." Kendra smiled at Vy, and walked back towards the center bar.

The background noise was a combination of laughter, people's stories, and the jukebox playing a Stevie Ray Vaughan song. The different conversations drowned out Stevie Ray's guitar licks. At that instant, Vy felt arms circling her waist and heard, "Yes! I'm so happy that you guys are here tonight!"

"Tracy, how have you been, girl? I haven't seen you here in a few months." Tracy reminded Vy of a lost little girl. She was in her thirties, trying to find her way in life. She had a good heart, but men stepped over it, or so she would tell Vy.

"I know. It's been a while since I could go out and spend money," Tracy explained. "The company that I work for downsized, and decreased my salary. Can you believe that? But I'm here and ready to dance! I can't wait to hear you sing."

"Well, I'll make sure to make it worth your buck."

"I'll see you later." She gave Vy another hug and took off.

Vy walked around the bar greeting the regulars and giving away what seemed like a hundred hugs. She liked analyzing the people at the bar. This would give her a sense of how the night was going to turn out. She would know what kind of night a person was having by their facial expressions, or the drink they held in their hand.

There was a woman sitting alone at a high table located by the center bar. She was staring off towards the stage area. She was unfamiliar to Vy. Her gaze seemed sad. She sat there slowly absorbing the alcohol and not caring who was judging her. In this line of business, Vy learned that sometimes liquor was a person's best friend. Vy proceeded to head towards the main entrance of the bar.

There were three antique-looking pool tables lined up in a row. Each pool table was designed differently. The first pool table closest to the back entrance had a red velvet lining. In the center of the table, it read in gold letters, *Budweiser*. There was a handsome guy dressed in a button-down dress shirt and nicely fitted pants. He was shooting pool with his GQ model-like friend. Their facial expressions were meant to make you think they were concentrating on the game, but they were really concentrating on the game of picking up women.

They both looked at Vy at the same time and smiled. "The singer's in the house," said Mr. GQ.

"Who's winning?" Vy asked.

Mr. GQ smirked and answered, "Who do you think, sweetheart?"

"Have fun, boys." Vy winked at them, and continued her way to the main entrance.

The second table was like the first, except the lining was black with no writing on it. The wooden border was polished, but chipped in a few different places. There were two men shooting pool, while their girlfriends sat on a long wooden bench alongside the mirrored wall. The girlfriends were checking out Mr. GQ and his buddy. Who could blame them; those two women were bored out of their wits. Those were the women Vy would eventually bring up on stage to give them a boost of confidence.

The third pool table closest to the main entrance of the bar, was the newest of the three. It was called Brazza Arch. It was made of Maple and Oak. It had a velvet red lining, solid wood rail and legs, and a beautiful high gloss finish. The inside of each pocket was a vibrant red. People were waiting in line to play on this table.

Three women occupied the table, with almost identical outfits on. Two of the women waved at Vy, as one continued to bend over trying to make that one impossible shot. One of the three women came up to Vy and asked, "Can you sing that new Pink song? I just love it."

"Of course," Vy said and the woman did a little hop, and walked back to the other two women. Vy faintly heard her say with excitement, "She's going do it, girls."

Vy finally made her way to Kyle, the door guy, bouncer, and her personal bodyguard. He was sitting on a stool, carding those who looked like they were under twenty-one.

Kyle was six-four, bald, and covered in tattoos. He reminded Vy of Stone Cold Steve Austin from the WWF. On a personal level, Kyle's face radiated a kind demeanor. On a non-personal level, he looked like a vicious man.

"Hey, sweet thing, how's it going tonight?" Vy asked.

He looked at her with those intense blue eyes and a devilish smirk on his face, "I'm keeping an eye on some schmucks who've been here for a while now. You let me know if they cause any trouble. I'm looking for a good reason to kick them out, and you're normally that reason."

"Thanks. Wait, is that a compliment or an insult?"

Kendra appeared to Vy's side. "Here's your shot, hon. Sorry it took so long. It's busy tonight, thanks to the band."

Kyle smiled at Kendra. She then walked away with her butt sashaying from side to side. Vy caught Kyle staring.

"What?" he asked.

"Nothing," Vy said smiling.

Vy glanced over to the lonely lady. "Kyle, who's that lady sitting at the high table? I've never seen her here before."

Kyle followed Vy's eyes. "Oh, that one; she came in here already buzzed. I felt sorry for her, so I let her in. I'm keeping an eye on her too."

"Well, she looks really depressed."

"Kendra cut her off already, so I think she's just nursing that drink. And before you say it, don't worry, I'm not letting her go anywhere like that."

Vy briefly recalled the one night that Kyle carried out a drunken, heavy-set woman over his shoulder. He looked at her license to see where she lived, called her a cab, paid the taxi cab driver, and had her taken home.

"I wasn't worried," Vy said.

Rob started checking the microphone, "Testing, one, two, three." Vy knew it was time to start cranking out some tunes. "That's my cue. I hope you enjoy the show." She gave Kyle a quick hug.

"Rock it, woman," Kyle said with a smile.

TESTING 3

"Thank you, we're going to take a short break. Don't forget to take care of your bartenders and servers. We'll be right back!" As Vy walked down the steps, she saw Ricky, the owner of the Steel Horse Bar. He was a ragged, older version of Andy Garcia. It had been about six months since she'd last seen him.

Ricky was standing by the kitchen door speaking to Dave, the general manager of the bar. It seemed like they were arguing about something, but then again, Ricky liked arguing about every little thing that went wrong or did not go wrong at his bar. Vy was trying to eavesdrop, but the background noise made it difficult to pick up on their conversation. She was curious to know what they were bickering about. Dave's facial expression was tense and projected a defeated look. Ricky continued jabbing Dave's chest with his index finger, as if he was threatening him.

"Another drink, honey?" A voice from beside her asked.

"Jesus!" Vy, surprised, placed her hand on her chest.

"Sorry, I didn't mean to startle you," Kendra said giggling.

"Yes, please."

"I knew once I started you on one, you'd loosen up," Kendra said elatedly.

"Kendra, I'll be right back, I have to go the ladies room," Vy said. "Just leave the drink at the table where the rest of the band is."

"You got it." Kendra hurried off to another customer.

As Vy was walking to the restroom, she was checking her phone for any missed calls or text messages. She ran directly into someone. "Oh, I'm sorry," Vy said.

Her eyes slowly made her way up from the man's feet to his eyes. He was a human version of a Ken doll, blonde hair, about six-five, with intense hazel eyes. She could just imagine how nicely built he was under that Steel Horse Bar t-shirt. As he looked down at her, she admired his perfect smile, which would make any woman feel like she was the most beautiful woman in the place.

"It's cool. I'm Shawn. I was heading your way to introduce myself. I heard that you guys always rock the house, and you sure killed your first set. Tonight's my first day, so I'm excited to hear some more great music."

Honestly, Vy was delayed in her response only because she was so enthralled with his eyes. She was writing a song in her head as he was speaking: *I don't know what you're saying to me. I don't care. I just want to breathe your air.*

"Thanks. I appreciate it. It's nice to meet you; I'm Vy. So, you started tonight? Is everyone treating you alright?"

"Yeah, I used to play here a few years ago. I'm a guitarist and a vocalist. But times are tough now, so I had to get another job. I've known the staff for a long time."

"Cool," was all that Vy could manage to say.

"I don't want to keep you. Looking forward to your second set." Shawn smiled at Vy, threw a small towel over his shoulder, and walked away.

Vy finally made it to the restroom. She looked at herself in the mirror. She wet her index finger and attempted to remove the already smeared eyeliner. She touched up her lipstick, and headed back out to the bar.

James and Cassandra were bartending at the center bar, which they did every Friday night. James was six-two, brown hair, with vibrant brown eyes. His smile was pure and sincere. Unfortunately, there were no attempts to sweet talk him into a free drink, although Vy had been able to a few times. Not because she was charming, but only because he felt like she deserved a free one after a four-hour gig.

"Hi, guys." Vy waved to James and Cassandra.

"Hi, Vy. It's good to see you," James said.

"You too. Why are you covering your cool Mohawk with that UM baseball cap?"

"You know, change it up a bit. Keep the ladies on their toes." He gave a mischievous smile.

"You ready for a shot?" Cassandra asked.

Cassandra was five-five, and skinny as a toothpick. She had long, blond hair and green eyes. She didn't have a beautiful face, but her sweetness gave her a hint of visual beauty.

"Kendra's on it. Thanks though," Vy replied.

"Figures you're the one I'm making that girly shot for. I'll change that one day," James said.

"It's nice to know what your mission is. See you in a bit."

As Vy made her way to the table, she ran into Shawn once again. "Hey there. Are you following me?" Vy attempted flirting.

"Maybe. I meant to tell you earlier, they were right about the band, you guys are really tight," Shawn said enthusiastically.

"They who?" Vy asked.

"The regulars, the waitresses, everyone I've spoken to."

"Good. I don't want to let the fans down. The bar's paying us big bucks for this gig you know." She was slowly becoming her sarcastic self again. Shawn chuckled. Suddenly, Vy heard Ricky's voice vibrate through her bones.

"Shawn! Stop talking and get to work!" Ricky was still standing by the kitchen, yelling across the bar.

Shawn shrugged his shoulders. "Sorry, I have to get back to work."

Vy walked up to Ricky, completely forgetting that there was a nice cocktail waiting for her at the table. "Hi, Ricky; it's great to see you here tonight. It's not often that I'm blessed with your presence," Vy said facetiously. Ricky gave her a quick hug.

That's what I like about you, Vy; you say what you mean," Ricky said. If he only knew what she meant.

Ricky wasn't the nicest person to deal with, especially when he'd been drinking. Vy was once told that an owner of a bar shouldn't be drinking at his or her own bar. But she figured this rule didn't pertain to Ricky.

Ricky had once booked her band for an event that was being held on a Monday night. They usually didn't gig during the week. The band was scheduled to play from eight to midnight. After they were done with the gig, Ricky came up to Carlos and demanded—not asked, but demanded—that they play an extra hour. Considering that they all had day jobs and they were exhausted, the band declined. Ricky replied, slurring his words, "I pay you good. If you choose not to continue, I won't have you come back." The band didn't play that extra hour demanded, yet they were playing tonight. He never did apologize for his rudeness, but Vy blamed the alcohol.

"Listen, I started talking to Shawn, so don't be upset with him."

"If he gives you any problems, you tell me or Kyle," Ricky said annoyed.

"Why would he give me problems? It seems like you hired a really nice guy. You shouldn't worry."

"Vy, it's when I think I shouldn't worry, that I know I should. You know me. I don't trust anyone, not even my own parents." *He must have been such a wonderful son,* Vy thought to herself.

"Sorry, gotta run. By the way, you sound good." Ricky whisked away to the office.

"It's show time," Carlos said to Vy as he walked on to the stage.

"Great," Vy said sarcastically, since she was quite thirsty.

Vy made her way to the center of the stage. As she was adjusting her ear monitor, Vy saw her best friend Tina, enter the bar. She was a walking Victoria's Secret billboard—a mix of Pamela Anderson and Carmen Electra. When Vy and Tina had their girls' night out, men always lingered around them. At least their bill was cheap at the end of the night. Tina was very down to earth and naïve, but so was Vy, which was why they were best friends.

Carlos started strumming the introduction to "Big Girls Don't Cry." Every man and even some women turned to look at Tina walking towards the stage. She emanated this "I have arrived" vibe, without even realizing she was doing it. She walked right up to the stage and signaled Vy to give her a hug. Vy jumped off stage and gave her a big hug while she sang a verse. When Tina walked to the table, every man had that universal look of lust. Vy stepped back onto the stage, and looked at all the different faces that were having fun tonight. "Don't cry. La da da da da da." The applause from the audience, after the song, was comforting to Vy.

"I need some dancers on stage for this next song!" Vy said to the crowd. The strobe lights were shining right into her eyes. The red, yellow, blue, and white lights made it difficult to see faces in the audience clearly.

A few women jumped up on stage at the chance to dance against Carlos. At times, they forgot that he was playing a guitar, and the 'rubbing up against him' move didn't really work to his advantage. He didn't complain though. He enjoyed the beautiful women by his side.

"Okay, are you girls ready to shake it?" Vy shouted

"Yeah!" The women yelled back.

"I can't hear you! Are you ready?" The women fixed their hair, adjusted their boobs, and once more yelled, "Yeah!"

"Then let's go crazy!" Vy shouted.

Carlos started to play the opening riff to "Pour Some Sugar on Me." The women went wild. They were dancing as though they'd all morphed into strippers. Because Vy didn't know the lyrics to this song yet, she stood behind Carlos reading the lyrics off her cheat sheet. Luckily, no one noticed because the women on stage were distracting the audience. As she skipped a few words here and there, Vy looked to her left and saw the Brad Pitt look-alike. This time, he was standing closer to her side of the stage.

Vy kept her eyes on him. He remained expressionless. Then Tracy started dancing against him. Vy's mom always taught her to follow her gut instinct. Her gut was telling her something weird was going on with this guy. Unfortunately, at that moment, Vy couldn't do anything about it.

"Go, Sugar," Carlos whispered. Vy missed her cue to come in on the song. She smiled at Carlos, and mouthed the words, "I'm sorry", and started singing. Once the song ended, Vy placed the microphone on its stand and stepped off stage. It was Rob's turn to have the spotlight. Rob started to sing the eighties tune, "I Melt With You." Vy was looking for the Brad Pitt clone, but he was nowhere to be found.

Tracy ran, rather skipped, up to Vy and hugged her again. "This is turning into one of the best nights I've had in a long time. I'm so glad you played that song. It encouraged me to dance my sexy dance, if you know what I mean."

"Who was that guy you were dancing with?" Vy asked.

"I don't know, but he is hot!" Tracy said excitedly.

"Tracy, about that guy—"

"Hold that thought; I have to answer this call." She pulled out her cell phone from her back-right pocket, placed it on her ear, and covered her other ear with her index finger. "Hello, yeah, are you on your way?" Tracy started to walk away.

Vy had about a minute left before she had to get back on stage. She decided to sit with Tina.

"Hey, girl, as always, you guys sound great," Tina said.

"I'm so happy you're here tonight."

"Hey, you girls want a d-drink?" asked a drunken man, pulling up a chair, and sitting next to Vy and Tina.

"I don't think so, buddy. Let's go." Kyle tapped the man on the shoulder, grabbed his arm, and escorted him to the exit.

"Thank you," Vy said to Kyle.

"One of those nights, huh?" Tina always knew when she was having a rough day. What Vy didn't know was that the night was going to turn out even worse than she thought. The break was over soon and Vy returned to the stage.

"Thanks for being here tonight! I want to take a second to introduce the gorgeous men, and woman, I have on stage with me tonight." As Vy introduced the band, she started to look around the bar, not knowing what she was looking for. She finished the introductions, and the applauses echoed throughout the bar. "We're going take a short break. We'll be right back."

Vy jumped off stage and went to the office to talk to Dave. She knocked, pushed the door slightly open, and peeked inside. Dave was sitting at the desk drinking a glass of red wine. He was flipping through his calendar, jotting down some notes.

"Come on in and have a seat," Dave said. "I'm almost done."

All four walls of the office were comprised of shelves of different liquors and wines. All labels faced forward. The bottles were in alphabetical order. It was like a mini liquor store, but without the grumpy cashier. Vy was always amazed at how many different types of liquors existed. Her taste palette restricted her to Malibu Rum and pineapple juice, watermelon jolly ranchers, and if she was feeling frisky and fun, then an Apple Martini was her signature drink.

Vy sat in a big, old brown leather chair. It would let out a deflation sound every time Vy sat in it. At first, she was embarrassed by it, but she got used to it over the years.

Dave was seventy years old, with thin, silvery hair. Vy knew his exact age, only because this year, she'd jumped out of a cake for his seventieth birthday. She had dressed as a sexy gangster, and sang him the Marilyn Monroe rendition of "Happy Birthday."

He probably weighed one hundred pounds and was fragile looking, but at the same time he was one of strongest men she knew. She could tell by his eyes that he'd had a life well lived. Dave had shared many delightful memories with Vy. She loved listening to him reminisce about the 'good old days' as Dave would say. He once told Vy that this bar had become his life, and he wasn't sure if that was a good thing.

"Thanks, Dave. How's it going for you tonight?"

"Good so far, but then again, the night is just beginning. What's up, kiddo?" He placed his pen down, removed his bifocals, and leaned back on his reclining chair.

Dave had a huge fish bowl of candy behind his chair. Vy got up to get her usual Blow Pop, and sat back down. "Have you noticed anyone weird lingering around the bar tonight?" she asked casually.

"Besides the usual, no. Why? Is someone bothering you? You know we'll get rid of him." He had a slight look of concern.

Dave was the best at what he did. A fight could break out, and no one in the bar would know. He kept everything under the radar. He was casual, collected, and very conscientious when it came to his surroundings. So, if he hadn't noticed anyone out of the ordinary, then Vy was probably overreacting.

"No one's bothering me, Dave." Vy gave him a sweet smile and got up. "I was just asking. It's been one of those nights where something feels off."

"No worries, kiddo; we have it all under control." He looked at six little black and white monitors that were above her head. With that gesture, she felt better.

"Where is she?" Vy heard Rob's voice through the sound monitors. "Does anyone know where she might be?"

"I have to go, Dave." Vy blew a kiss at him and ran out of the office. Running in her four-inch heels wasn't easy, but she had become a professional at it.

Larry yelled to Rob from the pool table, "She's probably at the bar!" Everyone started to laugh.

"I'm right here!" Vy shouted.

Rob frowned at Vy, but she knew he wasn't bothered by the fact she was late for the third set. She jumped on stage knowing that her shin was going to pay for it tomorrow.

"Sorry, I was in the office with Dave." There were oh's and ah's coming from the crowd. "It's not what you think. I just wanted a Blow Pop is all." The crowd continued to laugh. Carlos started to strum the first song of the set. She closed her eyes, took a deep breath, and slowly reopened her eyes. Vy jolted back when she saw that the Brad Pitt clone was standing in front of the stage, barely reaching her mid-drift, holding up an Apple Martini.

"You're empty," he said, looking at her empty martini glass.

"Thanks," was the only thing Vy could utter. He walked away. Carlos continued to strum, and again she missed her cue to come in. Vy had a bad feeling about this man.

Vy's rule was that she didn't accept a drink from anyone other than one of the waitresses. She placed the Apple Martini beside the sound monitor located next to the steps. Carlos continued strumming the same three chords waiting for Vy to start singing the song. The words finally found their way out of her mouth.

The bar was alive tonight. Vy was feeding off the positive energy that was generated throughout each table, each person. That energy replenished her soul. The crowd sang along with Vy to "Sweet Child of Mine." Carlos went into the song's notorious, edgy guitar solo.

The women stood in front of him going ballistic. Vy belted out the chorus while she was on her knees in front of Carlos' guitar.

"Yeah! Give it up for Carlos!" Vy shouted into the microphone.

The song ended, and it was time for Vy to take a break. Rob was going to take over, and sing a few more songs. As she walked down the steps, Vy noticed that her martini had disappeared. Shawn walked up to her, "Vy, that was awesome!" Shawn turned her into mush.

"Thanks. You know, if you want to play a song, I'm sure that Carlos will let you use his guitar." His smile was vibrant, but it was soon cut off when Ricky approached them. Ricky had the tendency to ruin Shawn's every amazing smile.

"I know, get back to work," Shawn said mimicking him.

"Good boy," Ricky responded. Vy could tell Ricky had been drinking already, just by the tone of his voice. "I tell you, if he keeps slacking, he's gone."

"He was just telling me how great we sounded, relax." Apparently, that was the wrong thing to say. His eyes dilated, and his lips were about to say something to Vy, but Tina emerged next to her like an angel.

"Hi, Ricky," she said. "You're not giving my best girl here a hard time, are you?"

"Hi, Tina." His entire demeanor changed. She had him salivating.

"Um, no. I was just going to offer you ladies a drink on the house. By the way, Vy, I drank that martini you left by the monitor. You shouldn't leave your drink unattended, could be dangerous. You're lucky that I drank it." Ricky laughed. "Anyway, you want another one?"

Sure, you jerk, was what she thought, but what Vy said was, "Sure, thanks."

"How about you, beautiful? You want to have a shot with me?" Ricky asked Tina.

"I will have a shot, but I already promised Vy I'd have it with her. Next time, sweetie," Tina grinned. Ricky didn't even realize that Tina was belittling him.

He caught himself staring at Tina and quickly snapped out of it. "Kendra! Get these ladies what they want!" Ricky stormed off to the office without saying another word.

"Jack ass," Tina muttered as they walked back to the table. "How do you deal with that crap?"

"I usually don't. He usually isn't here when we play. But thanks for saving me."

"Honey, I saw that look you give when you're ready to kick someone in the gut. I wanted to save that man from excruciating pain."

"Was it that obvious?" Vy asked.

"Big time."

Kendra came over with two martinis and two shots. "Here you go, girls."

"Sorry that he gave you attitude," Vy said.

"Oh, sweetie, that's normal around here." Kendra smiled. "Let me know if you need anything else. Enjoy."

"Now, let's drink to friendship," Tina said.

"Here's to friendship." As they raised their glasses, they heard a loud scream, over Rob's Led Zeppelin song. Cassandra hysterically came out of the office, and ran over to Kyle yelling, "He's dead, Kyle. He's dead!"

TESTING 4

The band immediately stopped playing. Deep, long breaths filled the void of laughter. "Is this a joke?" yelled a man from the center bar. The chattering began immediately thereafter.

"Who's dead?" Larry asked the GQ guy.

"Dead, what!" a woman frantically said, and bolted for the exit.

"James, call 911!" Kyle said as he ran to the office.

Vy stood up, but lost sight of Kyle as soon as he closed the door behind him. Carlos rushed over to Vy. "Sugar, you okay?"

"Yeah, I'm alright."

Vy held Tina's trembling hand trying to calm her down, "It's going to be okay, sweetie. James called the police. Wait here; I'm going to try to find out what's going on."

"You're not going anywhere," Rob said as he came up from behind Vy.

"It doesn't sound good, Vy. We should get out of here. We'll come back for the equipment in the morning," Adrianna added.

"Thanks for taking care of me, but if something happened to Dave, I wouldn't forgive myself for leaving."

Although Vy was acting tough, she didn't want to let them know that she was internally freaking out. She thought something horrible had happened to Dave, like a heart attack, or maybe the wine had caused a bad reaction. She had a hundred million scenarios running through her mind.

"Fine, but we're staying at this table until someone arrives," Adrianna said.

Everyone waited patiently for the paramedics to arrive. Vy looked over towards the office, but the door remained closed. She noticed that the customers were using both the front and back entrance of the bar to leave. As people continued to hurry out of the front entrance, Vy saw red and blue lights from a distance coming from the parking lot. A uniformed cop approached the door and instructed the customers to remain inside. The police officer held the front door open, and the paramedics came in with a stretcher. She now knew something was seriously wrong.

"Okay, the police and paramedics have arrived. I'm going to try to find out what's going on." Vy didn't wait for anyone to reply. She just got up and proceeded towards the office.

She was slowly maneuvering herself in between people so that she wouldn't be seen by any police officers. She wasn't ready to hear the truth. She figured she could find Kyle, and get the story from him. She almost got to her point of destination when she saw two police officers situated in front of the office's doorway.

"Damn," Vy mumbled. She slowly turned her back to them to try to go unnoticed. She was trying to listen in on their conversation.

"Sir, we don't know the cause of death yet," she heard a paramedic say. Vy slightly turned her body to somewhat face them. An older police officer wiped his forehead. It was as though he had heard that phrase too many times in his career. He regained his composure and asked, "Do we know who it is?" Vy closed her eyes and tensely waited for his answer, fearing that the answer was Dave.

"Sir, the door guy Kyle identified him as the owner of the bar, a Ricky Callister."

"Oh, thank God," Vy said to herself. Unfortunately, it was loud enough that two sets of eyes were now looking in her direction. She smiled at them and casually made her way back to the table. Tina grabbed Vy's hand, "Did you find out anything?"

Before Vy could respond, a man yelled out, "Everyone, stay calm. I need everyone to take a seat."

The people lowered their voices and found seats. Another regular, who was completely inebriated, was dancing with himself on the dance floor, oblivious to his surroundings.

"Who's that singing?" he asked. He was imagining that the man's voice was coming from the jukebox.

"Sir, I need you to sit down."

Vy's heart stopped beating for a millisecond. The man who was keeping everyone calm was none other than the Brad Pitt look-alike. Now she needed a shot.

The man walked Tony over to a table and sat him down. Vy, Tina, and Kendra, were seated at one table, and Carlos, Rob, and Adrianna were seated at a table next to them. Vy still couldn't see what was going on in the office. There were now six officers blocking the doorway. She looked at her watch. It was twelve forty-five in the morning. This was about the time the band usually started their final set. Vy presumed that wasn't going to be happening anytime soon.

"No one is to leave the premises," another policeman yelled out.

The depressed woman whom Vy had seen earlier that night called out, "What's going on?"

Vy started to mentally sing the Four Non-Blonds classic tune, "What's Up." The woman's question was disregarded, but Vy knew the answer. She decided to do the one thing she always did in a dire situation, call her older sister Alexia. She was the one person who could keep her calm at a time like this.

"I'm going to the restroom; I'll be right back," Vy whispered to Tina.

"Do you want me to come with you?" Tina asked.

"No, stay here with the others. I'm going to call Lexi."

"Oh, good thinking."

Vy finally made it to the restroom. As she was about to push the door open, someone stopped her by grasping her shoulder.

"Where do you think you're going, miss?" Vy turned around, and the Brad Pitt clone appeared before her.

She looked towards the wooden door that had a poster of a woman wearing a jersey, cut off jean shorts, and drinking a Bud. There was a sign above the poster that read *Women*. "I'm going rock climbing," was the first thought that came to mind, but she simply answered, "To the ladies' room," in a sarcastic tone.

"Then why are you holding your cell phone in your hand?"

"Because I'm going to call my sister."

"Now?" The battle of the sexes began.

"Yes, I want to tell her what happened tonight. I need her to come to the bar."

"Why? Is she a lawyer?"

"A CPA," Vy retorted.

"A CPA? Then why are you calling her?"

"Look, officer," Vy said, emotionally exhausted.

"Detective Gunbar," he added.

"Look, Detective Gunbar, she's the one person right now who's going to keep me from screaming at the top of my lungs. I feel claustrophobic, I'm five seconds away from hyperventilating, and I have needed to pee for the last three hours." Her frustrations were articulated in one breath. Vy's vocal lessons were really paying off.

"Let her go to the restroom, Gunbar."

Vy's eyes scanned this man from his polished black dress shoes, to the top of his perfectly styled hair. She stared at him with her mouth slightly opened.

"It's not protocol, sir. We need to interview everyone," Gunbar said.

"Gunbar, she's only going to the restroom."

"To call her sister, sir."

"We're done here, detective."

Gunbar looked intently at Vy, then walked away.

"Thank you," Vy said exasperated.

"No problem. I'm Detective Houston; you are?"

He was a little over six feet tall, had electrifying blue eyes, a shaggy, yet trimmed haircut, and from what she could notice under his tight, black shirt with the Miami Police badge logo, a nice chest. "And you are?" he repeated.

"Sorry, um—Vy."

"Well, 'Um Vy,' please hurry out." He turned around and left.

Vy stood there staring at his firm butt as he walked away. When Vy entered the restroom, she checked the stalls to make sure no one was there. She called her sister, Alexia, and briefly told her what was going on. She asked her with urgency to come to Miami. As promised, Vy made it out of the restroom quickly, and returned to the rest of the others at the table. It was going to take about an hour before her sister Alexia arrived.

Vy passed the time by analyzing the individual faces that walked passed her. Some faces had somber expressions. Others seemed completely confused as to what had transpired. Vy felt confused and scared herself. Normally she liked to be in control of situations that happened in her life, but this was out of her hands. Even though it seemed like an eternity, Alexia arrived an hour later. Vy saw her walk through the front entrance of the bar, and immediately her sanity returned. Vy stood from the table and headed towards her sister. She hugged Alexia, and held onto her for a second longer than usual.

"Hi," Alexia said into Vy's ear. Vy pulled away and smiled at Alexia. "What a mission to get inside. But luckily this officer let me in as soon as I told him I was your sister. Odd though, he knew my profession." They walked back to the table, and sat down. "So, what's happened since you last spoke to me?"

Before Vy could answer, Detective Houston approached the table. Both Vy and Alexia starred up at him, "You ladies stay put, someone will be by shortly to question you." He walked to the next table.

Alexia snapped her fingers. "Matthew McConaughey!" Alexia said as he walked away.

"Not now, Alexia! Do you know how difficult it was to get you in here?"

Alexia shrugged her shoulders and whispered under her breath, "Well, he does."

Vy didn't disagree with Alexia. Detective Houston did look like Matthew McConaughey. But this wasn't the time to think about that, but now she was. "Thanks a lot, Lexi."

"What?" she innocently asked.

Vy caught up Alexia on the scenario. "So now, we wait."

I can't believe this happened. Poor guy. Okay, so what do you all know so far?" Alexia was now addressing Vy, Tina, and Adrianna.

"Besides what I overheard the police say, I know absolutely nothing. They are detaining everyone here until every single person has been questioned. Can you believe that?" Vy heard no response from Alexia. "Hello, are you listening to me?"

"Oh yeah, sorry—single person, detaining. Yep, got it."

Vy looked over to where Alexia's gaze was fixed. "Don't even think about it, Alexia."

"That's the officer who let me in. Who is he?"

"I call him Mr. Bah Humbug," Vy said with angst.

"But he looks like—"

"I know, Brad Pitt, but he isn't as charming." It was not like Vy would know on a personal level if Brad Pitt was charming, but she figured that compared to Detective Gunbar, a rock was probably more charming.

"He's the one who gave me such a hard time about letting you come to the bar," Vy said to Alexia, trying to knock some sense into her.

"Well, then, I should personally thank him for letting me in."

At two in the morning, Alexia looked like she'd stepped out of a *Fredericks of Hollywood* catalogue. She was a mix between Selma Hayek, Penelope Cruz, and Jennifer Lopez. She had the seductive, Latin look of Selma, the beautiful long brown flowing hair of Penelope, and the body and butt of Jennifer. Swaying her Latin hips from side to side, she walked over to Detective Gunbar. For the first time that night, he had a smile on his face. Vy knew he was a goner. Alexia gently touched his arm; she giggled and—three, two, one—he gave Alexia his card. She flipped her hair behind her right shoulder, turned around, and started walking back towards the table. He couldn't seem to stop staring at her butt.

"That's it!" Vy said to herself. She was frustrated and wanted answers. She walked past Alexia and approached Gunbar.

"Enjoying the view, detective?" Vy defensively crossed her arms.

He cleared his throat. "Please take a seat; we're going to get to you shortly," Gunbar said nervously.

What she wanted to say was, "I've been sitting here for over an hour, and you're telling me that you had time to stare at my sister's behind, but you don't have time to tell me what happened?" But what Vy actually said was, "I've been waiting for over an hour, and I still don't know anything. Do you know how Ricky died? Was it a natural death? Was it a homicide? If so, do you have any leads?" Vy continued to keep her arms crossed.

"Are you studying to become a cop?"

"No, I just read a lot of mystery novels."

Gunbar smirked. "We can't determine the cause of death yet. The medical examiner is in there as we speak."

"Thanks." Vy looked towards the office to see if she could get a glimpse of something.

"Vy?"

"Yes, detective?"

"Your sister? Is she? Well—"

"Yes, she's single." He smiled, and then it quickly vanished.

Vy shook her head, determined that she would never understand a man's mind. And they said women were the complicated ones. Vy questioned who 'they' were. 'They' were probably men.

"By the way," Gunbar asked, "how did you know who the victim was?"

"Like I said, I read a lot of mystery novels." Vy left it at that, and hastily left.

"What did he say," Alexia whispered to Vy.

"The medical examiner is in there as we speak."

"No silly, about me?"

"Lexi, I called you here for support."

Alexia hugged her. "Sorry, bug."

"How many times do I have to tell you not to call me bugger in public? I have a reputation to uphold."

Vy and Alexia sat in silence for a few minutes. Alexia placed her hand on Vy's. "Vy, I'm really sorry."

"Oh, Kyle's still here!" Vy interrupted, "Sorry, Lexi, I have to go talk to him. I'll be right back."

Kyle was sitting at his usual spot. She quickly walked up to him, hoping that he had some answers for her.

"Hi." She placed her hand on his shoulder. "I'm so sorry about Ricky."

Kyle firmly clutched her hand and pulled her close. What Vy thought was going to be a kiss on the cheek, turned out to be a whisper in her ear, "I'm not."

Vy's body became tense. She didn't know whether to respond or to run. He let go of her hand and continued, "There he was, faced down on the desk, with his arms dangling off the table. Can you believe his eyes were open? But Vy, the worst part of it is, is that I didn't feel one hint of remorse. Does that make me a horrible person?"

Vy stood there motionless searching for the right words. "No, I think that makes you human. Maybe you were in shock." She didn't really know if that was true, but she wanted to give him, as well as herself, some comfort.

"Did you notice anything strange earlier tonight?" Vy continued.

"Only Dave and Ricky arguing for like the tenth time. Then Ricky headed back to the office. Well, more like stumbled to the office. By then he was already drunk. Dave went home because he wasn't feeling well. The only thing I found strange was that Ricky was drinking an Apple Martini. He never drinks, or drank girly drinks. No offense."

"None taken. Thanks, Kyle."

After another half hour of not being questioned, Vy decided to ask Gunbar what the progress of the situation was. She walked over to him. "Hi. I've been very tolerant, and you still haven't spoken to me."

"It just so happens that I was just headed your way. I tend to leave the best for last."

Vy disregarded his last comment. "Well, can you tell me what happened to Ricky?"

"Why don't you tell me?" Gunbar said, with implication.

"Excuse me?"

"See, I've recently drawn my own theories, and it turns out that you're on the top of my list. You've been on the top from the very beginning. So now I'm giving you a chance to tell me your side of the story."

"What do you mean from the beginning? This horrible incident happened a few hours ago!" Vy yelled.

"Don't act all innocent. You know what I'm talking about."

"I—" She was confused and felt threatened. For the first time in all the years Vy had been singing at the Steel Horse Bar, there was silence.

"What's going on here?" Houston asked.

Vy looked up at him, "Apparently, I'm on the top of his list," she air-quoted. "And I definitely know what that means."

Alexia and Tina rushed over to Vy. "What what means?" Alexia asked.

"Ms.?" Houston intercepted.

"I told you earlier, just Vy," she answered defensively.

"Vy, let's go have a seat in the back, and I'll explain everything," Houston said.

For some reason, his voice calmed her down. "Fine, but Alexia is coming with me."

Vy turned to Tina, "Go home. And take Adrianna with you, okay? I'll be fine."

"Okay, but you call me when you get home, no matter what time it is."

"You got it." Vy gave Tina a quick hug.

"Gunbar, please escort this lady and her friend to her car," Houston said.

"But—"

"I said; escort this lady to her car. And you and I," Houston whispered in a harsh tone to Gunbar, "will discuss your behavior when we return to the station."

Gunbar groaned, and proceeded to the exit with Tina and Adrianna following him. "Hey, wait up! I thought you were supposed to be escorting me," Tina called out.

Vy, Alexia, and Houston sat down in one of the red booths located on the far back wall of the bar. The mirrors on the wall reflected the few remaining curious and tired faces still in the bar. The remaining band members had been questioned, so they had headed home.

"We've been investigating Ricky Callister for some time now. We believe he's been using this bar for a drug trafficking operation," Houston said.

"Are you serious? And you think that I'm involved? I can't even sniff Afrin when my nose is stuffed up." Vy then realized that sharing that unnecessary fact to the man of her dreams wasn't a good way to start a relationship. She was a singer, not a seductress.

"It's true; she can't. I have to trick her into it," Alexia added. Vy looked for a hole to fall into.

"We're not saying that you're involved. We just wanted to see if you were reliable enough to help us figure out who is."

"You need me already; how romantic." That's what she wanted to say. "Why did Gunbar say I was on the top of his list?" Vy asked.

"Because my partner doesn't know how to properly express his thoughts. Gunbar has been undercover at this location for some time now. You were the one person he constantly saw interacting with the staff. He figured since you've been here for a few years, you had to know something. Tonight, he was going approach you as a civilian."

"He's been on the down low? That's why I didn't recognize him. Better tell him that the next time he wants to approach someone as a civilian, he shouldn't look so pissed off. It scares a girl off."

Houston chuckled. "I apologize for his behavior. He's been on this case for a few months, and I think that it's starting to get to him. Be assured that I'll be speaking with him about his behavior."

"Thanks," Vy said.

"Now, I do believe that you would be a great asset to this case. You've been singing here long enough that these people trust you. Any information you can extricate from them would be helpful," Houston said.

Before Vy considered helping the police department, she wanted some questions answered. "So how did Ricky die?" Houston seemed puzzled.

"Vy changes topics constantly. You just have to learn how to keep up," Alexia said with a smirk.

"Okay," Houston said.

"So?" Vy asked.

"The cause of death has not been determined. We put a rush on the autopsy report."

"Do you have any theories?" Vy pressed.

"Yes, but they're irrelevant until we get the report back. Now, getting back to the initial topic, will you help with the investigation?"

"Can I think about it? The people who work here are my friends. I don't know how they would react if after three years, I started asking questions."

"You have no other choice," Gunbar rudely interrupted.

He was standing behind Vy. She turned her head around and looked up at him. "Excuse me?"

"You have no choice. So far, we've cleared everyone here. The tapes don't show anything. All I do know is that there's something going on here. Mr. Callister was involved, and someone is doing a really good job at covering it up."

Vy slid out of the booth. She stood on the tip of her toes, to be at eye level with him. "So that means that I have to be a snitch to solve your case? Did you notice the emphasis on the word *your*?"

"You want to know what I really think?"

"Bring it on!" Vy hissed.

"I swear you two are like an old married couple." They both looked at Alexia. "Vy, let's go home and talk about it. Detectives, we'll call you tomorrow afternoon. It's already four in the morning. Everyone's agitated. There's no need for this hostility. Gunbar," Alexia winked, "back off my little sister."

"Good night, ladies," Houston said.

"I swear Lexi; you are the only one who could get away with that," Vy said.

"Gunbar and I had some words prior to your little explosion."

"I don't even want to know," Vy said.

As Kyle and Shawn escorted Vy and Alexia out, Vy saw Kendra through the Plexiglas crying inside the DJ booth. "I'll meet you guys outside."

Vy opened the door to the booth. Kendra was looking at a picture, which she immediately put in her back pocket. “Honey, are you okay?” Vy asked.

“It’s all too much to handle right now, Vy. I can’t believe he’s gone,” Kendra sighed.

“I’m sorry. I don’t know what to say. Do you have any idea what could have happened to Ricky? Did he have any health issues? Did he feel ill tonight?” Vy asked.

Kendra looked at Vy with a confused look. “You sound like the cops. But like I told them, no, I have no idea what could have happened to him.”

That was a strange reaction from someone Vy considered a friend. But did she really know Kendra, or anyone who worked at the Steel Horse Bar, for that matter? She’d been singing here for three years, but that was the extent of her association with the staff.

“I’m going home. I’m really tired, and I still have to come in tomorrow night,” Kendra said as she looked down at her untied sneaker.

“Okay, K. Drive safe and I’ll see you in two weeks,” Vy said. Kendra hurried off without saying anything further to her.

Alexia, Kyle and Shawn were hanging out by the car. “How are you boys doing?” Vy asked.

“The question is how are you doing?” Shawn asked Vy.

“I’m tired and shocked. This was the longest gig we’ve ever had.”

Alexia put her arm around Vy’s shoulder, “I guess you didn’t get paid tonight, huh?”

“Kyle, Shawn, thanks for the escort to the car, have a good night. Call me if you guys get any more news.”

“Will do, love,” Kyle said. Both Shawn and Kyle headed back to the bar.

Vy and Alexia were finally driving to Vy's apartment. She couldn't wait to arrive to her haven. "Alexia, thanks for coming to my rescue. I know that it's an hour-long drive, and it was really late."

"Are you kidding me? I have to take care of my little sister. And besides, I got a hot date out of it."

"What! Are you seriously going out with Gunbar?" Vy was appalled.

"Let's approach it from this angle. You know him already, so we don't have to go through the introduction stage."

"Lexi, for one, he's a pain in my neck, and secondly, I was on the top of his list," she air-quoted, "and thirdly, I don't even know what his first name is. And, did I mention I was and still may be on the top of his list?"

"First, stop air quoting. Second, grammatically speaking, that came out wrong. And third, I'll straighten him out. No one puts my little sister on the top of their list," Alexia giggled. "Get it, like *Dirty Dancing*, but instead—"

"I get it. When's the date?" Vy asked.

Alexia looked at her cell phone, "Tonight. Want to go shopping with me?" Vy hesitated. "I'll buy you shoes," Alexia added.

"I'm in." Vy was a sucker for shoes and for Alexia.

TESTING 5

Vy woke up to one of life's greatest aromas, French Vanilla coffee. She looked at the clock, and closed her eyes again. She had only slept for five hours. After a late-night gig, waking up before noon was uncommon for her. But then again, Alexia slept over. She was an early riser. Vy took a deep breath and forced herself out of bed.

She closed the restroom door and looked at herself in the mirror. Because she didn't remove her mascara before passing out last night, Vy looked like she was punched in the eyes several times, and a semi-truck ran her over five times. She heard Alexia shout from the kitchen, "I cooked burnt bacon for you." She knew that burnt bacon helped with Vy's morning grumpiness.

"Thanks. I'll be right out."

Vy finally made her way to the kitchen. Alexia was going back and forth from the stove, to the coffeemaker, to the refrigerator, resembling a mini tornado. Marilyn was sitting on the bar counter staring at Alexia with amazement.

"We have a full day ahead of us," Alexia said.

"More cream," was all that Vy grumbled.

"I took a shower already. So, I just have to get dressed, wait for you to get ready, wait for Adrianna and Tina to get here, and then we're off to the mall," Alexia explained, laying out the agenda for the morning.

Vy still couldn't put sentences together, so Alexia continued speaking. "I called the girls to help us with the investigation."

Vy finished taking her sixth gulp of coffee and finally conjured up a sentence, "Help with the investigation? Am I still dreaming, or am I just hearing things?"

"Gunbar told me that the Steel Horse Bar will not be opened for business until Ricky's case is closed," Alexia explained. "Notice I used the proper term 'closed'."

"You talked to Gunbar already? This early?"

"I had questions for him."

"What questions?" Vy asked as her stomach grumbled.

"What time was he planning on picking me up? Which restaurant did he have in mind? I have to make sure I wear the appropriate outfit. Then, we started talking about what happened last night, and that's when he told me about the bar."

Vy looked at her empty coffee mug. Alexia was already pouring her another cup, and handed her a plate of turkey bacon. She finally sat down across from Vy.

"Alexia, that is why detectives exist; they are trained to solve these kinds of cases. By themselves. Without us. Get what I'm saying to you?"

"First of all, you have to brush your teeth again. Look, Vy, we need your help. I think that if all four of us put our heads together, we can solve it in no time. Anyway, you love this stuff. You read mystery novels all the time. You have the most knowledge of all of us to solve this case in a timely and fashionable manner."

Vy saw Alexia's lips moving, but she couldn't comprehend what she was saying. Vy mentally recalled the movie line from *Rush Hour*, 'Do you understand the words that are coming out of my mouth?' Vy laughed to herself.

"What are you laughing about?" Alexia asked.

"Nothing. Listen, Alexia, reading mystery books and watching *Lifetime* movies doesn't make me a crime solver. That sounds ridiculous. Besides, if Ricky died of a heart attack, let's say, then there's no mystery to solve."

"I picked up from my conversation with Gunbar this morning that he doubts that Ricky died of natural causes. But that was all I could get out of the man. Anyway, I drafted out a plan. Like a business plan, but one you can actually understand."

"Too early for jokes, Lexi."

"I know. I just love bugging you when you're half asleep. Your defenses aren't up yet," Alexia replied.

"It does suck that Dave's temporarily closing the bar. I love playing there, and the extra income definitely helped," Vy stated.

"This is why we're going to help solve this case. It's like we're the A Team, or is it the Fantastic Team? Well, you know what team I'm talking about, the one with Superman in it. The only difference is that we're going to wear cuter outfits."

"How do you know about the Justice League of America?" Vy inquired.

"While you were sleeping, I watched an episode of *Smallville* you'd recorded."

"Goodness, woman, how long have you been up?"

Vy was about to rebut Alexia's insane idea, when someone knocked on the door. "Saved by the bell," Alexia sang and went to answer the door. Adrianna walked in with her gadget, also known as her laptop. She never left home without it.

"Hi, Adrianna." Vy gave her a hug. "I take it you're going to be Information Woman?" Vy laughed at her own joke and proceeded to the restroom. "I'm going to jump in the shower; I'll be right out."

Vy heard Adrianna whisper, "Is she still grumpy?"

After Vy's refreshing shower, she found herself in front of her closet. She didn't want to put too much thought into what she was going to wear. She wanted to go for the comfortable look.

Alexia yelled from the restroom, "Do you have a brush? My hair is disheveled." There was a slight pause. "My hair is a mess." Vy noted her vocabulary word for the day. Again, Alexia yelled, "It's your vocabulary word for the day, isn't it?"

"Stop that! And yes, it's in my left drawer."

"Found it! Okay, are you ready yet?"

"Getting there."

"Wear those tight jeans I like on you. I want to get a discount at that one store your crush works at." There went Vy's idea of comfortable apparel.

Marilyn was sitting on Tina's lap enjoying having her ears scratched when Vy walked out.

"Hey, girl," Vy said.

"Oh my God, are you okay? Are you still freaked out? Talk to me," Tina said in one breath.

"I would, if you'd give me a second to squeeze in some responses."

Tina smiled. "Are you still sleepy? Is that why you're grumpy?"

"That must be it, because I fed her this morning," Alexia replied.

"Hello, I'm right here," Vy said. "I'm not grumpy or hungry. I'm fine. I'm just tired from last night's activities. Let's go to the mall. That will definitely give me energy."

Unfortunately, Tina was driving, but fortunately it woke Vy up. Vy was sitting in the front with Tina. Alexia and Adrianna were in the backseat of Tina's

Land Rover. Adrianna was wrapping a hair curl with her index finger. "So any updates on last night?"

"Not yet. This is frustrating, being left out in the dark," Vy said.

Tina pulled into the mall's parking garage. "I know you just had breakfast, but can we have an early lunch at Riozani?"

"Who can say no to their spaghetti?" Alexia said.

"Just thinking about it makes me hungry," Vy added.

"Yes, let's go," Adrianna concluded.

*****

Vy, Alexia, Tina, and Adrianna arrived at the restaurant and got seats at a round table near the back of the restaurant. The smell of Italian tomato sauce permeated the air.

"I'm so happy you finally came to visit, Lexi. It's been too long," Adrianna said.

"I know. I shouldn't wait for something bad to happen to visit my little sister."

"Girls, what you don't know is that I talk to Lexi every day, multiple times a day. Trust me, it makes up for her not visiting as often as she should," Vy said sarcastically. Alexia smacked her hand.

"Ladies, are you ready to order?" The waiter took their order. "The bread basket will be coming shortly. Thank you."

"So now that we are officially settled, I want to talk about part one of the plan," Alexia started to explain.

"The stage is all yours, Jill," Vy chimed in.

"Oh, good one! A *Charlie's Angels* reference. I just loved Farah Faucet on that show," Tina gushed.

Vy, Alexia, and Adrianna were staring at Tina. "What? I don't say anything when you continuously talk about Rob Thomas."

They giggled, but soon after, Alexia continued, "Okay, so here's part one of the plan." Alexia brushed her hair from her eyes, and scooted up to table.

"Adrianna suggested that we stop by the Spy Store. And before you ask, Vy, let me finish. From the Spy Store, we're going to purchase a listening device that I can use during my dates with Gunbar. So, for example, if he mentions a certain name regarding the case, Adrianna can run an instant search on that patron, and pull up any information available. We're now one step ahead."

Vy turned to face Alexia. "Okay, patron? And, how do you expect to get any information out of that man? Furthermore, how do you expect to hide this so called 'device'? Have you seen your dresses? They're the equivalent of body paint," Vy said.

Alexia cleared her throat. "Yes, patron until proven guilty. And, I'm great at probing for information. And furthermore, Gunbar will subconsciously speak because he will be hypnotized by the sexy dress I'll be wearing tonight. And if you must know, I will be hiding the device in the cleavage area. It will work for the first and second date, but after that, we may have to buy a different device." Tina looked at Alexia quizzically. "The device only works twice?" There was silence then laughter erupted. "Oh, I get it," Tina said and commenced to crack up.

"So that's part one. What do you think, Vy?" Alexia asked excitedly.

"Okay, let's say part one works, then what? And what happens if Gunbar catches on to our little investigation?"

"Then I work my magic," Alexia said.

"Please spare us the details on what constitutes magic," Vy said, flinching at the thought.

"This all sounds so exciting," Tina said.

"No, Tina, this sounds ridiculous and risky," Vy stated.

"Risky, as in we will be swimming in treacherous waters?" Adrianna asked.

"Risky, as in we will be singing our last notes," Vy responded.

There was silence among the four of them, "You did not just say that, bug?" Alexia asked.

TESTING 6

"How do I look?"

"Breath-taking as always."

Vy was lying on the couch watching a recorded episode of *Ghost Whisperer*. Alexia looked at her, "How come you're not ready?"

"Ready for what?"

Alexia glanced down at the tiled floor, and looked back up at Vy biting her lower lip, "Crap."

"Crap what, Alexia?"

"I knew I forgot something from my to-do list."

"Oh God, Lexi, you didn't?"

"I thought it would be fun."

One of the few flaws Alexia had was to conveniently forget certain things Vy wouldn't agree she should do.

"What would be fun?" Vy sat up and pressed pause on the remote control. There was a freeze frame of Jennifer Love Hewitt about to cry because she'd just crossed a ghost over to the other side.

"A double date." Alexia sat across from Vy.

"I can't believe you didn't run this by me first." Vy exited out of her show, turned off the television, and sat up.

"It's been a while since we've been on a double date. It's been a while since you've been on a date. You went on my first dates all the time. Besides, your date is Detective Houston, and you love Matthew McConaughey."

"First of all, I was thirteen when I went on your first dates. And I had to go because mom didn't want you to be alone the first time you went out with a guy. And, I have no problem getting a date on my own, Lexi!"

"Right, like that one who talked about himself most of the night? Or the one who took you out to dinner, but conveniently forgot his wallet. Then it turned out that he was living in his car, in hopes of moving in with you that same night. Or the one who became psychotic, because you fixed his lopsided collar. Yeah, you do a really great job getting fantastic dates." Vy hated the fact that Alexia had a point, but she couldn't back down.

"And newsflash, he's not Matthew McConaughey, Alexia, he's a detective. You know that I don't care for cops."

"He's better than a cop. You said it yourself, he's a detective. Now stop arguing and get ready. They're picking us up in thirty minutes." Vy stomped to her bedroom to get ready.

"Wear that black halter dress I like."

"Why, so I can get you guys a discount at the restaurant?" Vy blurted out.

"Oh, stop whining; you'll thank me later."

Thirty minutes later their dates arrived. Vy forgot how to breathe for about three seconds. Houston was wearing dark blue jeans, with a nice black collared, semi-tight shirt. His smile would melt iron. Vy momentarily closed her eyes, and engulfed herself in Houston's cologne. Alexia cleared her throat, and Vy quickly snapped out of the trance.

"Detectives, you both look very handsome," Alexia said.

Gunbar started to blush. "Alexia, Vy, please call me Anthony."

"Anthony Gunbar? I would have never imagined," Vy said mockingly.

Alexia smacked Vy's arm and whispered, "Vy, behave." She gave Alexia the 'you made me come with you' grin and looked at Houston.

"So, Houston, what's your first name?" Vy was hoping it wasn't corny.

He smiled. "Don't worry; it's not Sparky or anything like that." Vy was thankful this one had a sense of humor. "It's Bryan, with a Y. My parents wanted to be semi-creative with my name."

"Bryan with a Y is a nice name." Vy had to keep in mind that this date was strictly for business. Alexia grabbed onto Gunbar's arm. Houston gave Vy his and said, "Shall we, ladies?"

*****

After the meal, Vy patted her stomach and leaned back on the chair. "I'm stuffed like a turkey on Thanksgiving Day."

"Like you would know, bug." Vy gave Alexia the evil eye. "Well, you eat like a bird, and you don't cook at home."

"Bug?" Gunbar said.

"Don't ask," Vy replied.

"So, I take it you don't like to cook?" Houston asked.

"No, I like to cook, but unfortunately the outcome never turns out the way it's supposed to look and taste," Vy said embarrassed.

Alexia and Gunbar started to laugh. At least they had one in thing common; they found humor in Vy's inability to cook.

"Since you're cracking yourself up over there, Anthony, I suppose you know how to cook?" Vy asked defensively.

Gunbar replied with a grin, "Actually, I went to culinary school before I went into the academy." Vy just wanted to reach over the dinner table and smack his mouth.

"A cook, impressive. Why did you decide to change careers?" Alexia asked.

"I became bored with the kitchen and cooking. Every woman I dated expected me to cook for them. It became vexatious."

Vy didn't know what *vexatious* meant, but from Alexia's reaction, she knew it wasn't a good thing. Strike one for Gunbar. Vy knew this one wasn't going to stand a chance with Alexia.

She gave Vy the, "I'll tell you the definition of vexatious later" expression, and then gave Gunbar a disappointed look. Vy felt Houston kick Gunbar under the table.

Houston automatically changed the subject. "So, Vy, how long have you been singing?"

Before Vy could answer, Alexia answered proudly, "She's been a performer from the moment she was born. My mom always made both of us sing when we were kids. Vy and I were the entertainment for every party my parents threw."

Vy continued reminiscing, "Yeah, we hated it. But I've always been into music, whether I was playing the piano or singing along to the radio. I realized at an early age that music was and continues to be my true passion in life."

"How did you get started?" Houston asked. Vy enjoyed the fact that he was very intrigued by her story.

"I guess you can say that my professional career began when I was eighteen years old."

"Only a year ago?" Houston said.

"Kiss ass," Gunbar said under his breath.

"I wish! Anyway, I was signed with an independent music label. I was going to school at night, and I had a full-time day job. I spent the weekends and my free time composing, singing and recording my first CD in the studio."

"That's a lot for an eighteen-year-old."

"Not for me. I was trying to live my dream. I used to go to this place called The Warehouse Café. It was constantly packed with artists, writers, musicians, anyone who had anything to do with the arts. One night, I sat on a couch that faced the stage. A girl sat on a bar stool with her guitar and played her song. I remember sitting there thinking to myself that I could do that very thing she was doing. I wanted the people to feel what I felt, to see what I'd seen, and to know what I'd learned. I've been able to accomplish my dream slowly with the two CD's that I have out. I just want my music to be the window to my soul for the world to peek in. It's more than just listening to the songs; it's breathing in the words."

There was silence. Vy didn't realize that she had gone off about the love she had for music. Two sets of eyes were looking at her with adoration, the third set of eyes, which were Gunbar's, were staring at Vy with the 'Are you done yet?' look.

"I told you she was amazing. And, she draws really well too," Alexia said.

Gunbar finally joined in on the conversation, "You two seem really close."

"I don't think I'd be where I am without Lexi's support," Vy said. "She's like my second mom."

Gunbar sarcastically responded with an, "How sweet," then he became sincere, "On a serious note, I can now understand why you called Alexia last night."

Vy saw a glimmer in Alexia's eyes. Alexia knew this was the perfect time to start talking about the investigation. "Speaking of last night, any leads regarding the investigation?"

By the book, Gunbar wouldn't release any juicy details to a half-naked woman. "Sorry, we can't disclose any information to you," Gunbar said in his official tone. "You're a civilian."

"Let me guess; it's not protocol to share information with a civilian?" Vy said. Houston chuckled at her remark. Vy could tell that Alexia's brain was working overtime.

"I think I have every right to know if my little sister is in danger." Alexia used the protective card.

"I understand your point of view, Alexia, but—" Houston cut in, "the autopsy report stated it was a lethal dose of the foreign chemical, cyanide. In addition to the cyanide, Mr. Callister was heavily intoxicated. The ME is under the assumption that the alcohol was laced with the cyanide."

"Houston, can I talk to you outside for a second?" asked Gunbar.

"What is it with you and stepping outside every time you have to say something to Houston?" Vy asked, "At least he's being honest."

A light bulb went off in Vy's head, "Wait a second." The three of them were now focused on Vy. "Alexia, switch places with me." Alexia did what she was told, no questions asked. Vy was now sitting next to Gunbar.

"So, Ricky was poisoned?" Vy asked.

"Yes," Houston answered for Gunbar.

Vy kept her focus on Gunbar. "Oh my God! You! You gave me that drink!" Vy looked directly into Gunbar's eyes.

"Excuse me?" Gunbar responded.

"Kyle said that Ricky was drinking an Apple Martini when he headed back to the office. You bought me that Apple Martini that Ricky was drinking. You were trying to drug me!" Vy didn't know what had come over her, but she smacked Gunbar's chest hard. At least she thought she did, but he didn't seem to flinch.

There was silence in the restaurant. "Let's take this outside," Houston said. Alexia explained to the waiter that they would be returning. She left him a credit card, and the four of them went outside.

"Okay, what is she talking about, Gunbar?" Houston asked. Gunbar started to take Houston aside to talk.

"Oh no!" Alexia practically yelled. "You do not just walk away without an explanation. And I expect one now." Vy was thankful that Alexia was there to defend her.

"You were my main suspect," Gunbar told Vy straight to her face.

"What!" Vy and Alexia said in unison.

"What do you mean a suspect?" Alexia asked.

Vy looked at Alexia and murmured, "I can handle this."

"What do you mean a suspect?" Vy asked Gunbar.

"I thought you were in cahoots with Mr. Callister and his operation. I was keeping tabs on you, considering that you've been singing there for three years. With reason, I couldn't rule you out. Then I saw you speaking with Ricky several times last night. I've been undercover at this location for four weeks, and I've only seen you twice. I was trying to get a feel for who you were. So, I figured—"

Alexia couldn't contain her anger any longer, so she interrupted Gunbar. "So, you figured that by buying her a drink, you were going to—quote, unquote—'get a feel' for who she was?"

"Yeah," was the only word Vy could think of to back Alexia up.

"I didn't poison your drink. Think logically," Gunbar said.

Alexia was on a roll. “Think logically?” Neither Vy nor Houston were about to interrupt Alexia’s monologue. “Okay, here’s some logic for you. I just found out that Ricky was found dead, apparently murdered, at a place where my sister sings every other weekend; you don’t have any leads, and now you want to somehow pin this on her? Listen here, detectives,” Alexia was pointing to Gunbar and Houston, “if your precinct doesn’t have any leads by tomorrow, or an inkling of an idea of what happened to Ricky, I guarantee you’ll be hearing from my attorney.”

Houston was about to rebut, but Gunbar raised his hand to stop him from saying anything. Gunbar took a hold of Alexia’s hand. “Listen, Alexia, yes I was wrong to accuse Vy without any evidence, but it’s my duty to consider all angles on a case.” He looked at Vy. “I’m sorry that I said it the way I did. And obviously, *I* didn’t drug you. But that does add another angle to this case.” Gunbar looked at Houston. “Who was the drink intended for? Ricky or Vy?”

“That’s just great,” Vy said as she ran her fingers through her hair.

“Oh, my goodness,” Alexia added. She grabbed a hold of Vy’s hand.

Gunbar locked eyes with Alexia again, “I know you’re concerned for your sister’s well-being, but we need time to investigate this case. In the meantime, Houston and I will make sure nothing happens to Vy.”

“Why would something happen to me? I’m just a freaking singer!”

“Bug, calm down.” Alexia gave Vy a reassuring smile. She then turned to Gunbar and whispered, “You promise nothing will happen to her?”

“I promise,” Gunbar said.

“I guarantee it,” Houston added.

Even though Vy didn't mesh well with Gunbar, what he said gave her comfort. And the way Alexia was smiling had the same effect on her too.

"By the way, Alexia, you'd be a good interrogator," Gunbar said.

The four of them went back inside the restaurant. A few people looked at them with inquisitive eyes. "Can we just talk about something else for the remainder of the evening?" Vy said.

"Definitely," Houston said.

They took their seats and proceeded with the evening. Vy caught Houston staring at her with what she thought were seductive eyes. But then again, her imagination often ran wild. The Pinot Noir was kicking in, so her confidence level was in high gear. "What do you think, Bryan?"

"About what?"

"About the murder? Ever since I started reading murder mystery novels, I've been intrigued at how a detective's mind works."

"I thought you no longer wanted to talk about it," Houston said.

"Oh, right." Vy snapped her fingers. "But I'm intrigued to know how your mind works. Upon the scene of a crime, do you instantly assess the situation?" Vy and Alexia laughed hysterically in unison. Gunbar and Houston looked at one another.

"Okay. Yes, we assess the situation," Houston said. Vy and Alexia continued to choke back a laugh.

Vy told Gunbar and Houston about the comedian Dane Cook. He had a skit relating to the assessing the situation comment. By this point, the second bottle of Pinot was empty. Even though Alexia only had two glasses of wine, for her that was the equivalent of five tequila shots in a row. Vy on the other hand, was feeling extremely relaxed. Houston's blue eyes were hypnotizing her as he was speaking.

"I'm glad that you ladies are having a good time. And I apologize for the misunderstanding earlier," Houston said.

Vy got close to his ear and whispered, "I'm having a really good time." She then realized that she sounded more like a youthful Meg Ryan than a sexy Kathleen Turner.

With enthusiasm, Alexia exclaimed, "Hey, do you guys want to go to a karaoke bar?" Houston and Gunbar reacted as if another murder just occurred. "Oh, come on," said Alexia, "it should be fun."

"Yeah, it would be fun if your sister doesn't sing," Gunbar said.

"Why, Gunbar, that sounded like a compliment." Vy said.

"It was. I've watched you sing twice and you're pretty good at it."

"Could you at least say that with a smile?" Vy asked.

TESTING 7

They ended up at the jazz bar Moonstruck. Saturdays nights were popular because it was karaoke night. "How do I live without you?" shrieked through the sound monitors. Vy imagined fifty wine glasses breaking behind the bar. The woman singing sounded nothing like Leanne Rimes, but at least she was feeling the song and was having fun.

The interior of the bar was a nineteen-forty's design. The quaintness inspired Vy to talk to the people next to her, raise her glass of wine, and toast to the night. The ambiance changed Vy in a way. Moonstruck was her escape from Miami. There were no superficial people. It was a genuine place to sit, relax, and escape the reality of the world. The lights were dim, yet bright enough to acknowledge the atmosphere. This was one of the few bars that didn't permit smoking, so the haze didn't distract Vy from the beauty that surrounded her. The only element lacking was the piano player Sam, from the movie *Casablanca*, or the raspy, yet desirable vocals of Kyle Legend.

The hostess seated the four of them at a small, round wooden table; their knees touching one another. "So Gunbar," Vy said, "aside from cooking and solving crimes, can you do a little Frank Sinatra?"

Alexia had her elbow on the table, resting her chin in her palm, leaning in towards Gunbar. Because Alexia's exotic look can make any man do anything, he simply nodded yes to Vy's question without realizing what she had just asked him. "I'll be right back," Vy whispered to Houston.

Vy made her way to the high table top. There was a stack of little, white request slips. She casually filled one out, and happily handed it to the karaoke host, and made her way back to the table.

"Thanks for giving in, guys. I rarely go out," Alexia said.

"Are there any good bars in Fort Lauderdale?" Gunbar asked.

"There are many, but unfortunately, Vy is the only one I like to go out with. And with her constantly gigging, and me constantly working, we haven't been able to get together."

"Well, thanks for inviting us, Alexia," Gunbar concluded.

"Vy, I'm curious," Houston leaned in closer to Vy, "being a Cuban American, how is your name Vy?"

Vy was distracted by Houston's remarkable beer breath. "Can you hear me?" Houston asked.

Vy nodded and there was a slight pause. She was trying to formulate a sentence, but for some reason this distraction caused her to go mute.

"Violeta or Violet. I absolutely hate my name, the Spanish and English versions. So, Alexia nicknamed me Vy."

"Yeah, unfortunately I was only four years old when Vy was born, so I couldn't talk my mom into giving her a better name."

"Well, I think all three versions of your name are beautiful," Houston said.

Vy felt her cheeks getting warm. Luckily there was minimal lighting. "Thanks," Vy barely vocalized.

Suddenly, the host said, "Next up, Anthony Gunbar singing, "Fly Me to the Moon." Oh, and he wrote a small dedication to his friends, 'To the most beautiful women in the bar—Alexia and Vy. There's love for you too, big boy Houston.'"

"Go, Gunbar; they're calling you," Vy said.

Houston broke out laughing. "Good one," he said to Vy under his breath.

For acting like such a tough guy, Gunbar appeared as though he was going to pee in his pants. He looked petrified. Color had escaped his cheeks. He walked up to the stage very slowly, grabbed the microphone, and stared at the small television. Alexia was completely enamored of Gunbar. Vy saw trickles of sweat descending from Gunbar's forehead to his nose. He would look at the crowd, then at the television, and then back to the crowd. He did that same maneuver about a hundred times in a matter of one minute.

"Oh, how great," Alexia said as she applauded. Gunbar glared at Vy. "Did I miss something?" Alexia asked.

"Let's go," yelled an elderly man from the bar.

The instrumental version of the song began, but Gunbar was frozen stiff and missed his cue to start singing. For a moment Vy felt guilty for putting him on the spot, but that feeling quickly disappeared when she recalled being on the top of his list of suspects. Gunbar finally started to sing halfway through the first verse. Although he sounded terrible, the audience was supportive. Vy gave him credit for not walking off the stage. She scanned the bar, and caught sight of Kendra. She was sitting alone at a table closer to the stage. She seemed preoccupied by her thoughts.

"Lexi?" Alexia was devouring Gunbar as though he were a piece of meat. She was certain that by the way Alexia was staring at him; the listening device had just been decreased to a onetime usage.

"Lexi?" This time Vy smacked her on the arm. Alexia slowly turned to Vy with her eyes barely opened. "Kendra's here. I'm going to talk to her."

"Okay. I'll be here. You know I love you, right? You sleuth, you. Do you want me to define sleuth for you? It means—"

"I know what it means, Lexi. I'll be right back."

"Make me proud, little sis." Alexia was officially wasted, but Vy would deal with her later.

"Everything okay?" Houston asked Vy. He gently grasped her hand. Her skin took pleasure in every one of his calluses. She slowly sat back down.

"Do you work out?" Vy asked.

"Yes," Houston chuckled. "Where did that come from?"

"I was just wondering. Yeah, everything's cool. I'll be right back. Keep your eye on her."

"You got it." Houston smiled. Even though Vy didn't want to leave his side, she was on a mission.

She gradually approached Kendra. "Hi, Kendra; it's great to see you again." Kendra appeared startled by Vy's presence, but then quickly composed herself. Not that Vy was Dr. Phil, but she appeared to be rundown, confused, and lost.

"Oh, hey. What are you doing in this neck of the woods?" Kendra asked.

"I actually live in this area. The Steel Horse is the neck of the woods for me."

For some reason, Vy felt a little nervous. Sleuthing wasn't as easy as the mystery books made it out to be. "Have you heard any news regarding the mur—or what happened to Ricky?" Vy wasn't sure if Kendra had been informed about Ricky's cause of death.

"No, the police keep giving me the run-around. Apparently, they questioned everyone who was at the bar last night, but nothing came of that. Actually, I think that man on stage now is the jerk I've been dealing with." Kendra looked in Gunbar's direction. He was just ending his massacred rendition of "Fly Me to the Moon." Kendra was staring blankly at him.

"Actually, my sister and I are hanging out with Detective Gunbar and Detective Houston tonight."

"Is that so?" she said. Her response was cold and empty.

"Do you mind if I sit with you for a couple of minutes? Would you like a drink?" Vy asked Kendra.

"No, I'm fine thanks. Sit. You probably have a lot of questions for me."

"What do you mean?"

"You saw me crying in the booth holding that stupid picture. Isn't that what you're curious about?"

That had slipped Vy's mind, but now that Kendra mentioned it, she figured this was her perfect in. "You got me." There was a hint of uncomfortable silence.

"I guess you didn't know that Ricky and I were dating," Kendra said.

"What were you thinking? Were you that desperate?" were questions that crossed Vy's mind, but what came out was, "I thought that you and Kyle had something going on."

"No, he wanted to be with me, but I recently told him about Ricky and me."

"How did Kyle take the news?"

"Not very well," Kendra said, picking away at her purple nail polish. "His entire attitude changed towards me. But it didn't matter. I wanted to be with, and was devoted to Ricky. I loved him."

"How long were you two dating?

"Long enough." Kendra wiped away a tear that had formed under her right eye. She clasped her hands together. "His divorce was finalized last week. We were planning to elope in Vegas." Kendra started getting teary-eyed. "What am I supposed to do now, Vy? How can I go back to the Steel Horse and pretend that nothing happened?" Kendra looked around, lowered her voice, and leaned in towards Vy, "I know how Ricky died."

"Did the police tell you the cause of his death?"

"No. No one knows the truth but me. Vy, please help me. I can't come forward myself. Maybe you can tell your cop friend and he can look into it."

A woman sitting next to Vy unexpectedly yelled, "He's finally done!" Vy saw Gunbar get off stage, then instantly turned her focus back on to Kendra. Kendra immediately stood up and grabbed her purse. "I have to go," she said.

"Please don't go. Tell me how he died. I can help you."

Something spooked Kendra during that one second that Vy turned her head, but she had no clue as to what it was. "No one can help me now, Vy. Don't worry, I'm a big girl. I can take care of myself." Kendra gave her half a smile and walked away. Vy watched her head towards the restroom. She was struggling as to whether she should go after her. Kendra looked scared. Vy was determined to find out why, and what she knew about Ricky's murder.

Vy took a step towards the restroom, and ran into Gunbar. His face was red, and his nostrils were expanded, "Well, I hope you're happy. Why on earth would you put me up there like that?" Gunbar asked.

"Not now, Gunbar. I have to go to the restroom."

Gunbar side stepped in front of her. "What were you possibly thinking?"

Vy finally gave in. "I thought you wanted to serenade my sister. I figured this was the perfect way to do it." Without a reply, Gunbar marched back to the table. By this time, Vy figured Kendra had left the bar.

She made a mental note to get her telephone number from Dave, and call her tomorrow.

She headed back to the table. Houston watched Vy's every step. Her knees were trembling.

"Is everything okay?" Houston asked.

"Kendra, the waitress from the Steel Horse Bar, was here. I went over to speak with her. I don't know if this will help with your investigation, but it turns out that Ricky and Kendra were dating."

That amazing smile appeared. "She told us last night when we questioned her. Thank you though."

"I'm really worried about her. She said she knew how Ricky died. But then her mood changed, and she left abruptly. This is considered a big break in the case, right? And I totally blew it."

"Listen, Vy, usually the victim's significant others are so hurt, that they start to assume how that person died. *Assume* being the key word. Ninety-eight percent of the time, their emotions exceed the facts. But, yes, this could be a break in the case. By the way, that was really cute." Houston smirked. Vy felt her cheeks get red. "But I'll call her first thing tomorrow and bring her in for further questioning. Hopefully, what she assumed is factual, and we can find out the truth behind Ricky's death."

"So, I shouldn't try calling her?"

"No, leave the investigating to the professionals." Houston winked.

"Okay."

"You're a good friend, Vy."

"But that's just it. I don't really know any of the staff on a personal level. So, does that make me a good friend?"

"A friend is a person that shows concern, so, yes, you are a friend." Houston's eyes were giving her tingles in indefinable places.

Gunbar was practically holding Alexia up. “Excuse me. I know you two are having a Hallmark moment, but can we go?”

Houston looked at Vy. “Are you ready?”

Vy whispered in his ear, “The question is, are you ready to ravage my body?”

Vy did say that, but she drew a blank as to the why part. She felt her entire body getting red. Houston responded with a smile. “I think it’s time to take both of you home.”

“Home, yes. Sounds good.” Vy decided to keep her sentences short.

“Do you want to go to the restroom with me?” Alexia asked Vy.

“Why do women need to go to the restroom in pairs? It’s a single-handed task.” Gunbar said.

“If you must know, there were two reasons why. We have someone to talk to when we’re in line, and we make sure we don’t walk out with tissue paper stuck under our heel.” Not waiting for a response from Gunbar, Vy simply walked away, guiding Alexia to the restroom.

On the way there, Vy told Alexia about the conversation she’d had with Kendra. “So, you couldn’t get any more information from her? You didn’t get to ask her who would want Ricky gone for good?”

“I’m sure there were a lot of people who didn’t want Ricky around. But I still can’t imagine someone wanting him gone for good.” Alexia pushed the restroom door open, but it wouldn’t budge. “I can’t push it all the way; it’s stuck.”

“Let me try. We both know you’re a little tipsy,” Vy said.

“Please, I can still push a door open.”

Vy pushed with all her body’s strength. She cracked the door just a tiny bit, and managed to squeeze herself into the restroom. Vy's scream would surpass Mariah Carey's highest note. There was Kendra, lying on the tiled floor in a puddle of blood. What was it with Vy, bars, and dead bodies?

TESTING 8

After two hours of being questioned by the Miami Police Department, Vy was ready to crash into bed. Alexia sobered up quickly after they found Kendra's body.

"What is it with you and dead people?" Gunbar said to Vy. She didn't want to admit that earlier she had asked herself that same question.

"Gunbar," Houston snapped, "Vy has nothing to do with what happened here tonight. Don't take out your frustrations on her."

Should Vy passionately kiss him now, or wait until he walked her to the door? The second option logically trumped the first. "Thank you," Vy simply said.

Vy and Alexia sat at the bar waiting for Houston and Gunbar to wrap up the interviews. While she watched Houston do his thing, Vy realized that he did everything sexy. He wrote sexy, he nodded sexy, even his eyebrows were sexy. Vy's trance was interrupted when Alexia hugged her.

"What was that for?" Vy asked.

"I don't want anything to happen to you. Lately, it does seem that wherever you go, well, there's a dead body. It turned out Ricky was murdered, and now Kendra was hit on the head with a heavy object. How am I not supposed to worry?"

"Nothing is going to happen to me. It's just bad timing on my part," Vy said.

"This horrific episode only motivates me to focus on our investigation. I know it sounds outlandish, but it's my duty to protect you. If it means getting down and dirty with Gunbar to get something out of him, then that's what I'll do."

"Down and dirty huh?" Vy said.

Alexia smiled then got serious. "I mean it, Vy. I just sent Adrianna a text. I asked her to research Ricky's background. I figured we should start there. But I need Kendra's last name, so we can start researching her as well."

"I don't know it, but I'll find out for you."

"But Vy—really, that's it?"

"That's it. I've always agreed with you. You're the rational one. Why wouldn't I trust your judgment?" She hugged Vy again.

"What are you two brewing up?" Gunbar asked.

Alexia stared him down, "Why would you ask that?"

"Because I've been a cop long enough to tell when a person has intentions."

"If you're so brilliant, then why is there another deceased person?" Alexia was the only one who could get away with using the term 'deceased,' instead of dead, solely for the respect of the recently departed.

"I think it's time to take you girls home," Gunbar scolded.

"Girls?"

"Houston," Vy yelled from the bar. He immediately called Gunbar over.

"He had the audacity to call us girls," Alexia said.

"Are you going to see him again?"

"Yes."

"That's what I thought," Vy said mockingly.

"For the obvious reason, of course. What about you, are you going to see Houston again?"

"I don't know. I don't even know if he's interested." Vy wanted to see Houston, but under different circumstances.

“He’s interested,” Alexia said giddily.

“How would you know?”

“I just do.”

“That’s the same line you used to use with me when I was a kid. Whenever I didn’t want to taste the food, you would say, ‘it’s good’. You hadn’t even tasted it, yet I fell for it every time.”

“Did you end up liking the food?”

“Touché,” Vy responded.

When Vy saw Houston walking in their direction, she was relieved that they could finally go home. The death of Ricky and now Kendra had really taken its toll on her.

“Are you all wrapped up?” Vy asked Houston trying to sound official, or so she thought. He was quiet for about one second, and for some unknown reason, Vy felt nervous.

“What’s wrong?” Alexia spoke the words Vy was hesitant to ask. Houston placed his hand on Vy’s shoulder, “We need to step outside for a minute; you and Alexia.”

Gunbar proceeded to follow them outside. Houston turned to him, “You stay here.”

“Of course,” Gunbar responded sarcastically, giving Vy a wicked smile.

The night was warm and breezy. It was one of those nights that Vy could sit outside her balcony, admiring the stars while strumming the tune of a love song.

Vy was ripped out of her reverie as soon as Houston said, “Someone left an anonymous note on the bar stating that they saw you go into the restroom.”

“I did, with Alexia. Hence, finding Kendra’s body.” Vy was defensive.

“No, Vy. The note stated that the person saw you follow Kendra into the restroom.”

"That's absurd, Houston! I didn't go near that restroom until I found her. Anonymous, great! So, it's my word against a ghostwriter who evidently knows who I am?"

"We sent the note to the lab to test it for fingerprints," Houston said.

Alexia was fuming. "So are you implying that Vy is responsible for Kendra's death based on this note?"

"Calm down, Alexia. I know that both of you are upset and shocked. I'm not implying anything. I wanted to give you a heads-up before—" Houston paused.

Vy took the lead, "Before the crap hits the fan? Is that what you were trying not to say?"

"Pretty much, Vy."

"So, what happens now?" Vy asked.

"We wait for the fingerprint results. We may have to question you further at the station. But I spoke to my Captain about waiting a day or two for that."

"Question, meaning I could actually be a suspect?" Vy felt her hands shake.

"You're not considered a suspect, more like a person of interest," Houston clarified.

"Being considered a person of interest does make me feel a whole lot better," Vy said sarcastically.

Houston stepped closer to Vy. "Listen, Vy, you asked me about my theory and here it is. Ricky was murdered because whatever it was he was working on backfired on him. Now, Kendra was found murdered, which makes me believe that these two murders are somehow connected. You unknowingly got in the middle of it. It's my job to find out what you got in the middle of and take you out of it. But there was a note left on the bar putting you in the time and place of Kendra's murder." Houston lowered his voice, "I know you didn't do it, Vy, but I can't be biased. Please understand that."

Vy felt her eyes well up. "I do understand."

"Don't worry; we'll get to the bottom of it."

"You bet your cute hiney, you will." Vy wanted to say that, but she just nodded. Houston patted her shoulder and walked back inside. Alexia took her into her arms and hugged her. Vy wanted to wake up from this never-ending nightmare.

Eventually, the four of them arrived at Vy's apartment. No words were exchanged on the way there. Houston and Gunbar walked Vy and Alexia to the door. Vy felt awkward trying to have a moment with her dream guy, when there were two other people standing next to her.

"Oh, Gunbar, I think I left my hair clip in the car. Can you walk me back to the car to find it?" Alexia took hold of his arm and dragged him away.

"I guess that's my cue," Houston said.

"Your cue for what?" Vy asked shyly. She knew she was blushing, and her body was losing its balance.

"My cue to kiss you good night."

And there it was, the perfect kiss. His lips were soft, and his breath, which she inhaled so effortlessly, was like an instrumental melody that flowed gracefully. His kiss was like the perfect song. But like every song, it came to an end. His lips disconnected from hers. Her body felt numb.

"Please play on—" Vy whispered with her eyes still closed.

"You're going to have to explain that one to me on our next date." Houston moved her hair from her face. "Vy, I don't want you to stress over this. I can imagine how terrible it's been for you. I'm still not used to being around dead people myself, so I can imagine how dreadful you feel. But I'll get you out of this mess. Now, do you have any questions for me?"

Vy was on the next date comment, and trying to recover from the kiss. "Just one."

Houston straightened his posture, and focused on Vy. "Shoot."

"Can I still call you by your last name although I know your first name?"

He flashed that Colgate smile and kissed her forehead, "Sure. Now get inside."

Alexia strolled in a few minutes later, and sat next to Vy on the couch. "He did a number on you."

"What? No, he didn't," Vy adamantly denied.

"Don't you start doing that."

"Doing what?"

"Acting cool and collected when you start to have feelings for someone. Let this one happen. He seems like an amazing man."

"I know," Vy said. She still felt his lips on hers.

For about three seconds, they stared off into oblivion. Quiet moments like these proved that they were related.

"You had a moment with Gunbar," Vy said.

"Of course, do you think that the hair clip scenario was all for you?"

"I'm glad you're staying over."

"Me too," Alexia said.

"What's step two of your plan?"

"I'm going to make coffee, you're going to get us two notepads, and we're going to start dissecting these two murders."

"I love your train of thought."

"I know. I practically raised you, remember?"

For the next hour, they were giggling on and off, jotting ideas down, and pigging out on chocolate chip cookies.

"Okay, what do you have?" Alexia asked.

"This is my list of potential suspects for Ricky's death." Vy ripped out the paper from the notepad. "Kyle, the doorman; and—I hate to say it—but Dave, the general manager of the Steel Horse Bar."

"That's more than I have. Actually, I don't have any suspects."

"I figured you wouldn't, but that's okay."

"Let's start with Kyle first. Why is he on your list?"

"Okay, two reasons. First reason, Kendra had mentioned that she'd told Kyle about Ricky and her. Evidently, he wasn't happy with them being together. And second is when Ricky was found dead, Kyle confessed to me that he really didn't care," Vy said remembering the tone of Kyle's voice.

"I would unquestionably have him on my list. Have you shared this information with Houston?" Alexia asked.

"Not yet. I don't want to jump to any conclusions. And I don't want to blame someone based on my own theories," Vy replied.

"You're right. I'm sure they'll question Kyle again. What about Dave?"

"Kyle mentioned to me that Ricky and Dave had been constantly arguing that night. This is more of a long shot than an accusation, but maybe Dave finally lost his cool. But then again, it turns out Dave left early because he wasn't feeling well. So, I just realized that suspect is a dead-end."

Alexia looked at Vy with pensive eyes. "What? What are you thinking?" Vy asked.

"Write this down. Step one; we need to do some research on Kyle. Do you have his number?"

"Yes."

"Okay, you need to call him and somehow find out about his relationship with Ricky and Kendra."

"Got it."

"Vy, you have to be extremely careful how you ask questions."

"I know; don't worry. We chat all the time."

"Step two; we need to research Ricky's life insurance policy, if he even had one. Maybe Dave somehow benefits from Ricky's death."

Alexia pulled out her cell phone from her purse, pressed a few keys, and put the cell phone back in her purse. "What was that about?" Vy asked.

"I sent Adrianna a text to call me as soon as she wakes up." Vy looked at her watch; it was already two thirty in the morning. "That's why I sent her a text," Alexia responded.

"I didn't say anything. How do you do that?"

"I know what you're thinking most of the time. We should go to bed; we have a long day ahead of us tomorrow."

"Don't you have to leave tomorrow?" Vy asked.

"I decided to take the week off from work. I needed it. The merger has been stressful. Besides, we haven't spent this much time together since we were kids."

Alexia was right; they were lacking sister time. Vy decided right then and there to e-mail her time-off request in tomorrow. She was aware what the employee handbook stated about vacation requests, and she'd only be giving her firm a day's notice, but saying that it's a family emergency should save her from losing her job. Technically, Vy wasn't lying. Needing some quality time with Alexia was a family emergency. But attempting to solve two murders in Vy and Alexia's one-week vacation was going to be a challenge. Vy missed playing with Barbie dolls on her days off from school.

TESTING 9

"Sunday Fun day! I brought bagels," Adrianna said wide-eyed. "And Dunkin Donuts coffee. I know that I can't come into the battlefield without it."

"Funny, ha-ha. Come on in, woman. I just love the smell of coconut coffee," Vy said, taking in the aroma.

Alexia was in the kitchen preparing breakfast. Once Adrianna placed her laptop on the dining room table, she went to the kitchen and Vy followed. Tina was sitting at the small coffee table watching Alexia. "You know, girls, all of you being in this tiny kitchen will not make the food cook any faster," Alexia said. She was flipping the bacon over in the skillet.

"Okay, call us when you're done," Vy said.

Fifteen minutes later, the four of them were sitting at the dining room table with their plates loaded with scrambled eggs, turkey bacon, and toast. Vy didn't even know she had this much food in her refrigerator.

"I went out this morning and bought groceries for you. You were completely out of everything," Alexia said.

"Thanks, that explains all the food."

The silence among them signified hunger. Finally, Adrianna typed in a few characters on her laptop, and shared her discoveries. "I was able to retrieve some information regarding Ricky and Kyle. Vy, thanks for getting me their last names."

"You're welcome," Vy said.

"Okay, let's start with Ricardo, also known as Ricky. He did have a life insurance policy. But Dave wasn't the one who benefited from it; Ricky's wife is the main beneficiary."

Vy briefly stopped chewing her bagel. "But Ricky was divorced. From what Kendra told me, the paperwork was finalized last week."

"No, he was still married."

"Holy crap," Vy said with a mouthful of bacon. She knew that speaking with your mouth full was rude, but this was an exception.

"After some extensive research, I found out that Ricky had his life insurance through American Life Insurance. It just so happens that I stumbled across the company's computer files."

"You stumbled upon this information, how convenient," Vy said. They giggled, and Adrianna continued.

"Ricky's wife's name is Margarite Chaster. Although Ricky lived here in Miami, her current address is in West Palm Beach. They were married, but not living together."

"That poses the question of whether it was an amicable separation," Vy said mainly to herself.

Tina finished chewing her bagel and said, "I'm going to see Kyle tonight; I'll probe him for information."

"You're going to see Kyle?" Vy said. She and Alexia briefly looked at each other.

"What's wrong?" Tina asked.

Tina's doe eyes had Vy feeling guilty. She didn't want to ruin her best friend's excitement with her theory that Kyle might be the bad guy. She didn't have any kind of evidence to implicate Kyle or anyone for that matter. Vy cleared her throat, "Nothing's wrong. It's just that I didn't know you two were dating."

"We've been casually dating for about a week. It's just with all this going on; I couldn't seem to find the right time to talk to you about it."

"Where are you going tonight?" Alexia asked

"To his place. He wanted to cook for me. Isn't that romantic?" Tina smiled.

Tina was happy and Vy wasn't about to burst her bubble. There was a sparkle in Tina's eyes that had been lacking for some time now. "Okay, but make sure that you call me first thing tomorrow morning to tell me how it went," Vy said.

"Yes, and if she doesn't answer, call me," Alexia added.

"You two are nosey, aren't you?" Tina asked.

Vy and Alexia's true intentions were to make sure that Tina got home safely after spending the night with a potential murderer. "Yes," Vy said, "extremely nosey."

"What else did you find out, Adrianna?" Alexia asked impatiently.

"Since we're on the subject," Adrianna looked at Tina, "I'm sorry to have to tell you this, but Kyle served one year in jail."

"I know," Tina said. "He assaulted a cop, and off he went to the slammer." And with that she continued to chew.

"What? You knew and you're still dating him?" Vy said.

"You kissed my boyfriend in fifth grade, and I'm still friends with you, aren't I? All I'm saying is that you can't justify who a person is by something they did a really long time ago."

"How long is really long?"

"When he was like eighteen or something."

Vy looked at Adrianna, and she gave Vy a nod of approval. "Okay, I get your point. I just worry about you is all."

"I know you do Vy."

"That's the only information I got on Kyle. Aside from that minor discrepancy, he's clean," Adrianna said.

"Okay, Tina, aside from enjoying your dinner, you know what to do."

"Yes, I do." Tina smirked.

"At least try to get a few words in tonight," Vy said sarcastically.

"I won't let you down," Tina winked.

"As for Kendra, unfortunately, I haven't been able to get any information on her."

"No problem, Adrianna. You did enough as it is," Vy said.

"That doesn't mean I'm giving up. This has officially become a challenge for me, and I will prevail," Adrianna said.

Vy was happy to have her closest friends and Alexia there with her. She just couldn't get over the fact that a dead man and a dead woman had brought them together for breakfast.

While Vy was taking a shower, she was going over the details in her head. Kyle was upset about Kendra and Ricky being together. Kendra thought that the divorce papers were finalized, but what if she found out they weren't and killed Ricky out of rage? But what was the reason Kendra was killed? Did she have something on Ricky? And how does Ricky's wife Margarite come into play? This thought process was giving Vy a headache. If Vy were Angela Lansbury, she would have tied up all the details in one hour. But unfortunately, this was reality and fortunately, Vy was not that old.

After Vy's shower, she lay in bed for a minute mentally exhausted. Vy's Sundays were usually her lazy days. But this past weekend's events had altered her agenda. Alexia knocked on the door, and cracked it opened, "Mom's on the phone."

"Did you tell her?" Vy whispered as she took the phone from Alexia.

"What do you think? Good luck," Alexia's ponytail hit Vy on the face as she walked away.

"Hi, mama."

"Violeta, how many times have I told you to be careful?"

"I am careful."

"Bueno, Alexia told me everything that has happened. That's doesn't sound like careful. You and Alexia are sleeping here, with me and your papa."

"No, mama. We are fine. I promise."

There was a slight pause, and then a sigh, "Okay, for now. But you and Alexia will have dinner with us tomorrow.

"Okay, mama."

"Te quiero."

"I love you too, Mom."

Vy placed the phone on the pillow, and lay back down for another minute.

Alexia knocked on the door, and let herself in. She sat on the bed next to Vy's head. She was fixing Vy's hair. "How did it go?" Alexia asked.

"I was able to get both of us out of sleeping at mom and dad's house, but we have to have dinner with them tomorrow."

"Oh good, that was easy."

"For you, you weren't the one being lectured at and sighed to."

"Hey, payback sucks. I did it for us a million times. So, get ready."

"Okay, I'll be right out."

"Well, hurry up." Alexia closed the bedroom door.

Vy decided to wear something comfortable. She put on loose-fitted blue jeans, a white t-shirt, and flip-flops. She looked in the mirror, and chose not to straighten her hair out with the flat iron. She wasn't trying to impress anyone today. She touched up her face up with a little bit of blush and lip gloss. As she walked out of the bedroom, she sprayed on her Pink perfume and headed to the living room.

"What's the rush?" Vy asked. She abruptly stopped walking, closed her eyes, and slowly opened them hoping that she was hallucinating. But Vy wasn't hallucinating; *he* was sitting on her couch petting Marilyn.

"Hi, Houston; what are you doing here?" Vy was slowly turning her attention to Alexia.

"I just wanted to stop by and see how you were doing."

"Fine, thanks. How long have you been here?"

"Ever since you stepped into the shower. I guess I was a few minutes late." Houston winked. "So, what kind of snooping are you two doing today?" Houston asked as he continued to pet Marilyn. Vy wanted to desperately switch places with her cat.

She joined him on the couch and placed Marilyn on the floor. "What gives you the idea that we're snooping?" Vy asked discreetly.

"Right. Well, then, I'll join you ladies today. I have the day off." He stood up and headed for the door.

"I don't think so," Alexia said. "You're only going to cramp our style. Who's going to want to talk to us with you hovering around looking like you want to beat someone up?"

"So, you are snooping?" Houston smiled. Vy was gazing at his gorgeousness. The words, "Right, Vy?" came slowly into her hearing spectrum. "Right?"

"Right, Alexia."

"Alright, ladies; be careful. Call me if you need me." When Houston left, Vy remained on the couch. She was waiting for her heart to start beating at a normal pace.

"You could have told me Alexia."

"What? And miss that look on your face. Not a chance."

Vy went to the kitchen and poured herself another cup of coffee. "By the way, you look great."

Alexia was standing at the doorway of the kitchen entrance. She was wearing a black business suit, with a white collared satin blouse underneath the jacket. Her hair was straighter than usual, and her make-up was impeccable. She carried her black, leather briefcase in one hand and a bottle of Zephyr Hills water in the other. She saw the look of bewilderment on Vy's face and simply responded with, "Get your iPod, Vy; we're going on a road trip. I'll explain on the way there."

"Should I change?"

"No, you look perfect to be my personal driver and assistant for the day."

"And where is it that I'm driving you to?"

"West Palm Beach."

*****

"So, how are you going to introduce yourself to Margarite?"

"I don't have a strategy yet, but by the time we get there, I will."

"It's Sunday; do you think she'll buy whatever it is you're selling, Alexia?"

"I'll tell her that it was imperative to get the paperwork in by Monday morning."

Obviously, this plan of attack worried Vy. After an hour and a half of driving north on I-95 it was too late to turn back. Vy and Alexia were two exits away from finding out or not finding out anything. Alexia was reapplying her lipstick, "Do you think this pink-colored lipstick makes my skin look pale? I'm going for the fresh look."

"It doesn't really compliment your skin color or your facial features."

"I knew you'd be honest. You always did know more about make-up and fashion than I did. Do you have that reddish lipstick in your purse?"

Being that Vy always looked up to Alexia, her comment had her smiling inside, "Yes, side pocket."

When they exited the expressway, Vy's nerves started to kick in. Her bladder was signaling to her brain that the holding it in method wasn't going to last long. "Alexia, I have to pull into the BK. I really have to go the restroom."

"Okay, but hurry. We're in a time crunch."

Vy pulled into the BK's parking lot, parked, and left the car running, so that "Crash Into Me" by the Dave Matthews Band would keep Alexia preoccupied.

Alexia yelled out from the car, "Can you please get me a Coke Slurpee?"

Vy finally relieved herself, washed her hands, and made her way to the register. Standing before her was a sixteen-year-old, pimpled faced boy, with neon-colored braces. He was wearing the BK logo hat and t-shirt. Vy couldn't help but stare and wonder what had gone wrong. "Ma'am, can I take your order?"

"Can I please have a Coke Slurpee?"

"Make that two, and large fries please," shouted a man's voice giving the back of Vy's neck goose bumps.

When she turned around, Houston was giving her his Colgate smile. "What are you doing here? Alexia is going to freak out if she sees you."

"I made sure she didn't see me come in. Besides, a man can eat wherever he pleases."

"So, you're telling me that you drove two hours for a Slurpee and large fries from this particular BK?" Vy asked.

"I heard this particular BK is rated number one in the nation," Houston said with a smirk.

"That will be five twenty-seven," the pimple-faced boy said to Vy.

"Please, let me." Houston took out his wallet, pulled out a ten-dollar bill, handed it to the boy and waited for his change. Houston had his wallet opened and she saw his badge. Even though she didn't care for police officers, to feel protected from the uncertainties of this world, she had to believe in the badge.

He suddenly closed his wallet. "Don't look at the picture. It was taken a long time ago, and I've been too lazy to get the photo updated." Before she could tell him what she was really thinking, Vy heard a car horn going ballistic in the parking lot. Alexia was getting edgy. "I have to go. Please don't let Alexia see you leave. She's going to think that I asked you to come."

"No worries. Go do what you have to do. I'll be incognito," Houston reassured her.

"Something's up. How come you haven't schooled me on my snooping?"

"Because if I tell you and your sister to stay out of it, you're going to do the opposite. Besides, maybe you can get something out of Margarite that we won't be able to get tomorrow."

"How did you know that's where we were headed?" Houston answered with his eyes.

"Right, you're the professional," Vy said.

"Exactly. But I figured you can't get into trouble talking to her."

The honking of the horn commenced. "I really have to go." Vy waved good bye and headed to the exit. Houston called out to her. She immediately turned around, "Yes?"

"You know, if you want to be a detective, one of the first rules is to make sure that no one is tailing you."

"Noted." She proceeded to walk to the exit door feeling sexy. That was until she pushed the one side of the door that didn't open. Why torture your customers with double doors if one door was always going to be locked? There went her sexy Natalie Imbruglia moment.

"What took you so long? Isn't it supposed to be fast food, right away, your way? Or something like that?" Alexia asked impatiently.

"Okay Miss Walking Billboard. There was a long line. Here's your Slurpee. Did you think of a plan yet?"

"Yes. Adrianna gave me a copy of Ricky's life insurance policy. I reviewed it, and it seems that Margarite gets a hefty sum."

"I don't want to know, but I do. What's the hefty sum?"

"One million dollars."

Vy slammed on the brakes. "Holy crap, Lexi, that's motive right there! Why didn't Houston or Gunbar pick up on that?"

"Be careful. I almost spilled coke on my suit. And I don't know why they haven't questioned her. Or maybe they did," Alexia said.

Vy already knew the answer to that. "Yesterday, I was able to get in contact with an agent from the life insurance company. I called on behalf of Ms. Chaster."

"Let me guess? You were Margarite's attorney?"

"Bingo. When a life insurance company hears the word *attorney*, they tell you anything and everything, just to get you off the phone quickly."

"You're keeping me in suspense. What happened?" Vy asked.

"It turns out that Margarite didn't sign the insurance forms that granted her the one million dollars. Ricky overrode her signature, and granted it to her anyway."

"So, Margarite had no idea about the money?"

"Maybe, maybe not. That's what we must find out. I also need to see a copy of Ricky's will, if he even had one. We need to find out about the bar."

"What makes you think that Margarite would have a copy of his will?"

"It's a guess at this point," Alexia speculated.

Vy was getting a headache. Her stomach felt nauseous. She felt like she was about to perform in front of fifteen thousand people at Madison Square Garden for the first time. She visualized it. Vy was the opening act for Matchbox Twenty. She was standing on this huge stage, with her guitar in hand. Her fingers were trembling with the anticipation of strumming that first chord. The lights were dim, acknowledging the silhouettes of the people that were there for the concert. Then suddenly, the bright lights came on. There were now fifteen thousand people silently staring at her. She tried to sing, but nothing came out.

"Snap out of it, Vy. You're having that Madison Square Garden anxiety daydream again."

"I can't help it, Alexia. This is insane. I'm not willing to go to jail to get a hundred-dollar gig back."

"First, this became personal the moment you were labeled a person of interest. Second, Houston or Gunbar would not let you go to jail. And third, just follow my lead," Alexia explained.

"I can't believe I'm saying this. Tell me the rest of your plan."

"Great! While I'm conversing with Margarite, you're going to be looking around her house for clues."

"You want me to sneak around her house! You have officially lost it."

"When I signal you by dropping my pen, you ask to go to the restroom. You accidently get lost on the way, and, voila, you have a rational explanation if you get caught. Oh, turn left here."

They arrived at a high-end residential neighborhood, reminding Vy of the movie, *The Truman Show*. All the houses were identical, with stucco roofs painted white, each with perfectly trimmed hedges. All that was missing were the white picket fences. One house had a Maserati parked in the driveway. Another house had a white, brand new 325i BMW. Vy dreamed of that extravagant life brought upon by her music career.

"Here it is, 523 Hemmershee Street." They pulled into Margarite's driveway. Alexia turned to Vy, "Are you ready?"

"No."

"Great, let's go."

Margarite's house differed from the others. Architecturally, it was remarkably unified. It had red roof tiling; the windows were long and rectangular shaped, opening towards the outside. The landscape was beautiful, with matured palms and rose bushes along the sidewalk entrance. Her home was *Dwell* magazine beautiful.

Margarite's neighbor to the left was a sixty-something-year-old man, who had a Frank Sinatra resemblance. He was waxing his Harley Davidson motorcycle. He flashed his perfectly false teeth in their direction, and gave a head nod hello. Vy smiled and waved.

Vy and Alexia walked up to an arched door. She looked over her shoulder and saw a dark blue, 1967 hardtop Mustang parked alongside the street. Vy knew that an amazingly hot detective was sitting in that amazingly hot car.

"Okay, you know the plan," Alexia whispered as she rang the doorbell.

"Ten-four, captain," Vy saluted her.

"Shush, be serious." Alexia rang the doorbell once more.

A dog started barking from inside the house. Vy envisioned the final moments of her life being mauled by a Rottweiler. A Hispanic Eva Longoria lookalike answered the door. She was wearing a light blue maid outfit and her hair was in a ponytail.

"Hello, how may I help you?" Eva said with a heavy Spanish accent. Her voice was so faint; Vy barely understood what she asked. Vy was relieved to see that the dog sitting next to the maid was a Shih Tzu.

"Good afternoon, I'm attorney Roberta Thomas, and this is my assistant Gwen. We're here to see Ms. Chaster," Alexia said.

"One moment please." The maid closed the door.

"Roberta Thomas and Gwen, really?"

"I forgot about the fictitious name part. It was the only name that I could think of at the last minute. Besides, I thought you would be happy. It's the female version of Rob Thomas. And who wouldn't want to be named after Gwen Stefani?"

The door opened again, and the maid let them in. "Please, follow me."

The interior of the house was as fascinating as the exterior. There were Spanish tiled floors that highlighted the entire house. The maid walked them through a grand entry hall, which led to the living room. The chandelier resembled continuous falling rain drops.

The palm leaf ceiling fans added the touch of a Spanish villa. The home was a combination of southern and modern living.

"Please take a seat. Ms. Chaster will be right with you." Vy carefully sat down on the very expensive looking white couch, which seemed to be consumed by a thousand throw pillows.

"Thank you," Vy and Alexia said at the same time.

Alexia snapped opened her briefcase and pulled out some documents. "Courtesy of Adrianna." Alexia smiled proudly.

"I thought you weren't coming until tomorrow?" Margarite looked like a younger version of Elizabeth Taylor. She was stunning. Her facial features were flawless. Even if it was from the miracle of plastic surgery, Vy gasped at the first site of her.

Alexia rose from the couch. "I apologize for the confusion. I was under the impression that my secretary called to reschedule for today."

"I didn't receive any messages regarding the appointment." Margarite spoke with authority. Vy could tell that Margarite was an intelligent, sophisticated woman. Why would she end up with a man like Ricky?

"Again, my apologies, but it's critical to have the documents in by Monday morning. But if you'd like, we can return first thing tomorrow." Alexia sounded so professional. Alexia collected her briefcase and turned towards the door to leave, and Vy followed suit.

"No, let's get this over with. Please have a seat," Margarite directed.

"Thank you."

"I'm surprised you work on Sundays."

"I was in the area this weekend. It worked to my advantage," Alexia said.

"Tell me where to sign." Margarite took a seat on the couch adjacent to Vy and Alexia.

"I'm sorry to be so blunt, but you don't seem very upset about your loss."

"He hasn't been my husband for many years." Margarite looked at Vy then at Alexia. "And she is?"

Before Vy could answer, Alexia answered for her, "She's my intern and driver for today. I hope you don't mind. She wanted to learn from the best."

"That's fine," Margarite addressed Vy. "Sorry that you're not taking on a more intriguing case. So, where were we?" Margarite asked Alexia. Alexia dropped her pen and Vy knew that was her cue.

"Excuse me, may I use your restroom?" Vy meekly asked.

Elena? Elena?" Margarite sounded exasperated. "She's never around when I need her. The restroom is down the hall, second door to your right. You can see yourself there."

"Thank you." Vy headed towards that direction. The left side of the hallway had stunning oil paintings of landscapes, sunsets, and horses. The right side of the hallway was bland, except for the hooks from where the pictures or paintings used to hang.

There was a door slightly opened on Vy's right hand side. She peeked in. It seemed to be an office. "Here goes nothing." She slowly pushed the door open enough for her to slide in. Her stomach growled. She didn't know if it was because she was nervous or because she hadn't eaten anything since this morning.

It was an office and a library. The left-hand side of the room had built-in cedar shelves. The smell of the cedar wood and the old books was overwhelming. She closed her eyes and took in the scent. She quickly opened her eyes. "Focus, Vy," she murmured to herself.

There was a cherry wooden desk located in the center of the room. Vy hesitantly walked over to it. "What a mess," she whispered to herself. She began skimming through scattered letters, bills, and miscellaneous receipts. Nothing seemed to be out of the ordinary. But then again, she didn't know what she was looking for. On the right-hand corner of the desk, lay an opened checkbook. "I guess she's not too worried about privacy. Look at me. She's not worried because I'm not suppose be in here. Why do I keep talking to myself?" This whole snooping idea didn't work well with her personality.

As she scanned through the checkbook, she quickly calculated that once a week, a five-hundred-dollar check was made payable to cash. It couldn't be for the housekeeper because there were weekly checks made out to Elena's name. She suddenly heard a sound in the hallway. She quietly placed the checkbook down, walked briskly to the door, and slid out. Vy now faced Elena, who was staring blankly at her.

"I was looking for the restroom. I guess this wasn't it," Vy said. She chuckled, hoping that Elena didn't catch on to her lie.

"Don't worry; it happens all the time. I won't tell Ms. Chaster. She gets very angry lately." Elena's English was rough, but Vy did her best to follow.

"Has she had a lot of visitors recently?"

"This way please. Yes, I don't know who they are, but when they leave, she is very angry."

"Here you are." Elena had led Vy to the restroom. But by this time, she really needed to go.

"Thank you, Elena. By the way, where are you from?"

"I from Brazil."

"So, you speak Portuguese?"

"Yes, ma'am." She bowed her head and walked away.

Vy eventually made her way back to the living room. Margarite was signing a document.

"Ms. Chaster, I appreciate your time. I apologize if today was inconvenient for you," Alexia stated in an apologetic tone.

"Actually, you were a lot easier to work with compared to the previous lawyers Ricky had contracted. As I mentioned earlier, he wasn't an easy client to work for," Alexia said.

"Thank you, Ms. Thomas. Should you have any additional questions, or need any further information, feel free to contact me directly. It was truly a pleasure to work with you." Vy was astounded that Alexia had pulled it off.

"Thank you," Alexia said and shook Margarite's hand.

Elena came from the hallway. "I walk you out."

Margarite also followed them out. She had a neutral expression on her face. Elena opened the door, and Vy and Alexia were on their way out when Margarite stopped them, "Wait."

Vy and Alexia turned around. Vy felt her palms sweating. No need to call the cops, there was one already outside ready to take them into custody.

"Yes?" Alexia asked casually.

"Do you have a business card? I wanted to get a new lawyer, and I think you would be ideal."

"Unfortunately, I ran out of business cards. I placed a reprint order. But I'll be more than happy to have my intern mail you a few when I receive them," Alexia adlibbed.

"That would be splendid. Thank you again. Drive safely."

"Thank you. Have a great day," Alexia said pleasantly.

As Vy and Alexia were making their way back to the car, she noticed that Houston was no longer parked alongside the street. After a speedy departure, Vy reached the stop sign and looked at Alexia. "Let's eat, I'm famished!" Alexia simply said.

TESTING 10

"I feel like Italian. Is that okay with you?" Alexia asked.

"You're not going to tell me anything until we get to the restaurant, are you?"

Alexia was looking at herself in her compact mirror. She snapped it shut. "Nope."

They found a charming Italian restaurant in a shopping center called The Red Snapper. They sat at a table far from the entrance. Alexia needed a pair of Jackie O. sunglasses, and a shawl that wrapped around her face to complete her undercover look.

The waitress immediately came to wait on them. "Welcome to Pazianno's. What would you ladies like to drink?"

"May we please have a bottle of the Frances Coppola Merlot and two glasses of water, no ice? Thank you." The waitress nodded and walked away.

"Okay, spill it, Alexia."

"Not until we order. I don't want anyone overhearing our conversation, and I don't want any interruptions." Vy looked around and realized that they were the only ones in the restaurant. Either Alexia was going blind, or she was being paranoid. Vy chose the latter of the two. They placed their order, chit-chatted about various things, and their food finally arrived. Alexia took one bite, swallowed and started talking.

"Evidently, Margarite found out yesterday that she was the sole beneficiary of the policy. She stated that at first, she was very upset by the fact that Ricky had gone over her authority. But then it occurred to her that she, quote, 'deserved every penny for putting up with that asshole', end quote."

"That's if she's telling you the truth."

"Let me finish," Alexia continued. "Anyway, it just so happened that she had a copy of Ricky's will. It turned out that Ricky's actual attorney's assistant mailed the copy to her on his behalf. I had to think of a quick way to get a copy."

"So, what did you say?" Vy asked curiously.

"I said that my intern, you, mailed the only copy we had in the office. Margarite said she understood how amateurs worked, and she willingly gave me a copy."

"Thanks, Lexi. Now Margarite thinks I'm incompetent. I wonder why Ricky was so concerned about Margarite having a copy of all his documentation. Usually, it's the other way around."

"I was wondering the same thing," Alexia confirmed.

Vy and Alexia took a quick break from speaking to eat their spaghetti and take a sip of the wine. "I briefly looked at the will, and Margarite inherits the Steel Horse Bar as well."

"Alexia, she has to be the murderer. It's so obvious!"

"Keep your voice down. Anyway, Margarite asked me to draft up a deed transferring the bar over to Dave," Alexia said.

"This is as strange as an episode of the *Twilight Zone*."

Vy heard the theme song playing in her head. The narrator appeared, dressed in a pristine, black suit. He began with the introduction to the episode: The year is 2017. Picture this—a scorned wife, a dead husband, and a dead mistress. Who did it, and why? Was the general manager in cahoots with the wife? Was it—"

"Vy, are you listening to me?"

"Yes. Sorry. Continue," Vy said, snapping out of her *Twilight Zone* sequence.

"Margarite wants nothing to do with the bar. She didn't want anything to do with Ricky period. Margarite said that Dave primarily ran the bar, plus he handled the accounting, the hiring and firing of employees, booking the bands, etcetera. She stated that Ricky would only show up to drink. It just made sense to her to leave the bar to Dave."

"Wow," Vy said.

All this information was overwhelming to Vy. She didn't know why Kendra was involved, or her for that matter. Vy assumed that someone must have seen Kendra speaking to her at the jazz bar the other night, and figured she now knew something that could incriminate him or her. Vy had many assumptions but no concrete answers.

"How did it turn out on your end?" Alexia asked.

"I don't think that I came across anything that would be relevant to the investigation."

"You never know. Think," Alexia said.

Vy told Alexia about the office, and explained what had happened with Elena. "Elena mentioned people were visiting Margarite, and apparently she wasn't very happy with the visits."

"Do you think that has anything to do with the drug trafficking allegations? Maybe they were looking for Ricky. Maybe Margarite is in on it. Maybe Margarite was being threatened. Maybe—"

"Maybe we're jumping to conclusions. Houston doesn't even know if the drug trafficking allegation is concrete," Vy explained.

"Dang it. I thought we were on to something."

"I'm sure the police department was on to it way before we jumped to these crazy conclusions. We're good, but we're not that good."

"Thanks for spoiling the moment."

"Anytime. Oh, there were weekly checks made out to cash in the amount of five hundred dollars."

"Hmm, the weekly checks could be Elena's paycheck."

"No, there were checks made out to her name. So those checks for cash could be for anything. So basically, I got nothing," Vy said disappointingly.

"You don't know that yet," Alexia said.

"I'm glad that Margarite warmed up to you, Lexi."

"She said she enjoyed working with a strong independent woman like herself." They started to laugh. "She's got that right," Vy said in the middle of her snorting.

When the laughter ceased, reality set in, "Where do we go from here, Lexi? Whoever did this, wants me to go down. I'm getting scared. Don't you think that we're in way over our heads trying to take on this investigation on our own?"

"I know that you're perplexed, but I don't want you to be scared. What we did today was a step forward to an answer. We just have to figure out what the question is."

"I guess we should call Houston and tell him what we found out," Vy said.

"But then he'll know what we've been up to."

"Well, he already knows." Vy told Alexia about the run-in she'd had with Houston earlier that afternoon at the Burger King.

"I figured something like that would happen." Alexia tapped on her right breast, "It's a good thing that I used my listening device to record the meeting. Isn't that exciting?"

Vy just smiled at Alexia. She knew that Alexia somehow had this situation under control. At least that's what Vy wanted to believe. It was called positive thinking.

*****

Vy and Alexia arrived at the apartment late that afternoon. "You want to watch a scary movie since it's raining?"

"Great idea. I'll go make the popcorn," Alexia said.

They found a B-rated flick on Netflix and situated themselves on the couch with Marilyn in between.

"Do you hear that?" Alexia paused the movie.

"No. What?" Vy said with a mouthful of popcorn.

"That," Alexia pointed to one of the dining room table chairs.

"Oh, my phone's vibrating." Vy got up and retrieved her phone from her purse. She didn't recognize the number, but answered it anyway, "Hello?"

"Hi, Vy; this is Shawn. The bar back from the Steel Horse Bar?"

"Hey! How are you?"

"Fine, thanks. I hope you don't mind, but I asked Dave for your number," Shawn explained.

"No, I don't mind at all."

Alexia looked at Vy and mouthed, "Who is it?"

Vy covered the receiver and whispered, "Shawn."

Alexia nodded in agreement and continued watching the movie.

"Vy?"

"Yes, Shawn; I'm sorry."

"I hope that I didn't interrupt anything."

"No, it's okay. I was watching a movie with my sister," Vy said.

"Great. Well, I called to ask you for a favor."

"Shoot."

"Have you heard of the new venue, Sugar Shack?" he asked.

"Yeah, evidently it's a difficult venue for a band to get into. I submitted our press kit to the manager last week. But who knows."

"Tell me about it. My band, the Steller's, have been trying to get in for at least three months. But luckily their house band canceled, and they called us to fill in and to test us out. That's the good news. The bad news is that our lead singer is out of town. Do you think you can fill in for her tonight?" Shawn asked. "We know all the songs you do with your band. It should be a piece of cake for you."

"Sure, that sounds like fun. What time do I have to be there?"

"Awesome! By nine. All you have to do is walk on to the stage. We'll be set up by the time you get there."

"Great, I'll see you there."

"Thanks again. Oh, and bring your sister and friends. I know it's a Sunday night, but the more people, the better we look. But of course, you already knew that."

"Alright, see you there. Bye."

Vy felt a rush of excitement. "I have a gig tonight," she told Alexia.

Alexia got up from the couch and hugged Vy. "Great! What should I wear?"

"Anything looks good on you. The question is what should I wear?" Vy headed straight to her closet.

A couple of hours later, Vy and Alexia stood in front of the mirror admiring each other. "Gosh we look good," Alexia said.

"Yes, we do. Are you ready to go?"

"I sure am. I can't wait to see people fall off their bar stools once you start to sing."

"Thanks, Lexi."

"No, I mean it. That's why Shawn called you. He knows you're a great performer and singer. By the way,

I invited—" Vy heard a knock on the door. Alexia's face glowed immediately.

"Let me guess. Houston and Gunbar?" Vy said.

"I'll get it," Alexia said. She walked briskly to the door with the speed of the Road Runner.

When Vy walked out to the living room, Houston and Gunbar were standing by the door.

"Wow," Houston said immediately. Gunbar echoed his comment as he stared at Alexia.

"Why, thank you, Detective Houston. I can say the same about you."

"Let's go, beautiful ladies. The chariot waits," Houston said.

*****

The first set seemed to go by a lot faster than usual. Vy was surprised by the crowd's positive feedback. Tina and Adrianna were seated by the stage.

Vy stepped off stage, and Shawn followed behind her. "That rocked, Vy! What a rush, huh?"

"Completely. Thank you again for thinking of me to fill in."

"I've been doing that a lot—thinking of you, that is. This gave me the perfect opportunity to see you again."

Vy was completely speechless. She felt her skin getting warm. Shawn kissed her cheek and walked away. "And what was that little exchange?" Tina said to the back of Vy's head.

"Tina, you scared the crap out of me!"

"Sorry. Okay, so what was that?" Tina asked again.

"I honestly don't know."

"Alrighty then." Tina smirked. "By the way, I spoke to Kyle."

"Great, let's go sit and you can tell us about it."

Vy and Tina joined Alexia, Houston, Gunbar, and Adrianna. Vy sat next to Houston. He leaned in, grabbed her hand and whispered in her ear, "You really do look and sound amazing." He gently kissed her forehead and leaned back.

Houston's kiss caused Vy's pulse to race, but Shawn's kiss had just had the same effect on her.

"Sweetie," Alexia addressed Gunbar, "would you be so kind as to bring us girls a few cocktails?" Alexia brushed her hand over Gunbar's.

"My pleasure." He flashed a smile at Alexia. "You should go with him, Houston. That's a lot of drinks to carry at once."

"I'll be right back, rock star." Houston whispered in Vy's ear.

Tina's voice interrupted Vy's train of thought. "Are you ready?"

"What?"

"Are you ready?" Tina asked for the second time.

"Yes, tell us what happened with Kyle. By the way, you forgot to call me when you returned from your date."

"She called me. Sorry, I forgot to tell you," Alexia said.

"Hurry up, girls, before they come back," Adrianna said. They wanted to stay incognito about their conversation.

"Kyle doesn't know anything about Ricky's personal life. The only thing he did mention was that Ricky and Kendra were dating. That's it. Kyle mainly kept to himself about what happened that night. I didn't want to push it, so I didn't ask any more questions."

Vy recalled the twinkle in Kyle's eyes when he'd looked at Kendra that night. Maybe Kyle somehow found out that Kendra and Ricky were planning to elope, and he became so upset by it, that he killed Ricky, or maybe even Kendra, out of rage. Vy shook her ill thoughts away. Kyle didn't seem like the hostile type, or was he?

"Tina, one more question. Do you remember his facial expression when he spoke to you about Ricky and Kendra?"

"He wasn't looking at me. He was cooking while he was talking to me about it. Why?"

"Just wondering," Vy said.

"An Apple Martini for the rock star, and three Malibu and pineapple drinks for the beautiful groupies," Gunbar said with flourish, putting the drinks on the table.

"Thanks, boys," Adrianna said, as she took her drink from Gunbar.

Houston sat closer to Vy. "I have to go back on. Thanks for the martini." Vy didn't even know if it was time to take the stage, but she had to escape somehow.

*****

As Vy was putting away her tambourine, Shawn approached her. "Not bad for not rehearsing as a band. You're a pro," Shawn said.

"You guys aren't bad yourselves. You guys followed me really well." Vy was moving the microphone stand out of the way. "You're easy to follow. I'm going to finish packing up." Shawn smiled.

Vy felt a sense of accomplishment when people approached her to tell her how much fun they enjoyed her singing. A cute playboy bunny-like woman stood in front of Vy's boobs, and flashed a big smile.

"Thanks for singing 'Happy Birthday' to my husband. He definitely enjoyed you rubbing his bald head." She started giggling.

"It was my pleasure," Vy replied.

"So, when do you guys come back?"

"Oh, I'm not with this band. I was just filling in for tonight. You might want to ask the guitarist when they're coming back."

"That's disappointing. You're fun. Well, thanks again." She waved goodbye and walked away.

Houston came up from behind Vy and put his muscular arms around her waist. "What was that?" he asked softly in her ear. She was lost in thought. His arms around her body immobilized her verbally. He must have felt the slight tension. "I'm sorry. Is this too much?"

Vy turned around, and faced his masculine, sexy face. She wanted to tell him exactly what she was thinking. "I, uh. You see, it's that—" Tina walked over to Vy and Houston. "You were awesome tonight!"

"Thanks, Tina."

"I'll leave you two to chat," Houston said, looking disappointed. "I'm going to get a drink. Vy, Tina, would you like anything?"

"No thanks," Tina said. Vy nodded no.

"I'm sorry, Vy, did I interrupt something?"

Vy was somewhat relieved that Tina had appeared when she had. She needed to get a hold of what she was feeling. "No, Tina, everything is cool."

"Right." Tina said.

Shawn approached them. "Vy, thanks for filling in tonight. You're a lifesaver. I've only heard great things."

"You're going to have to stop thanking me. Like I said, it was my pleasure."

"I was buttering you up for this next favor that I'm going to ask of you. Although the gig went great, there is a slight problem."

"What's that? We're not getting paid tonight?" Vy laughed at her own joke, which she often did.

"No, the venue wants us back next Friday."

"That's great! Why would that be a problem?"

"Because they'll only book us for next Friday, if you're the one singing."

"Did you tell the owner that I was only a fill-in?"

"Yes, I did. But that's what he said. He needs to know by tomorrow first thing. He has a lot of bands lined up. I really don't want to lose this gig. But I would totally understand if you can't do it."

The problem wasn't if Vy could do the gig, it was the loyalty she had to her own band. Vy would have to get their blessing first, and make sure they didn't have a gig themselves.

"Let me touch base with my band, and I'll let you know tomorrow, hopefully, in the morning."

"Thanks, Vy."

Tina put her arm around Vy's shoulder, "You're in high demand, my friend. Don't stress. I'm sure the boys will be fine with you filling in one more time. And Adrianna won't care at all."

Vy sent a mass e-mail through her iPhone informing her band about the gig. She didn't want to forget to do it the next day. She knew the boys would be fine with her filling in because they weren't booked on that Friday, and Vy had no intention of quitting of her band. It was time for her to go home. She went looking for Shawn to bid her goodbyes.

Vy went up to one of the other band members. "Do you know where Shawn is?"

"He's probably out back loading the gear into the trailer."

"Thanks."

Vy went outside but didn't see Shawn by the trailer. She faintly heard his voice coming from behind the wall of the building. It appeared he was talking to another person. "I know what I said man. Give me a little more time. It's not that simple."

The other person's response was more of a mumble. Vy was making her way closer to the two voices, when the drummer came outside.

"Sorry Vy, I got to get through." The poor guy was carrying all the drum cases at once.

"You need help, Ned?"

"No, but is it possible you can order a beer for me before last call?"

"Sure." Vy walked back inside wanting to know what that secret conversation was about. Who was Shawn was talking to? What was going to take time? What was not simple? So many questions were running through her head. She went to the bar to order Ned's beer. Alexia joined her.

"Spill it," Alexia said bluntly.

"Spill what?" Vy knew what Alexia was referring to.

"I can read it in your eyes. What's going on?"

Vy finally gave in. "Shawn was talking to someone outside—rather suspiciously."

"Vy, don't let your imagination get carried away. Maybe it sounded suspicious because of what's happening. Not everyone can be a suspect. Now, what else?"

"Nothing else," Vy replied too quickly.

Alexia lovingly stared at her, and Vy gave in once more, "Fine. Houston is what else. I don't want to rush it."

"Him putting his arm around you is rushing it."

"How did you know?"

"I just do. Don't over analyze it, like you normally do. Now go talk to that hunk of a man and do what you do best."

"What is that?" Vy asked smiling.

"Charm the pants off him. Well, not literally. At least not yet." Alexia stood up from the bar stool. "I have a little charming to do myself. Let's meet at the entrance in about twenty minutes. I'm exhausted."

"Okay."

Vy agreed with what Alexia said. It wasn't as if Houston and Vy were exclusively dating. He was just being affectionate. But was Houston aware that she wanted to keep her options open? Did Vy want to keep her options open? She had no idea what she wanted. "Just take it one day at a time," she said to herself.

After giving Ned his beer, Vy looked around for Houston. She spotted him talking to a drop dead gorgeous brunette. Go figure. Vy had hesitated for one second and he'd moved on.

She walked over to him anyway. She didn't feel intimidated, yet. When she approached them, the brunette was laughing at something Houston had said.

"Hi, there," Vy hesitantly said.

"Hey," Houston said. "Vy, this is Amy. She's an old friend of mine."

"It's nice to meet you, Amy."

"You were great tonight. Houston told me how talented you were, but I was honestly blown away." As Amy was speaking, she was rubbing Houston's chest with her index finger. For Vy to restrain herself from knocking Amy out, Vy tuned her out, nodded, and smiled politely.

Suddenly, a drop dead gorgeous redhead came up to them and stood next to Amy. "Are you kidding me?" Vy said under her breath.

"Houston, Vy, this is my girlfriend Melinda."

Vy's shoulders dropped. "Girlfriend? As in you two are a couple?" The model-like women started laughing. Houston smiled at Vy, and stepped a little closer to where she was standing.

Amy looked at Houston. "You're right, she is adorable. It was nice to meet you." Amy and Melinda gave Houston and Vy a kiss on the cheek and left. Houston looked at Vy and said with a smirk, "You do care."

Vy smacked him on the chest. “Uh. Men!”

TESTING 11

Alexia finally let Vy sleep in. Marilyn was lying at the foot of the bed. The sunlight crept in through her thin, wooden horizontal blinds. She felt well rested. "When It's Over" from Sugar Ray was blasting in the living room. What a sweet sound to wake up to. Vy headed to where the music was blaring from.

Alexia was on the floor using Vy's Ball Bender. "This little green ball is amazing! I can feel it in my abs already."

"I'm glad that you like it. I haven't used it in a few weeks. I have to start back up again."

"I—made—you—a—sandwich. It's—in—the—oven." Alexia exhaled after every word.

"Lexi, you're spoiling me. I'm not going to want you to leave."

"Enjoy it while you can."

Vy went to the restroom and prepared herself a bubble bath. She soaked herself in the bubbles pondering last night. Houston was such a sexy, smart, affectionate gentleman, with a rewarding profession. What was there not to like about him? But at the same time, Shawn made her feel weird, but in a good way. He was a musician, and even though she didn't date her own kind, it felt nice being able to talk to someone who knew what she was talking about. Vy kind of liked the mystery about Shawn. Houston, on the other hand, laid all his cards on the table. She felt as though she'd known him for years, even though it had only been a few days.

There was a knock on the restroom door. "Come in."

Alexia walked in with a cup of coffee. "I thought you drowned in here. Here, I brought you coffee, although it's already past noon."

"Thanks. It smells great."

"I buy the same coffee you do, but for some reason, it doesn't smell this good in my house." Alexia said, "Isn't that weird?"

"No, it's the same with an Apple Martini. It tastes better when it's made at a bar, than when you make it at home."

Alexia laughed. "You always seem to agree with me."

"That's because to me, you always make sense, even when you think you don't."

Alexia placed the coffee mug on the floor next to the tub. "I'll be in the living room. Hurry up; I don't want you to wrinkle." She started to close the door. "By the way, Houston called. He said he had something important to tell us regarding the case."

"Thanks." Vy's mind was not even on the case; it was on her love life, if she could call it that.

Vy didn't have anywhere to go, but she wanted to dress up anyway. When she finished getting ready, she went to the kitchen to eat her sandwich. Alexia popped up behind her. "Don't eat that sandwich. I decided to take you out to lunch and have a few martinis. What can I say; you got me in the mood with that theory of yours. Oh, I sent for an Uber. It should arrive in five minutes. It's safer that way."

"You just think of everything, don't you?" Vy said. She was not going to argue. They were on vacation.

They went to Vy's favorite restaurant, Marina Bay. She didn't know why she bothered looking at the menu when she already knew what she wanted to order. Alexia immediately ordered their drinks. "Two martinis, two waters, and an order of chips and salsa please, and thank you." The waitress walked away without saying a word.

Alexia pulled out a miniature notepad from her purse. "We have to regroup, and write down what we have collected thus far. By the way, did you call Houston back?"

"No, I haven't."

"Why not?"

"Because I was hungry, and I didn't want to lash out at him because my stomach needed food."

"Good point. But I know that you're not telling me the absolute truth. But I'll let it go for now. I'll be right back."

Alexia went to the restroom, and Vy sat there with her martini, contemplating the word *love*. There have been so many songs written about love: "Head Over Heels," by Tears for Fears, "Truly, Madly, Deeply," by Savage Garden, "Friday I'm In Love," by The Cure. Vy had even written songs about this specific word that somehow defined a part of her existence.

Vy leaned back in her chair and people-watched. She focused on one table where the couple held hands while waiting for their food to arrive. The woman was smiling at the man. She was holding his hand, and was listening to his every word. She seemed to be in complete awe of him. To that woman, they were the only ones in the restaurant.

But the table past them displayed the opposite end of the love spectrum. This couple were not speaking to each other, let alone looking at each other. The man was staring at his cell phone, and the woman was staring at him looking at his cell phone. There seemed to be absolutely no sparks. Vy wondered why even go out together if they were going to sit there in agony.

Vy wanted the sparks. She wanted to be with a man at a restaurant and forget that there were people around them. She wanted to be with a man who knew what she was saying and feeling without her having to explain it in detail every time. Vy wanted her soul mate. The problem was that it was much easier for Vy to express her emotions with her guitar.

She constantly pulled away from every amazing man who crossed her path. Maybe it was because she was afraid, or maybe it was because she wasn't really in love but was in love with the idea of being in love. Whatever the reason, Vy created a barrier and left it there until he—whoever he was at the time—simply gave up on her. She often heard, 'Vy, I don't get you. That's it, I give up.' But when that occurred, ironically, Vy was okay with letting him walk away. Maybe Alexia was right; she should give Houston or Shawn, or some man a chance.

Vy's thoughts were interrupted with Alexia repeating, "Are you here with me, space cadet?"

"Sorry, what did you say?"

"I said, I can't believe you took a sip of your martini without toasting first."

"Oh, sorry. What shall we toast to?"

"Sisters and reading their minds." Vy smiled at Alexia, and took that much-needed sip.

Two hours and a few martinis later, Vy and Alexia came up with nothing regarding both cases. "Leaving on a Jet Plane" played on Vy's cell phone. Vy had the option to either accept or decline the call.

"Hello."

"Hi. Where are you?" Houston asked.

"At Marina Bay restaurant in the mall."

"For how much longer?"

"For a while."

"Please wait for me. I need to speak with you."

"Okay. See ya, bye."

"Bye."

"Houston's on his way. He was short with me. But he says he needs to speak to me and to stay put," Vy said.

Alexia was taking the cherry out of her martini glass. "See what happens? You didn't call him back and now he's tracking you down. I'll give it to him. He's persistent."

"Drink water, Lexi. You need it."

"I'm just saying," Alexia said, giggling.

Vy and Alexia killed time reminiscing about their high school days, and the first boys they'd ever kissed. Vy was pleasantly surprised by Houston's voice, "I found you."

"Yes, you did," Vy said as she slowly turned around. Her smile disappeared at the sight of Gunbar. "Oh, Houston, you brought along your sidekick. Sorry, Gunbar, I didn't grab a chair for you. I didn't know you were coming," Vy said obnoxiously.

"Sorry to disappoint you, Vy, but I'm here on official business." Houston looked at Gunbar sternly, and whispered from the side of his mouth, "Don't even think about telling her. We discussed it on the way here."

"Telling me what?" Houston and Gunbar were still standing. Gunbar went to go grab a chair. Houston sat next to Vy. Alexia scooted her chair over to make room for Gunbar.

"Hi, Alexia. How are you?" Gunbar sweetly asked.

"Fine, thanks. But stop stalling and tell us what's so important. And what's with the look of vengeance, Gunbar?" Alexia was looking at him straight in the eye.

"Go ahead," Gunbar said to Houston.

Houston faced Vy. "Do you want the good news or the bad news first?"

"Bad," Vy and Alexia responded simultaneously.

Houston seemed to be getting used to the Siamese talk because he didn't even flinch that time. "Okay," Houston took a deep breath, "let me start by saying that you can't leave town until you are cleared of Kendra's murder."

Suddenly, Vy's vision became a blur. Her palms started to sweat profusely.

"Vy, can you hear me?" was the last coherent phrase she heard before the back of her head hit the ceramic tile at her favorite restaurant.

"She's coming to. Everyone, clear the way!" Houston's blue eyes pierced into Vy's green eyes. For one moment, she forgot there were people around them. For one moment, she forgot that she was sprawled on the floor of the restaurant. It was a good thing she'd won jeans today.

"Vy, say something." Houston's breath smelled remarkable. "Vy, please, say anything."

"What kind of toothpaste do you use?" The entire restaurant started to clap. Vy slowly sat herself up.

"I need you to take it easy. The paramedics are on the way," Alexia said to Vy. She was sitting next to her on the floor. She brushed Vy's hair from her face and whispered, "You scared the crap out of me."

"What happened?" Vy asked.

"You fainted, bug."

"I told you not to call me that."

"At least I know you're not suffering from amnesia."

Houston was demanding everyone to walk back to their tables. "There's nothing to see here, folks. Please go back to your tables and enjoy your meals."

A waitress came up to Vy and handed her a cold, wet dish towel, "I hope this alleviates the pain until the paramedics arrive."

"Thank you."

*****

After the paramedics checked her out and determined that she was okay, they reconvened at the apartment. Vy was safely situated on her couch with her fuzzy blanket wrapped around her, and Houston snuggled next to her with Marilyn on his lap. Alexia and Gunbar sat on the loveseat across from Vy. "I think that I'm ready to hear the news without fainting," Vy said comically.

"Are you sure? We can wait until you're one hundred percent recovered," Houston said, concerned.

"No, we can't, Houston. Tell her the details now," Gunbar stated.

"You're just a bucket full of sunshine, Gunbar," Vy said.

"What is with you?" Alexia added.

"What's with me is that your little sister is a suspect in Kendra's murder," Gunbar stated. "Luckily, she knows the detective in charge, who I might add, is keeping her out of jail, which goes against protocol."

"Do you have a personal vendetta against Vy?" Alexia demanded.

"How dare you waltz into my tiny apartment and falsely accuse me of murder!" Vy concluded Alexia's statement angrily.

"I want all of you to stop bickering at each other," Houston interrupted.

There was a long pause. Alexia got up from the couch and headed to the kitchen. "I'm making coffee for everyone, whether you drink it or not. Then maybe we can all have a civilized conversation."

Alexia was right, the coffee and the chocolate cookies calmed everyone's nerves—most importantly, Gunbar's. Vy broke the silence, "Houston, just tell me."

Houston scooted up to the edge of the couch facing Vy. "Remember when I told you about the note that was left on the bar stating that you were last person seen going into the restroom right after Kendra?"

"Yes, I clearly remember."

"We had the note tested for fingerprints and it came back negative. Unfortunately, that makes you the only lead suspect that we have for Kendra's case. You were the only one seen speaking with her that night."

"But Houston—"

"I know you had nothing to do with her murder, Vy. But this is—using Gunbar's terminology—protocol. Now, I did pull some strings with the Captain. He agreed not to bring you in, but under one condition."

"What is that?"

"That you're under my supervision at all times," Houston smiled, "which doesn't seem like such a bad thing."

"No, it doesn't," Vy blissfully agreed.

"This is making me sick," Gunbar spat out.

"No one's asking you to stay, Gunbar," Vy said.

Gunbar took in a deep breath. "Truce?"

They were all looking at Vy, awaiting her reply. She also took in a deep breath, "Fine."

"Great, now that we're done with that, Vy you need to come to the station and give us a formal statement."

"I have no problem with that."

"And I'm going with her," Alexia quickly said.

"I didn't doubt that," Gunbar said with a smirk. "Now, let's focus on the problem here. Who committed these murders and why?"

"So, does this mean that I'm not on the top of your infamous list?" Vy asked.

Gunbar sighed, "Listen, I just get fueled up on these types of cases. I don't have anything against you. I want this person put away."

Vy knew that was Gunbar's way of apologizing, so she left it at that and gave Gunbar a comforting smile.

Houston pulled out a small notebook, and started flipping through some pages. He switched to his official tone. "I've been digging into Ricky's background. There was a police report regarding Ricky. It turns out that he was in a car accident two years ago. A woman, who was unidentified in the report, was driving him home. Both were under the influence of alcohol. She was driving at an excessive speed, lost control, and drove into a tree."

"That's awful," Alexia said.

Houston continued, "The report stated that she died instantaneously. The officer in charge reported that Ricky was coherent enough to take the woman out of vehicle, with the intent of resuscitating her. But by the time the paramedics arrived at the scene, it was too late."

Gunbar added his two cents in, "Who was the officer in charge?"

"Thomas Avery."

"Wasn't he relocated to Tampa?"

"Yes, one week after the report was filed," Houston said.

"Interesting."

"That was my same exact thought," Houston said.

Alexia cleared her throat. "Excuse me, but what are you two insinuating?"

Gunbar smiled. He put his hand on Alexia's knee and said, "There's something off."

"Oh," Vy and Alexia said mutually.

"Do you two always do that?"

"Yes, but you get used to it," Houston said.

Vy remembered Shawn's intense conversation with that unknown person last night at the gig. She told Houston and Gunbar exactly what she'd heard and exactly how she'd heard it. "I don't know if that will help at all, but I wanted to tell you anyway. It gave me an eerie feeling at the time, and since Shawn is somewhat connected with the Steel Horse, I thought it was pertinent information."

"That's good, Vy. Any information we get could be important to the case, even if it turns out to be a dead-end," Gunbar said.

That was the first time Gunbar had ever spoken to Vy in a calm manner. She couldn't argue the fact that Gunbar was a good detective, but she couldn't get over how annoying and hard headed he was.

Vy's cell phone played "Push" by Matchbox Twenty. That was the ringtone she set for the Steel Horse Bar. Since Ricky liked pushing people around, the ringtone suited him perfectly. Alexia answered for her, "Hello?"

"Vy?"

"No, this is her sister Alexia."

"Hi, Alexia, this is Dave. Can I please speak to Vy?"

"Sure, one moment." She placed her palm on the receiver and whispered to Vy, "It's Dave." Alexia handed her the phone, and resumed her comfortable position next to Gunbar.

"Hi, Dave, it's great to hear from you. How are you holding up?" Vy felt three sets of eyes intensely staring at her. She got up and went to the kitchen.

"Oh, I'm hanging in there, doll. I know that it's short notice, and it's a week night, but can you guys play tomorrow night?"

"So, you re-opened?"

"I had to," Dave simply answered.

"Sure, let me call the band, and I'll let you know as soon as I can. It was good talking to you."

"Let me know. Thanks. Bye."

"Bye, Dave."

As Vy was replenishing Marilyn's food bowl, she yelled from the kitchen, "Dave just called to book the band tomorrow night, nosy bodies."

Vy found it odd that Dave had decided to re-open the Steel Horse. Her train of thought was interrupted by nice, firm hands massaging her shoulders. Houston smelled so good; like a chocolate chip cookie that had just come out of the oven. He turned Vy around to face him. She looked up at him, completely enamored by the look in his eyes. "I'm glad that you're okay," Houston said.

"Of course, I'm okay. You were there to catch me. You did sort of catch me, right?"

"Sort of." Houston kissed Vy. She felt like she was about to faint again, but this time it would be for a good reason.

TESTING 12

"It was great to see mom and dad. I have to come down to Miami more often," Alexia said.

"Yes. I ended up having a one-on-one with mom. You know how she is."

"She psychoanalyzed you, huh?"

"Yes, but it felt good to talk about it, even though I was completely hesitant. But she always finds a way to break you down. I still can't fathom what's happened these pasts few days," Vy said.

"I'm sorry that you have to go through this, Vy. I know that Kendra was kind of your friend."

Vy gripped the steering wheel, and let out a sigh. "Thanks for being here for me, Lexi. And thanks for coming with me to the station."

"Of course. Anyway, I've always wanted to check out a police station. There must be a lot of cuties there."

"Alexia!"

"What?" She innocently answered as she applied lip gloss.

Vy and Alexia made their way to the front desk. A Latino woman with a petite, heart-shaped face looked up at them, "Yes?" Her hair was slicked back in a ponytail; she had on very light make up, and a touch of pink lipstick.

"I'm here to see Detective Houston."

"You must be—"

"Vy!" Houston called out.

She turned around. Houston was making his way to her and Alexia. He was wearing beige dress pants, a well-ironed blue dress shirt and a tie. He had his holster on, with a gun dangling from it, and his badge clipped to his leather belt. In other words, he looked very handsome.

"Dang he looks good," Alexia said from the side of her mouth. Vy simply nodded.

"Thanks for coming in on such short notice." Houston was very proper in his workplace, and she respected that.

"Of course."

Houston led Vy and Alexia through a narrow corridor. He stopped at the end of the corridor, swiped a card, and opened the door. "After you, ladies."

The office was the size of Vy's kitchen. Brown storage boxes were stacked up one on top of the other. The office itself smelled like old paper books. Each box was labeled with names and dates. Some labels were typed, others hand-written with big lettering. "Please have a seat. I know there isn't much room."

"I give her about ten minutes before she has a claustrophobia attack," Alexia said with a grin.

"Yes, can you leave the door slightly opened?" Vy said with a shiver.

"Sure." Houston propped a door stopper at the bottom corner of the door.

"Thanks," Vy said.

The box placed on Houston's desk was simply labeled *Kendra Williamson*. Another shiver ran through Vy's entire body. "There's no date on her box."

"You're very perceptive," Houston smiled. "We haven't solved her case yet."

"But you will," Vy said faintly.

Alexia held on to Vy's hand. "Okay, let's get this cranking before you get claustrophobic."

Houston asked basic questions. How long had Vy known Kendra; did Vy know anything about her personal life; and what type of person was Kendra? Vy also retraced in detail the events of the night of the murder, from when she spoke to Kendra, up until she and Alexia found her body in the restroom. The questioning took about half an hour. "Thank you, Vy and Alexia. This information helps."

"Anything we can do to help," Alexia said.

"And if I remember anything else, I'll call you," Vy concluded.

The three of them stood from the chairs and headed to the door. Houston lightly grabbed Vy's arm. "Do you have plans for tonight?" Houston whispered.

"She has a gig tonight, remember?" Alexia whispered back.

"You can come if you want to," Vy said with a smile.

"That's right, okay. Then I hope to see you later," Houston said.

*****

"I still can't believe he decided to have this anniversary party," Alexia said to Vy when they got back to the apartment, questioning the motive for a party when so much had happened.

"Yeah. I'm wondering if he knows about Kendra. I mean, to lose two people who worked for you in one week, and then throw a party? It just doesn't make sense."

"Maybe you can ask him tonight. He may know more than he's letting on. Use your Nancy Drew skills. This is the time to start asking questions. Dave likes you, so I'm sure he'd tell you something," Alexia said while applying her blush.

Vy put on her stilettos and looked in the mirror for a final inspection. It was time to find out what the heck was going on.

Vy felt strange walking into the Steel Horse Bar. The environment seemed odd, at least to her. Kendra who normally tended to the band was literally gone. There were more unfamiliar faces tonight. She stood at the back entrance taking the atmosphere in. Dave stepped out of his office, and put his hand on her shoulder. Vy jumped at the touch of his hand.

"I'm sorry; I didn't mean to scare you," Dave said.

"It's okay. I was just spaced out."

Dave looked at Vy with sad eyes, and what seemed to be a fake smile. "Shall we go into the office?"

Dave had his usual glass of red wine on the desk. He locked the door, which was unusual, and waited for Vy to sit, before taking a seat. Dave rubbed his forehead and moved the wineglass aside. He looked at Vy. She felt like he was trying to tell her something with his eyes, but he couldn't say it with words.

She took the initiative. "Dave, can I ask you a question?" He nodded, glanced at the door as if to make sure that it was locked, and then focused on Vy. "Did you hear about Kendra?"

"Yes, how unfortunate. I can't believe that we lost her too," Dave said with sincerity. His eyes got watery. He took a sip of his wine.

"I'm sorry about your loss, Dave." There was a slight pause, "But why re-open the bar? Why throw this party with all that's happened?"

"I wanted to keep it closed, especially when I found out about Kendra. But when I looked at our finances, I realized that I couldn't afford to close the bar, not even for one day. Ricky made some financial decisions without my knowledge, and now we're struggling."

"But aren't you in charge of the books?" Vy asked.

"I was, until a few months ago. He didn't want to explain why the sudden change. He pretty much told me to stay out of it. Then he started planning this anniversary party. I reviewed the books without Ricky's knowledge, and that's when it all came together. There's more of a loss than a profit this year, which is strange. Ricky desperately needed the extra revenue to cover the loss of the bar. Vy, we've put so much money into the vendors, sponsors, etcetera, that I can't afford to not have it. There was a DJ hired, but yesterday I decided that you guys would liven up the place." Dave looked at the door again.

"Wow," Vy said. There was a slight pause. "Dave, is there something you're not telling me?"

Dave placed his pale, arthritic looking hand on Vy's and leaned in towards her, "Vy, listen very closely to what I'm about to tell you. Whoever you think your friends are, they're not."

"Dave, tell me. Who should I be worried about?" Dave opened his mouth to say something, but someone was impatiently knocking on the door. Dave instantly stood up and unlocked it.

Cassandra walked in. "Dave, why did you lock the door? You never do." She fixed her eyes on Vy. "Oh, hi, Vy. It's great to see you again. Sorry, I didn't know you were in here."

She hugged Vy, but in a manner, that seemed like she wanted to asphyxiate her, or maybe it was Vy's paranoia, due to Dave's warning.

"I think Rob's looking for you. They were doing a sound check and he was calling for you," Cassandra said to Vy as she let her go.

"Thanks, Cassandra. Dave, like always, thanks for the candy." Cassandra looked at Dave then at Vy. For a reason unbeknownst to Vy, she felt like she had to protect Dave.

Vy headed to the door, but then turned around, "Oh, and Cassandra, I asked Dave to lock the door. I was talking to him about gigging at this new venue. I wanted to make sure that it was okay with him. I didn't want to step on anyone's toes. I know how bar wars start."

"Oh. I can understand that. Have fun tonight, girl. We always do when you guys are here."

Vy left the office and she suddenly felt minimal tension fall off her shoulders. She made a mental note to tell Houston what Dave had told her. But Dave did say that whoever Vy thought was her friend, was really her enemy. If she told Houston or Gunbar, would she put herself in danger? Who was Dave warning her about? What was Dave trying to tell her with his eyes?

Before Vy stepped onto the stage, she needed a shot of something strong. She saw Shawn bartending. Maybe she could nonchalantly ask Shawn who he was speaking to last night.

"Hey, Vy. Are you ready to give it all you've got?" Shawn asked excitedly.

"Hi, Shawn. Yes, even though it's a Monday and it's very weird coming back so soon, with what's happened. Don't you think?"

"Yes, I agree. But Dave needs us, and so here we are. At times like these, we have to work together."

Even though Shawn was trying to hide it with his smile, he looked mentally tired. She didn't want to make the night more challenging for him. "Luckily, I'm off work this week. So, behind the bar now?"

"It's great. One day a bar back, the next day a bartender. I can't complain."

"I'm going to start complaining if you don't stop socializing. No offense, Vy, but he's been talking more than serving," James scolded.

"No offense taken. I just wanted a shot."

"Watermelon jolly rancher it is," Shawn said.

Vy was so astonished that Shawn remembered what she drank, that she failed to tell him she wanted something stronger than that. He served her shot with such enthusiasm, that she didn't have it in her to ruin his mojo. "Thanks, Shawn, I'll be back for another one next break."

Shawn winked at Vy, and tended to another customer.

"Should I worry?" Houston was standing next to Vy.

"You came?" Vy asked, startled.

"If it's the only way I can see you, then yes, I made the time," Houston said with a smile. "So, should I worry?" Houston asked again, looking in Shawn's direction.

"I just came for a shot."

"I see that," Houston humorously said. "You okay? You seem kind of out of it."

"Is it that obvious?"

"It is to me. Is everything copasetic?" Vy figured this was her chance to tell Houston what Dave told her, but just then Rob called Vy up to the stage. Maybe that was a sign to hold off until she'd figured out what was going on and who she could trust.

"Everything's peachy keen. I must go. I'll see you in a bit," Vy said and scurried away like a frightened dog.

As the evening progressed, more people danced, laughed, drank, and forgot about the outside world. She felt at ease with each song she sang. For the first time in her many years of singing, she didn't want to take a break. The crowd had a positive energy tonight. The sound of people clapping was therapeutic for Vy.

"We're going to take a short break. We'll be right back."

Vy wanted to see how Kyle was holding up. She scanned the bar from the stage and spotted Kyle in the back corner of the bar speaking with Dave. Dave had his right hand over his heart region. He was looking down at the floor. At that very moment, Vy's heart sank. Something was wrong with Dave. She ran down the stairs of the stage, and headed towards Dave. Every now and then, she would lose sight of Kyle and Dave because there were so many people in the bar. She felt as if she was running in slow motion. She took her cell phone out of her back-pocket ready to dial nine-one-one.

Vy was almost to Dave, but suddenly Cassandra jumped in front of her. "Don't cause a commotion," Cassandra whispered in her ear. "Dave's fine. He doesn't want anyone to be alarmed."

"No, he isn't fine. Let me through!" Cassandra grabbed Vy's arm to stop her from moving an inch closer to Dave. Luckily, Houston was already by Dave's side. "Let me go!" Vy yanked her arm from Cassandra's grasp and finally got to him.

Shawn was now standing next to Dave who looked as white as a ghost. "What happened?" Vy was out of breath. Her forehead was trickling sweat down to her nose. She felt like she'd just ran a marathon.

Dave looked up at Vy, genuinely smiled and said, "It's okay, doll. I still have a lot of years left in me."

Vy heard the ambulance sirens outside. Houston and Kyle started walking Dave towards the entrance of the bar, "Stay here," Houston said to Vy and Shawn.

No one seemed to notice what had just happened. A group of people at the last pool table by the entrance heard the sirens outside. There was silence amongst them for a few seconds, and then they continued doing whatever it was they were doing. The jukebox was playing, "Working for the Weekend" by Loverboy, which Vy found ironic because that was Dave's favorite band. Vy and Shawn stood there motionless. She immediately started to cry. Shawn took her into his arms and hugged her tightly. Vy's ear felt the warmth of his breath as he spoke, "He's going to be okay. He's a strong man." Vy knew that she was getting snot on Shawn's t-shirt, but she didn't care.

Vy pulled back just a bit and looked deep into his brown eyes. "Why is all this happening, Shawn?" Shawn frowned and instantly pulled completely away from her.

Vy heard Cassandra's voice behind her, "The paramedics assured me that Dave will be fine. He's suffering from over-exhaustion. They're keeping him overnight for observation at Cedar's Medical Hospital. Shawn, Kyle will stay with him until you can get there. Dave specifically said to go on as if nothing happened."

Vy didn't want to deal with this anymore. She went to the women's restroom without acknowledging Cassandra. There were three women in the restroom re-applying their lipstick, fixing their hair, and talking about which men they wanted to take home with them. Vy felt as though everyone here was so consumed in their own world, that they didn't realize what had just happened.

The three women were walking out of the restroom together, when one of them stopped in front of Vy, "Like always, we're having a blast." Miss America flipped her hair over her left shoulder and continued talking, "Can you sing 'So What' by Pink tonight? That's my fave."

Vy had two ways of handling this current situation; she could slap her until she could no longer utter a word, or find Alexia because she would keep her from going to jail for assaulting Miss America. Vy chose the latter option.

TESTING 13

Vy and the band commenced with the second set. Their break was longer than usual because of what had happened earlier with Dave. Unfortunately, as they say, the show must go on. Alexia, Houston, and Gunbar were sitting at a high round table directly in front of Rob. Tina arrived at the gig as Vy was finishing her second song. To see her friends in the crowd gave her some peace. She was no longer alone.

The woman Vy almost slapped, was dancing with her friends in the middle of the dance floor. She skipped over to where Vy was, looked up at her and yelled, “Don’t forget to sing ‘So What’!” She raised both her arms up and added, “Woohoo!” Vy couldn’t help but notice her cakey deodorant under her armpits.

“You got it,” Vy said. She looked out into the crowd and started her personal dedication to her. “This next song goes out to the smashed Miss America look-alike who is stumbling in front of me, with her cakey armpits.”

The woman was too drunk to realize that Vy had just insulted her, but the band didn’t miss it. They all had the ‘what was that about?’ facial expression. After the song they took their third break and stepped out to the back alley. Vy sat on the curb, while the rest of the band stared down at her.

“Vy, are you okay?” Carlos was sincere and worried.

“Yeah, I’m sorry, you guys. What happened to Dave really hit me hard.”

"We understand," Adrianna said. "But try not to attack the people in the audience. The last thing we need is for the bar to sue us because the lead singer lost it, and whacked someone with her wireless microphone." Vy felt a lot better.

"Thanks, guys. Again, I'm sorry. I'll control my Cuban temper. It does come out occasionally."

Vy needed to go to her car to get her lipstick. The guys went back inside, but Carlos stayed behind, "I'll wait for you."

"Okay, I'll only be a second." Vy jogged over to the car, and as she was about to unlock the door, she noticed a white folded sheet of paper taped to the glass. She unfolded the paper. The note was typed and Vy read it aloud to herself.

"I'm not crazy, I'm just a little unwell. I know right now you can't tell, but stay awhile and maybe then you'll see, a different side of me. But this won't be a pretty side, if you keep sticking your nose where it doesn't belong. Watch your back."

After she read the note, Vy remained still. Her fingers went numb, and her face felt flushed. Carlos came over to her, "Sugar, are you ready?"

Vy couldn't speak. She turned to Carlos and handed him the note. Now she was angry. She wasn't angry because she was threatened. Vy was angry at the fact that someone had the audacity to threaten her with Matchbox Twenty lyrics.

The remainder of the gig was a blur to Vy. While Vy sang, she kept looking around the bar trying to figure out who had a grudge against her and why. Houston, Gunbar, and Carlos were on the lookout as well. They were the only ones who knew about the note threat. Vy didn't want to inform the others until after the gig.

As the guys were breaking down the equipment, Vy wanted to indulge herself in a game of pool with her friends. She changed from her four-inch heels to her flip flops, jumped off the stage, and headed to the table where her friends were sitting. "Do you guys want to shoot a game of pool?" Vy asked.

"I'm taking you to the doctor first thing in the morning," Alexia seriously said.

"What? Why?"

"Because you have just been threatened, and you want to linger around this place and shoot pool? Vy, you need a CAT scan done." The others present were smart enough to remain quiet.

"I guess you all know by now."

Vy looked at the four of them, and stopped on Alexia. "Lexi, first, getting a CAT scan is a call for a claustrophobic attack. Anyway, I'm with all of you. What can possibly happen to me while we're shooting pool together? Please, I need this. I need to feel normal for an hour. This is all getting to be too much for me to handle. First Ricky dies, and then Kendra dies; of which I'm being accused of doing. And now Dave is in the hospital. And here's the kicker, I was just threatened. I can't take it anymore!"

Vy was on the verge of breaking down into tears. There was complete silence. Alexia stood up and grabbed her hand. She looked at Vy and asked, "You want to be my partner? You know that I'm a terrible pool player."

*****

The next morning Vy woke up mentally exhausted. She'd dreamt that Dave came to her apartment and lined her doors and window sills with salt to keep the demons out. She probably dreamt that because she'd watched a re-run of "Supernatural" before she fell asleep.

The apartment was quiet. Marilyn was not lying next to her like she normally did. And what was strange was that Vy didn't smell the French Vanilla coffee aroma that usually lingered down the hall. She slowly and quietly got out of bed. Her maneuvers were those of Ethan Hunt from *Mission Impossible*. She grabbed a perfume bottle for protection. It was better than nothing.

Vy carefully opened the bedroom door and tip-toed out to the living room, holding up the perfume bottle ready to spray. Part one of the mystery was solved. Marilyn was lying on the armrest of the couch. Nothing in the apartment seemed out of place, and no one jumped out of the linen closet to try to kill her. Alexia was nowhere to be found. Vy went to the kitchen and saw a huge pink note taped to the refrigerator. This one had Alexia's handwriting on it: "The coffeemaker broke. Went to go buy you a new one. Bringing Dunkin' Donuts."

That solved the second mystery, the void of the French Vanilla coffee scent. Vy placed the perfume bottle down on the kitchen table. She went to the living room and laid on the couch waiting for Alexia to return. She glanced at the clock on her kitchen wall, "Nine a.m. Time for a nap," Vy said to herself. She couldn't believe that she was up this early of her own freewill.

"Don't you get it? I don't want to be the chosen one. I don't want to spend the rest of my life chasing after vampires." Vy slowly opened her eyes and her favorite movie *Buffy the Vampire Slayer* was on television. When she tried to stretch out her legs, Alexia was blocking her path.

"Don't you just love Luke Perry? You used to be addicted to *90210*," Alexia said smiling.

"I know. I was so infatuated with that show that I collected the trading cards. I thought I was Brenda Walsh." They started to giggle. "When did you get back?"

"About an hour ago. I didn't want to wake you up. You looked peaceful. And besides, I needed time to think about this mess we're in," Alexia said.

Vy once again glanced at the clock on her kitchen wall, "It's 11:48. That's quite a nap." Vy sat up and stretched out her legs. She looked outside through her sliding glass door. It was a beautiful day. Everything seemed serene, but Vy knew it wasn't. "Talk to me, Lexi."

"We have to retrace your steps, Vy. From the night Ricky was murdered up until last night. You pissed someone off along the way. By retracing your steps, we will catch our guy or gal."

"Maybe we should just leave it to the professionals."

"What, and wait for another threat? I don't think so."

"But you said it yourself, I'm pissing someone off. And they got real close last night."

Alexia smiled. "And that's where they screwed up."

"I'm not following."

"They know you on a somewhat personal level. They knew where you would be there, they knew what car you drove, where you would park, and as stupid as this may sound, this person quoted your favorite band."

Vy cradled her legs to her chest. "Alexia, everyone on our mailing list knows the show schedule. And after singing there for three years, everyone knows my car and where I park. And, I'm constantly quoting Matchbox Twenty lyrics on Facebook. It's a moot point."

"That's where I think you're wrong. We have a lead, I just know it."

Vy was worn out. "Fine, Lexi, let me jump in the shower, and I'll be good to go. By the way, I'm going to visit Dave at the hospital sometime today."

"Okay, I'll go with you. In the meantime, I have invited the girls, Houston, and Gunbar over for lunch. I ordered the pizza already."

"So basically, what I just said wasn't going to matter?"

"No, it matters. The only difference is that I'm finally letting Houston and Gunbar into our little investigation. This is getting serious, Vy. I'm thinking that if we all put our minds together, we can pick up on some clue we might have missed."

"Have I told you lately how lucky I am to have you as a sister?" Vy said.

"No. But after this is over, you owe me a spa day."

*****

At lunch, the six of them sat around the table eating pizza and chicken wings. They were talking about their quirks, favorite movies, and pet peeves. Alexia, the mediator of the group, decided it was time to get down to business. "Okay, we are now officially open for discussion. Who wants to begin?" Alexia asked.

Houston cleared his throat and took the stage, "Even though I shouldn't be sharing any details about the investigation, I brought Ricky and Kendra's crime scene photos. It might be gruesome for some of you to look at, so if you want to pass on this, that's fine with me."

The girls agreed to look at the photos. Vy was the only one left without answering. She had to suck it up if she wanted to clear her name.

Vy straightened out her back, cracked her neck, and looked at Houston, "I've seen plenty of horror movies to prepare myself for something like this. Let's get started."

Houston patted her leg and whispered, "Okay."

Houston began with Ricky's crime scene photos. He was passing the first photo out, starting to his left. Vy was going to be the last one to look at the photos. By the facial expressions that Alexia, Tina, and Adrianna were giving, Vy wasn't looking forward to it being her turn.

The first photo was of Ricky face down on the desk, his eyes looking directly into the camera. His lifeless body gave her chills. She examined the background of the photo. This angle showed only the liquor shelves. Vy noticed a bottle was out of place.

"Houston, Gunbar; did you notice that this liquor bottle is not aligned with the other bottles on the shelf?" Vy placed the photo in between Houston and Gunbar, and she pointed to the tiny bottle. They stood up and examined that section of the photo.

"What does that have to do with anything, Vy?" Gunbar asked.

"I've been in that office plenty of times to know that Dave never had a bottle out of place, and the labels always faced forward. But look," Vy pointed to the bottle again, "the label of this bottle is facing left. You can barely see the label."

Gunbar pushed the photo back in her direction. "Maybe Ricky took a sip from that bottle, and put it back the way it's seen in this photo."

"You have a point," Vy said disappointedly.

Houston remained quiet. Vy was wondering what kind of conclusions he was forming in his mind. Whatever they were, he didn't want anyone to know yet.

Vy proceeded to the next photo. This photo was taken at a different angle. The photographer was behind Ricky's body. She looked at the background once again. This angle showed the staff pictures on the wall, the autographed poster of the CD cover Vy had given to Dave, and the entrance to the office. There was nothing out of the ordinary in this photo, or the remaining photos from Ricky's crime scene.

The next round of photos were of Kendra's crime scene. Her photos were tough on Vy's stomach even with her vivid imagination. Because the background of the photos was of the restroom stalls, Vy figured the photographer had taken the shots from the restroom's entrance. Kendra's body was in a fetal position facing the photographer.

"Houston, is it possible that the assailant was already in the restroom stall when Kendra came in?" Vy asked.

"Why do you ask?" Gunbar intriguingly asked.

"It's just; in this photo, she's facing the entrance of the restroom. I automatically assumed that the assailant struck her from behind. So maybe she fell in the direction she was facing?"

"That's a great observation, Vy. Gunbar and I had discussed that possibility," Houston said.

"Kendra was probably leaving the restroom. The person, who was waiting for her in the stall, came out, and struck her on the head," Tina continued Vy's thought process.

"Those are all great points, but unfortunately, we can't base this case on assumptions," Houston said.

"I know, Houston. I just can't imagine why someone would want to murder her," Vy wondered out loud.

They all continued to share their theories with one another. Fortunately, for Vy, they were coming to an end. She couldn't look at any more photos. She was disgusted, upset, and scared that she may soon be a victim and would have her own crime scene photos.

The last picture Vy was holding was a four by six photograph. "Wait, where did this come from, Houston?"

"That's a photo that Kendra had in her back pocket the night she was murdered."

The photo was folded in half and a bit crinkled. Vy straightened the photo out a little more, and ran her index finger across Kendra's face. Vy was apologizing to Kendra in her mind, and remembering how distraught Kendra was the night Ricky was found dead.

"That's the photo," Vy faintly said to herself.

"That's what photo?" Alexia responded to Vy.

Vy looked at Marilyn who was now lying on her lap. "On the night that Ricky was murdered, I found Kendra in the DJ booth staring at a picture. This must be the photo she was looking at."

Vy looked at the photo intently. She foolishly thought that if she stared at the photo long enough, either Ricky or Kendra would tell her who did this to them. The photo was taken at the Steel Horse Bar on a night that she'd had a gig. Carlos was in the background talking to a blond-haired woman. Kendra was hugging Ricky. She genuinely looked happy, and so did Ricky. They did look in love. They were standing by the center bar.

Far in the background, by the kitchen's serving window, Cassandra was leaning against the wall and was staring at the back of Kendra's and Ricky's head. She looked troubled. Cassandra's arms were embracing herself, as if she was cold. Everyone in the background went about their business, except for her.

"Vy, do you see something?" Alexia asked.

"No." Vy felt like she was missing something, but didn't know what it was.

"Are you sure?" Gunbar persisted. Vy felt as though Gunbar thought she was deliberately hiding something from him.

"I'm sure, Gunbar. Now if you and Houston can excuse us, it's been a long afternoon, and I have plans to visit Dave at the hospital."

"I'll go with you," Houston said.

"No, that's okay. Alexia is coming with me." Vy was hoping that by visiting Dave, he could finally tell her who not to trust. If Houston was with her, he might not want to talk. Until then, Vy and Alexia were on their own.

On the way to Cedars Medical Hospital, Vy thought she saw a black SUV with tinted windows following her. But this was Miami; many people were driving in the same direction as Vy. Houston recently had taught her to keep her eyes open. The SUV seemed to be keeping its distance to about two vehicles behind Vy's mustang. She felt as though she was being followed, but for now, she kept that feeling to herself. She didn't want to alarm Alexia.

The SUV was no longer behind her when Vy made a left turn into the hospital's parking lot. Fear was the first step to insanity. She had to calm down and not jump to any conclusions, or she was going to drive herself crazy.

Vy and Alexia walked in through the automated glass doors of the hospital. Vy hated being in a hospital; but then again, she didn't think that it was a pleasant experience for anyone. The smell of the hospital, the beeping sounds coming from the machines from various rooms, and the beige walls depressed her.

"Did you call the hospital to see if Dave is still admitted here?" Alexia asked.

"No. It was going to take longer being on hold than to actually drive here."

Alexia wrapped her arm around Vy's. "Yeah, you're right."

Vy and Alexia headed to the gift shop first. She bought Dave a tiny brown bear that held a get-well sign. If Dave was still admitted, she didn't want to visit him empty handed. Vy and Alexia went to the information desk. There was a woman sitting behind the desk who looked to be in her sixties, with poufy, silver hair, and pink lipstick. She was squinting at the computer monitor. “Excuse me,” Vy said.

“May I help you?” Her Spanish accent was a lot thicker than Diana’s. If Vy switched to speaking Spanish, the lady might take offense. So, just to be on the safe side, Vy continued the conversation in English, “I’m here to visit Dave Campbell.”

“Please spell Campbell.”

Vy spelled out his last name. “Okay, one moment.” Her fingers typed rapidly. “Yes, he in Intensive Care on third floor. But only one family member at a time. Are you a family member?”

Vy stared at her blankly. The words *Intensive Care* had shocked Vy. Alexia spoke for her, “Are you sure? He only came in for something minor.”

“Yes, ma’am, I sure. You can talk to the doctor to find out what happen. But you have to wait, a family member is already here.”

“Who is here?” The words barely came out of Vy’s mouth.

The lady looked at the computer monitor, then at Vy, “Shawn Anderson. Now, can I have your license to check you in. You have to wait, okay?”

Alexia held Vy’s hand. “We’ll come back to check in. Thank you,” Alexia said. They slowly walked away.

“My God, Lexi, he’s in Intensive Care.” Vy placed her hand on her chest.

“Okay, breathe. I don’t need you hyperventilating. Why don’t you call Shawn and have him come downstairs? He can let us in on what happened to Dave.”

Vy pulled out her cell phone and dialed Shawn. “It went straight to voicemail. Now what?”

"Come on." Alexia grabbed Vy's hand and led her to the lobby. "Let's wait here for Shawn. Maybe he'll be down soon."

"Okay."

They sat facing the elevators. Vy was hugging the teddy bear. "I didn't even know that Shawn was related to Dave. Alexia, this is getting to be—"

"Weird," Alexia said, completing Vy's sentence.

About an hour had passed and still no sign of Shawn. "Alexia, I'm going to sneak up to the third floor. I can't wait any longer."

"No. What if you get caught?"

"Lexi, they can't arrest me for accidentally ending up on the third floor." Vy winked at Alexia.

"Do you want me to go with you?"

"No, stay here in case Shawn comes down."

"Be careful."

Vy barely made it past the pink lipstick lady. She walked alongside a tall, heavy-set man. Vy made it to the elevator and pressed the *up* arrow. She hated getting into elevators, but she had to do it. The elevator doors slowly opened. The man she used as her camouflage, let her get on the elevator first. This elevator was much smaller than the one at the building where she worked. She took a deep breath, and hoped that it was a fast ride to the third floor. Vy pressed the number three button.

"What floor?" she asked the man.

"Same. Thanks."

Vy felt as though he was staring at her from his peripheral view. The elevator couldn't get to the third floor fast enough. She was getting nervous.

"Excuse me, miss?"

"Yes," Vy said nervously.

"Sorry, but, um, you have a big chunk of something hanging from the bottom of your chin."

"What? Oh gosh." Vy started cleaning her chin. And sure thing, there was a big chunk of the chocolate chip cookie she ate in the lobby. "Oh gosh, thank you."

The man smiled, and the elevators doors opened. "Have a good day, miss," the man said, and walked out of the elevator. Vy felt so embarrassed by her paranoia.

Vy stood in the hall watching the nurses walk past her. One nurse stopped, and with her southern accent asked, "Can I help you, sweetie?"

"I need to find a patient's room. Who do I ask?"

"Follow that hall down to the end and make a right. They'll let you through to the Intensive Care unit."

"Thanks."

"Sure thing. And remember," she placed her hand on Vy's shoulder, "everything will be alright. God has a plan for us all." The nurse smiled, and she walked away.

Vy followed her instructions and ended up at another information desk. This time, there was a nurse sitting behind the desk. She looked up at Vy and smiled, "Hello. Can I have the patient's name?" Her demeanor was a lot different than the southern bell. This nurse faked her smile, and Vy could tell she was tired of asking the same question to different people.

"Dave Campbell," Vy replied.

"Your name?"

"Vy."

"Vy what?" the nurse inquired.

"Vy Blanco."

The nurse looked down at a clip board, sighed, and looked at Vy. "You're not on the visitor's list."

"I know. But I wanted to see if I could see Dave for a few minutes."

"No, sorry," the nurse said, and proceeded to look at her computer monitor.

"Miss, it won't be that long. He's a good friend of mine and—"

"No. You're not a family member," the nurse interrupted. "Therefore, you're not permitted. Now, if you can excuse me." She spun her chair around and answered the phone.

"Warden," Vy muttered under her breath as she walked away from the Nurse's station.

The entrance to the ICU was controlled by a swipe card, or the red button behind the nurse's desk. Vy started to walk away when she heard a man call out her name. She turned around and Shawn was standing by the double doors.

"Vy, what are you doing here?" Shawn asked as he advanced towards Vy.

"I came to visit Dave, but the nurse warden won't let me through. She made it very clear that because I'm not a family member, I can't see him. I called you, but it went straight to voicemail."

"He's in stable condition."

"What happened? I mean, I thought he was admitted for over-exhaustion."

"It turns out that he had a minor heart attack." Shawn rubbed his eyes.

"Is he coherent?

"No. I'm sitting there hoping that he'll wake up soon. I don't want him to think he's alone."

"That's nice of you." Vy started fidgeting, "I didn't know you two are related."

"I wasn't supposed to say anything at the bar. He didn't want people thinking he was favoring his nephew."

"Nephew?"

"Yeah, but he's more like a dad to me. Uncle Dave and my Aunt Linda pretty much raised me. My dad took off when I was a baby, and my mother couldn't deal with raising a child on her own. Uncle Dave and Aunt Linda took me in and raised me like I was their own son. They couldn't have any children of their own. Aunt Linda used to tell me that I was a Godsend."

Shawn was getting teary eyed. "Is your aunt here with you?"

"No, she passed away a couple years ago."

"Shawn if you need anything." Vy stepped an inch closer to him and held his hand.

"Thanks. I should go. Like I said, I don't want Dave to wake up and find no one there," Shawn said.

"Yes, of course. I understand."

"I'll tell him you came by to see him." Shawn gently squeezed Vy's hand. "Is that for him?" Vy had forgotten that she was holding the teddy bear she bought at the gift shop.

"Yes. Can you give it to him?"

"You're a really nice person, Vy. I'll put it on the table in front of him, so when he opens his eyes, that's the first thing he sees." He hugged Vy and walked back through the double doors.

The nurse buzzed him in. Vy stayed staring at the doors wanting to go inside. She wanted to comfort Shawn, and be there for Dave.

The nurse then cleared her throat, "Excuse me, but you're going to have to leave this area." *The hospital didn't hire based on personality*, Vy thought to herself.

On the way home, Vy explained to Alexia what had happened.

"How's Shawn holding up?" Alexia asked.

"He seems really sad. I can't imagine that Shawn is the only family Dave has left. He's alone."

"He's not alone. Shawn is there." Alexia said.

"Yeah, but it makes me realize how lucky we are."

"Yes, we are," Alexia said.

Vy pulled into her favorite gas station. "You want anything from inside?"

"Twizzlers."

"Good call. I haven't had those in a while."

Vy jumped out of the car, and went inside. "Hi, Diana. It's so nice to see you."

"Hello, my Coco Chanel. You are not working today?"

"I took the week off. My sister's in town."

"Oh, how nice," Diana responded with a smile.

"Damn, my purse," Vy said to herself. "I'll be right back, I forgot my purse in the car."

Before exiting the gas station, Vy saw a black SUV parked by the carwash. Obviously, there was more than one black SUV in Miami, but this was too much of a coincidence. Vy wasn't too keen on coincidences.

She walked up to Diana, "Can I please have a pen and a piece of paper?"

"Of course, my dear. Are you okay?"

"Yes, yes. Thank you, Diana," Vy said nervously. Diana tore off a piece of the receipt paper, and handed her a chewed-up pen. "Thanks."

Vy exited through the opposite side of the gas station. She walked around the building, making herself inconspicuous. She gradually and discreetly made her way to the SUV. She was now in a squatted position, quickly jotting down the license plate number. Vy maneuvered herself away from the SUV, and this time she power walked back around the building, and into the gas station. She let out a sigh of accomplishment.

"Everything okay?" Diana seemed concerned.

"Yes. My sister wants Twizzlers. Where are they?"

"Twizzlers are on the second row," Diana said.

On the way to her car, Vy saw that the SUV was no longer there. She leaned into her car, "You are aware that you left your purse. What took you so long?" Alexia said.

Vy grabbed her purse. "I know. I'll be right back."

Vy bought the Twizzlers, paid for her gas, and returned to her car. She was anxious to tell Alexia what she'd just done. As the gas was pumping, Vy joined Alexia in the car.

"Okay, hear me out before you freak out."

"What could you have possibly done in a matter of a second?"

"Just hear me out, okay?"

Vy told Alexia how she thought they were being followed on the way to the hospital, and how she just saw an identical vehicle parked by the carwash. Then she continued to tell her about getting the SUV's license plate number.

"Have you completely lost it? What if the car went in reverse, didn't see you, and ran you over?"

"I was squatted at a reasonable distance from the SUV," Vy said.

"You know that there are about a hundred thousand black SUVs in Miami, right?"

"Yes, that thought crossed my mind. But it's better to be safe than sorry. I was careful, Alexia."

"I know. But just remember, you're not one of those superhero characters that you read about in your comic books."

Vy heard the pump click off. "Hold on," Vy said. She went around the vehicle, and put the pump back in its place. She resumed her position in the driver's seat and started the Mustang. Before putting the gear into drive, she looked over at Alexia, "I know I'm not, Lexi. But please stop treating me like I'm five years old. I know what I'm doing."

"Fine," Alexia said.

"But," Vy put the car in drive and gripped the wheel, "if I did have super powers, I'd be invisible."

*****

Alexia threw her purse on the couch as they entered the apartment. "What a long afternoon. Want to lay out by the pool?"

"Why don't you go ahead? I have to call Adrianna and ask her a favor."

"What?"

"I want her to run that license plate number, and see if she can get any information from it," Vy explained.

"Okay, but don't take too long. I get bored if you're not there to talk my ears off."

Vy called Adrianna, and explained her situation. "Okay, here it is." Vy gave her the license plate number. "Thanks, A, I really appreciate it."

Vy changed into her favorite black two-piece bikini that had a small, hot pink butterfly on the right upper butt-cheek area. She applied lip-gloss and headed for the door. She heard her cell phone play, "Mamas Don't Let Your Babies Grow Up To Be Cowboys," from her bedroom. Vy wanted a break from any more drama, so she ignored the call and joined Alexia at the pool.

Later, Vy and Alexia returned to the apartment sporting a nice tan. "That was relaxing. Boy did I need that."

"Me too. Did you want to go out to dinner?" Alexia asked.

"Sure. I'll take a shower in the guest restroom, you can have my bathroom," Vy said.

"Okay, but let me check to see if I have any missed calls from the office. I left my phone here, because I didn't want work to bother me."

"Me too, I didn't want anyone bothering me either."

Alexia stayed in the living room, and Vy went to her bedroom. She had five missed calls from Adrianna. She also sent Vy a text message that read, call me now.

Vy called Adrianna immediately, but it went directly to her voicemail. Alexia came running into her bedroom. Her face was flushed, and she looked terribly upset. "Did you check your voice messages yet?" Alexia asked.

"Not yet. God, Lexi what's wrong?"

"It was Gunbar."

"What was Gunbar?"

"You were right; we were being followed—by Gunbar!" Alexia said.

TESTING 14

"Okay, calm down. I'm sure he has a reasonable explanation." Vy was trying to find the right words to calm Alexia down.

"I'm calling him right now!"

"No, Alexia. Let's sit. Take a deep breath. Pretend like you're in your Yoga class."

Vy didn't know why she was defending Gunbar. He did act strangely with her earlier that afternoon. Then he followed her. He'd better appreciate the fact that she just saved him from Alexia's rage.

Alexia took a deep breath, "You're right, Vy. I need to relax. I'm going to take a shower and calm my nerves."

Alexia looked at her cell phone, threw it on Vy's bed, went to the bathroom, and slammed the door shut. She had turned on the radio, and Good Charlotte's, "Anthem Song" was playing on the radio. Marilyn was sitting on Vy's bed staring up at her. She whispered to her cat, "What the heck is going on, Marilyn?"

Vy showered, got dressed, and waited for Alexia to get out of her bedroom. She was flipping through the channels, and ended up on the Lifetime channel. The movie was about a woman who kept seeing the ghost of another woman. Her husband thought his wife was going crazy. They were on their way to see a therapist. As the therapist was telling the woman she was going insane, Alexia came out to the living room. She looked refreshed, and calm. She had her wet hair up in a ponytail.

"I just want you to know that I called Gunbar, in a relatively calm manner I might add, and invited him and Houston to dinner." Alexia said.

"You're going to give him a piece of your mind in person, huh?"

"You bet I am. Are you ready to go?"

"Sure, but where are we going? I feel underdressed next to you."

"You look fine. We're going to Ralph's Diner." Alexia grabbed her purse, and headed for the door. Vy turned off the television, gave Marilyn a kiss on her head, and followed Alexia out.

"You were right about cops, Vy."

"I thought you said detectives were different," Vy sarcastically said.

"Oh, shut it."

*****

They met Houston and Gunbar at the diner. Houston looked extremely attractive, even in the Miami Dolphins t-shirt he was wearing. He would make anyone root for the team. Vy didn't care for sports, but maybe now she would consider backing up her home team.

Houston and Gunbar stood up as Vy and Alexia approached the booth. "Hello, ladies," Houston said. He walked over to Vy and hugged her. His aftershave smelled so good. She closed her eyes for a second and took in a quick whiff.

"Thanks for the invite, Alexia," Gunbar said. He couldn't stop drooling over her.

"It was my pleasure." Alexia smiled and they all sat down.

Vy and Alexia sat across from Houston and Gunbar. Vy personally loved eating at this diner. Every time she walked in, she felt as though she was transported to the fifties. It was like being in a scene from the movie *Back to the Future.* There were black and white framed photos of Marilyn Monroe, Dean Martin, James Dean, Frank Sinatra, and the Rat Pack just to name a few. The lives of movie stars in that era always intrigued Vy. She looked at the photos and wondered what was running through their minds the instant the camera took their picture.

"What'll it be?" The waitress was wearing a poodle skirt, a pink button-down collar shirt, and white sneakers. Her blue name tag read in white, engraved letters, *Amy—Nashville, TN.* She pulled out a pen from behind her ear, and a pad from her apron.

"Ladies first," Gunbar said, and gestured to Vy and Alexia with his hand.

"I'll start with a house salad, Ranch dressing, please. Then I'll have an order of six chicken fingers with garlic fries. That's it. Thanks," Vy said.

The waitress then looked at Alexia. "Just bring an extra plate please. I'll share with my sister. There's no way she'll eat all of that food." The waitress nodded, not caring if Vy ate her food or not, and proceeded to take Houston and Gunbar's orders. Alexia waited until the waitress walked away. "So, what have you two been up to since you left this afternoon?" Alexia wasn't hesitant to jump right into the cold water.

"Well, I have something interesting to share with the three of you," Houston said. He remained silent.

"Well, what is it?" Vy asked.

"I was just waiting for you to ask." He smiled and continued, "Remember how Gunbar and I thought something was off with Ricky's accident report?" Vy and Alexia nodded in sync.

"I was able to get the contact information for the Captain of the Fire Department who was at the scene that night," Houston said.

"House salad for you and here are your drinks. I'll be back shortly with your food."

Vy poured the Ranch dressing on her salad and split it in half. "I'll just eat the salad from your plate, Vy," Alexia said. Houston and Gunbar watched them inhale the salad.

"Oh sorry," Vy said with her mouth full, "do you want some?"

"No thanks," Houston and Gunbar said at the same time.

Vy started to laugh, "Now you two are starting to sound like Lexi and me." Vy placed the fork down and wiped her mouth, "Okay, Houston, tell us what happened."

"Considering what I have to share with you, I'm going to wait until we're done eating," Houston said.

After dinner, the four of them went outside and were standing in the parking lot of the diner. Vy was looking up at the red sign. Ralph's Diner flickered on and off. Houston leaned in, "It's like something from a classic movie, huh?" Vy smiled even more. Houston understood.

"Are you girls up for a nightcap?" Although the question was for Vy and Alexia, Gunbar directed the question to Alexia.

"We would love one. Let's go to Shooters," Alexia said without hesitation, and much determination.

Vy was getting anxious. She wanted to know what Houston had found out from the Captain, but more importantly, what Gunbar's intentions were this afternoon when he was following them.

They managed to get a quiet corner booth at Shooters. They placed their drink orders. Vy had her eyes on Houston, and Alexia was coldly staring at Gunbar. "Okay, Houston, I'm really curious about your conversation with the Captain," Vy said. Their drinks came, and Houston continued where he'd left off at Ralph's Diner.

"I went to the Fire Station and," Houston started to say.

Alexia interrupted, "Gunbar, you didn't go with Houston?"

Gunbar snapped out of the daze he was in, "No."

Houston continued speaking, "I showed the Captain the report and,"

Again, Alexia interrupted, "Why not? I thought you two were working together on the cases."

Houston appeared confused at Alexia's line of questioning. Houston answered, "Gunbar had something to take care of. Now, as I was saying."

"What were you doing that was more important than clearing my sister's name, Gunbar?"

Gunbar finally snapped, "What is your deal, Alexia? My world doesn't revolve around saving your sister's butt."

"Is that so?" Alexia took a gulp of her red wine and continued, "well, if your world doesn't revolve around saving my sister's butt," Alexia air quoted that line, "then why were you following her this afternoon?"

There went being discreet. Gunbar's face turned red. Vy didn't know if he was about to have a panic attack, or if he was just angry. Whatever the case, it wasn't good. Houston was surprised by Alexia's question. He turned and looked at Gunbar, "What's she talking about?"

Gunbar downed his beer. He slightly turned to Houston, "I thought Vy was hiding something this afternoon. So, I followed her. It's that simple. I'm doing my job."

"And what is your job?" Alexia asked.

"Following a lead," Gunbar stated.

Vy was now fuming. She was about to lay it on Gunbar, but Houston held up his index finger to prevent her from erupting. Gunbar then looked at Vy and asked, "How did you know it was me anyway?"

"I noticed a black SUV following me on the way to the hospital," Vy quickly winked at Houston. "Then I saw the SUV at the gas station. So, I simply snuck behind it, took down the license plate number, and the rest is confidential." Vy added a nod at the end of the sentence for emphasis.

There was silence, and then Vy gave in, "Why did you follow me Gunbar? Do you see me as a suspect, as a murderer?" Vy was trying to sound rational and calm. Maybe this type of communication would get her somewhere with him.

"I was watching you as you were looking at Kendra's photo. You saw something, didn't you?"

Vy was contemplating whether she should tell them about Cassandra in the background, but chose not to say anything. "I was just looking at the picture, Gunbar. That doesn't give you the right to follow me. You could have come to the hospital with me if you thought I was lying about where I was going."

"That's not the point, Vy," Alexia said. "He thinks you were lying. I can't be around a person who believes you're cold hearted enough to end someone's life." Alexia pushed Vy out of the booth. "Come on, Vy; we're leaving."

Houston got up and walked Vy and Alexia to the door. Vy looked behind her and saw Gunbar looking down at his empty beer mug.

Houston grabbed Vy's hand. "I'm sorry, Vy, Alexia. I had no idea what Gunbar was up to."

"I know you didn't," Vy said sweetly, "but Lexi has a point; how am I supposed to trust Gunbar, if doesn't trust me?"

"I'll talk to him." Houston kissed Vy on the cheek. "Call you later."

*****

Alexia slammed the door once they got back to the apartment. "Can you believe Gunbar? Vy, you haven't said one word since we left the bar. Talk to me."

"I honestly don't know what to say or think. I don't understand why this is happening to me of all people. Talk about being at the wrong place at the wrong time. But she knew something, Alexia."

"Who knew something?"

"Kendra, she knew something about Ricky's death. She almost told me. I wish I could go back in time." Vy let out a sigh. She was tired of thinking about Kendra, Ricky, Dave, and what Gunbar perceived her to be.

Alexia sat next to Vy and put her arm around her. "Everything's going to be okay. You'll see. Then, we can look Gunbar straight in the face and say, 'We told you so.' That will show him."

Vy smiled, but didn't feel content. "I'm going to go check the mail. I need the fresh air."

"You want me to go with you?" Alexia asked.

"No, I'll be fine. I just need a minute to myself."

It was a breezy night. The air felt good against Vy's skin. She followed the sidewalk that led to the mailboxes. She stopped midway, closed her eyes, and took in the scent coming from the gardenia bush. The scent reminded Vy of her mom. When she used to live with her parents, her mom would brighten Vy's room with a vase of gardenia roses from her own garden. Vy re-opened her eyes and continued walking, taking a short cut through the grass. She thought she heard someone walking behind her, but when she turned around, she didn't see anyone. She figured it was one of the neighborhood cats.

She proceeded to walk, but this time she heard someone stepping on a tree branch. Now she felt like she was in one of those scary movies where the damsel in distress knows she's being followed, and asks stupidly, 'Is anyone there?' Like that person is going to reply with, 'Yes, and I'm about to kill you.'

She increased her pace and finally arrived at the mailboxes. She looked around to see if anyone was there. "Maybe this wasn't such a great idea," Vy said to herself. She quickly opened her mailbox, retrieved her correspondence, quickly locked the mailbox, and headed back to her apartment. She heard the footsteps again and finally turned around and asked that stupid question,

"Okay, who's there?" She thought she had shouted it confidently, but her voice cracked.

She saw the shadow of a person coming toward her, so she started to run the opposite direction. She dropped her mail and ran as fast as she could, but she was wearing flip flops, so she wasn't going as fast as she wanted to. Suddenly, Vy barely heard, "Wait! Vy, stop!" She continued running, but slightly turned her head to see who was behind her, and then she blacked out.

"Vy, are you alright?" the man whispered. She slowly opened her eyes. Shawn was looking right back at her.

"Shawn?"

"Yeah, it's me. Sorry I scared you," Shawn whispered again.

"What happened?"

"You ran into a tree," Shawn said, smirking.

Vy slowly sat up and rubbed her forehead. "What is wrong with you? You nearly gave me a heart attack!" Vy smacked his arm.

"I have laryngitis, so I couldn't really yell out that it was me. When I tried to catch up to you, you started running," Shawn said. This time, he started to laugh hysterically.

She joined him. "Thanks a lot!" Vy finally said.

Vy stood up and brushed off the grass in her hair. "Here, you dropped your mail." Shawn continued to chuckle.

"Thanks. By the way, what are you doing here? And how did you know where I lived?"

"I wanted to talk to you about Dave. I saw you walk out of your building, and tried to catch up to you. I wanted to call first, but I can't really talk on the phone," Shawn was whispering.

"How did you know where I lived?" Vy curiously asked again.

"Dave has your contact information at the bar. I hope you don't mind." Shawn started to cough.

"No, I don't mind. You could have at least sent me a text. I don't like surprises, especially these days."

"Sorry." Shawn's eyes looked sad and confused. He looked like he hadn't slept in days.

"How is Dave?" Vy asked.

"The good news is that he woke up. The bad news is that he has to stay in the hospital indefinitely." Shawn coughed again, "Do you mind if we sit somewhere?"

"Sure, let's go to the pool. There's a water fountain there as well," Vy said.

Vy and Shawn situated themselves at a picnic table near the pool. He leaned back on the chair and put his legs up on another chair. Vy did the same thing. Although she was a bit nervous, she wanted to come off as relaxed. "I needed someone to talk to, and for some reason, Vy, I feel like I can talk to you about anything."

"Thanks, Shawn. That means a lot. Whenever you're ready, I'm listening."

Shawn started to whisper, "Like I said, Dave is awake, but he can't leave the hospital. He wants James and me to oversee the Steel Horse."

"Okay," Vy said.

"Here's the problem. When the staff finds out that I'm related to Dave, they're probably going to look at me differently, especially since I'll be managing the bar temporarily."

"Shawn, you have to do what you have to do. It's not like you chose this role. I'm sure that they'll support you, not ridicule you."

"You don't know these people. They put on an act for the crowd. But at closing time, everyone wants to be the main act."

Vy's mind was racing with thoughts. Shawn had just said the equivalent of what Dave had told Vy. She was in a predicament. She wanted to confide in Shawn, but she didn't know if she could. "Shawn, can I ask you a few questions?"

Shawn sat up and placed both feet on the floor. He leaned in towards Vy, and for some reason, her heart rate grew rapidly. Vy looked at her fidgeting fingers, took a deep breath, and looked back up at Shawn. "Go ahead," he said.

"The night that Kendra died, she started telling me something about Ricky's death," Vy said. Shawn leaned in closer.

"There you are!" shouted Alexia. Vy and Shawn jumped out of their seats. "What are you trying to do, kill me?"

"Lexi, calm down; what are you talking about?" Alexia disregarded the fact that Shawn was sitting across from Vy.

"What am I talking about? You tell me you're going to check the mail. You don't come back. I looked for you frantically, and I couldn't find you. So, I went back inside, and I called the police!" Lexi exclaimed.

"What? Lexi, I'm sorry. I should have checked in and told you that I was out here with Shawn. I didn't mean to worry you, but you shouldn't have called the police."

"Well, she did," Houston said. Vy looked up at Houston. He looked like he'd been dragged out of bed. His hair was messed up. He was wearing a wrinkled Def Leopard t-shirt, khaki shorts, and flip flops.

Shawn stood up. "I'm sorry, Vy. I didn't mean to complicate your night. Detective Houston, Alexia, have a good evening." Vy barely heard Shawn speak.

"No, Shawn, wait." Vy stomped her feet out of frustration towards Shawn.

"Don't worry; I'll text you tomorrow," Shawn said as he headed to the parking lot.

"What are you doing walking around at night by yourself?" Houston asked.

"I told her I'd go with her," said Alexia, "but you know how hardheaded she is."

"Next time—" Houston started to say.

"Stop, both of you!" Vy inhaled slowly, and then exhaled. "Both of you have to stop treating me like I'm a child. I have checked my mailbox a million times at night, by myself. I don't need you two breathing down my neck. I feel lucky that both of you care so much, but I'm starting to feel a little claustrophobic."

"Well," Alexia took a moment to gather her thoughts, "mom said that was psychological. You think we're suffocating you, but we're just protecting you."

Vy decided to give in. "Okay, let's just go inside. Houston, want to come up?"

"Sure. Do you have any more cookies?"

"We sure do. I bought two packages," Alexia said, as she wrapped her arm around Vy. "Oh," Alexia looked at the mail Vy was holding in her hand, "did you get *US Weekly*?"

*****

Once they got back to the apartment, Alexia yawned. "I'm going to bed, goodnight." Alexia gave Vy a kiss on the forehead, and waved a goodbye to Houston. Vy and Houston were alone for the first time since they'd met. He was sitting on the loveseat, and Vy was lying on the couch.

"Do you mind if I ask you a personal question?" Houston asked.

"Depends on the question."

Houston moved to the edge of the loveseat and clasped his hands together, "What was Shawn doing here tonight?"

Vy sensed a bit of jealousy. Houston's body language projected just that. She sat up and covered her legs with the throw blanket. "He stopped by to talk to me about Dave and the bar."

"Why didn't he just call you?"

"Because he has laryngitis and can't really talk."

"How did he know where you lived?"

"What's with the questions? Does Shawn coming over here bother you?"

Houston exhaled, "I don't like him, Vy. It seems like he's hiding something."

"And what would that be?"

"I don't know yet. I just—" Houston started to say.

The conversation was starting to get uncomfortable, so Vy took it upon herself to change the topic. "You never did tell me what the captain of the fire department said."

Houston seemed relieved with the topic change. He leaned back on the loveseat. "Okay, I'm going to make this as detailed as possible for you to completely understand the Captain's perspective."

"Go for it. I have all night." Vy smiled and laid back down on the couch.

"Once the captain reviewed the report, he remembered the incident instantaneously."

"That's impressive, considering that's it's been a couple of years, right?" Vy asked.

"Tell me about it. So, he said that when he and the crew arrived at the scene, the woman was lying on the ground on the driver's side of the vehicle. Ricky was sitting on the curb. When questioned, Ricky stated that the woman, who until this day remains unidentified, was driving Ricky home. They were both inebriated, but apparently, she was the soberest out of the two. She somehow lost control of the vehicle, and crashed into a tree. Ricky pulled her out, but apparently it was too late."

"Okay. That matches the police report."

"I know."

"There's a but, isn't there?" Vy asked.

Houston smiled. "Yes. The Captain told me that something about the scene didn't sit well with him."

Vy was now completely intrigued. She straightened her back, crossed her legs, and leaned forward. Marilyn jumped on Houston's lap and looked up at him with her big, brown eyes. At Marilyn's voiceless command, he rubbed her head.

"What didn't make sense to the Captain was that the passenger side of the windshield was damaged," Houston explained.

"Damaged how?"

"Where the windshield was cracked, there was an indentation the size of a basketball, maybe bigger. The indentation resembled a spider web. That signified that somebody's head hit the glass with tremendous force. The center of this spider-cracked glass had visible blood. The Captain assumed that the passenger wasn't wearing a seatbelt. The passenger would have had obvious bleeding to the forehead and scalp area."

"I'm still following you," Vy said.

"The woman had a deep gash on the right side of her forehead, which probably caused her death. Ricky was supposedly the passenger, but he didn't have any cuts on his head," Houston elaborated.

"Oh my God, was Ricky driving the vehicle?"

"That was the captain's assumption. But Officer Thomas Avery was already at the scene when the fire department arrived."

"Why didn't the captain report it to the police department?" Vy asked.

"He did. He reported it to Thomas Avery's supervisor."

"But by that time, Thomas had already been relocated," Vy added.

"Exactly. The supervisor told the captain that the report was already filed and closed. The supervisor made it clear that the department couldn't re-open a report based on an assumption."

"Holy crap, this sounds like a dirty job!" Vy exclaimed.

"Okay, Nancy Drew, you have been watching too many crime movies," Houston snickered.

Houston moved from the loveseat to the couch. He moved closer to her. His warmth felt amazing against her skin. He moved her hair from her eyes. It had been a while since a man had comforted Vy. She had so many questions to ask him about the case. Vy wanted to tell Houston about what Dave had told her. But Houston's touch had her motionless and speechless. She just wanted to take this moment in. Houston placed the palm of his hand on her cheek, leaned in and kissed her passionately. For that moment, nothing else mattered.

TESTING 15

Vy woke up feeling happy and exuberant. Houston's kiss left quite an impression on her mind and her body. Furthermore, she woke up early, determined and with a plan. Alexia was working out with the Ball Bender. She looked up at Vy and smirked, "Look who's glowing this morning."

"Stop," Vy responded.

"Details, please."

"Over lunch. Let's go to the Steel Horse Bar for lunch. I have some snooping to do."

Alexia stopped mid-stomach crunch, "I love your ideas," she said, out of breath.

Once in the car, they sang along to "Billie Jean." "You are aware that neither of us are singing on key, right?" Alexia said as she turned down the radio.

"I don't care. We're in the car. No one can hear us obliterate Michael Jackson's song."

"Yeah, but you don't have sound proof windows."

"True that," Vy said, giggling.

Vy and Alexia arrived at the Steel Horse Bar. This time Vy parked in the parking lot of the shopping center. They got out of the car and walked towards the entrance. The mid-afternoon heat somehow replenished Vy's energy. The sun's rays illuminated the red highlights in Vy's hair. She stopped suddenly and looked up at the crooked sign. "This is so strange to me. I've never been here in the afternoon. And I hardly ever come in through the front door."

"Look at that. Now you're like one of the customers," Alexia said sarcastically. "Come on. I'm sweating my butt off and I'm really hungry."

Vy slowly opened the rotted, wooden door. At night, this place seemed so vibrant, full of energy. But instead of being welcomed by a cloud of cigarette smoke, laughter, and loud music, what welcomed Vy was a jukebox that was barely audible, and loneliness. Kyle wasn't at the door carding customers. No one was shooting pool. The tables and the booths weren't occupied.

"This is like another time zone," Vy said. James was the only one working the bar. "Let's sit at the bar."

"Okay," Alexia said.

"Hi, James," Vy said. She pulled out two stools from under the bar and they situated themselves.

"Hey, Vy, I'm surprised to see you here on a Thursday afternoon."

"We were hungry, and we were in the area. Do you remember my sister Alexia?"

"I haven't properly introduced myself." James held out his hand, and Alexia placed her hand in his. "I'm James." He tenderly kissed her hand. Vy was impressed. She had never seen James' suave side.

"It's nice to meet you, James," Alexia said.

"Let me get you ladies a couple of menus."

Alexia was staring at James' butt as he walked away. "I think he's taken, Lexi."

"I can still look, can't I?"

"Here you are," James said as he handed over the menus.

"Thanks. Is it always so empty this time of day?" Vy asked.

"Yeah. Normally the afternoon crowd comes in at about four. Drink specials motivate the customers."

Vy and Alexia placed their drink and food orders. Since there was no one around, Vy took this opportunity to ask James a few questions. She inhaled, and smiled, trying to hide her actual goal of today's visit.

"James, how's Dave doing?"

James stopped wiping the bar down. "He's still at the hospital, but he's recovering slowly."

Vy had not seen Cassandra or Shawn around. "Where's Cassandra?"

"Out sick; she called in at the last minute."

Just as Vy was going to ask about Shawn, James became distracted by someone who walked into the bar. Both Vy and Alexia turned to see who'd come in.

"Crap," Alexia said. It was Margarite, and she stationed herself by one of the pool tables scoping out the bar.

Vy and Alexia quickly snapped their heads back, "Crap is right. What do we do?"

"Maybe she hasn't and won't see us," Alexia whispered through the side of her mouth.

"Lexi, we're the only ones sitting at the bar!" Vy whispered back.

"Can I help you, ma'am?" James asked.

Margarite now stood at the bar. She placed her handbag on the vacant seat next to Vy.

"Yes, is Shawn available? Roberta! What are you doing here?" Margarite said with surprise. James looked baffled. His eyebrows shifted downward, and he cocked his head sideways.

"I'm surprised to see you here," Margarite continued. Then she shifted her gaze to Vy, "Gwen, is it?" Vy nodded yes. "Well, I'm still waiting for Roberta's business cards." Margarite sounded annoyed, and then looked at Alexia.

"You know how it is with new interns," Alexia said, quickly changing the topic, "and what brings you to Miami?"

"Oh, I needed to speak to Shawn." Margarite looked at James. "Is he in?"

"No, ma'am; he comes in tonight at eight."

Margarite looked frustrated. "I need to head back to West Palm now." She looked around the bar as if she was trying to find a solution to something. "Thank you," Margarite told James, then looked at Vy. "And please do mail me the business cards. I'm in dire need of Roberta's assistance."

Margarite signaled for Alexia to follow her out. She grabbed her handbag and proceeded to the exit. Alexia followed behind Margarite, turning and quickly glancing at Vy as she shrugged her shoulders.

Vy watched Alexia and Margarite from the corner of her eye. They stood in front of the double doors. Margarite said something to Alexia, who nodded, and then Margarite handed her an envelope. She shook Alexia's hand and left. Alexia returned to the bar, sat down, and sighed heavily. James brought their food order, and looked at Vy and Alexia curiously.

"Don't ask," Alexia said to James. He smirked and walked away.

"Okay, spill it," Vy said as she ate a fry.

"Margarite needed to give this envelope to Shawn," Alexia whispered. She then pointed to an envelope inside of her purse, "but she didn't trust giving the envelope to James. I told her that since I lived around this area, I would be more than happy to drop it off tonight. She was more than willing to trust me with it. So, she gave me the envelope to give to Shawn."

Vy and Alexia stared at the envelope like it was going to instantaneously reveal the secret of life. "I have to go to the restroom," Vy said.

"Me too," Alexia replied.

They hurriedly went to the restroom, and locked themselves in a stall. Alexia pulled out the envelope from her purse. "Well?" Alexia was waving the envelope in front of Vy's face.

"Fine, I'll open it," Vy finally said.

It was an adhesive envelope. Vy carefully tried to open it without tearing the paper. She spent five minutes maneuvering the envelope. She finally succeeded. She expanded the envelope and glanced at the contents inside.

"Well, what is it?" Alexia asked impatiently.

"It's a check and a letter." Vy pulled out the check and Alexia took the letter. "Alexia, the check is made out to cash in the amount of five hundred dollars. Do you know what this means?"

"Margarite's been paying Shawn five hundred dollars a week?"

"Seriously, this cannot get any more confusing," Vy said.

"I think you might be wrong," Alexia said as her eyes focused on the words.

"What does the note say?"

"Shawn, you moved and failed to give me your new address. Here is your weekly check. Please email me your updated mailing address. Regards, Margarite."

Vy snatched the letter from Alexia's hand, "Lexi, this letter is typed!"

Alexia took the check and the letter from Vy, and placed the contents back in the envelope. She resealed it and situated it in her purse. Vy plopped down on the toilet seat. She was bewildered.

"We are back to square one," Vy said infuriated. "Okay, so now we know that the weekly payments posted in Margarite's checkbook, are for Shawn. But what does Shawn have to do with Margarite? Why is she paying him every week? How do they even know each other? And the million-dollar question is, did Margarite leave that note on my car?" Alexia was writing in her small notebook. "What are you doing?"

"Keeping track of what we have to find out. Those are great questions, Vy."

There were too many questions and no answers. They finished their meal and headed back to Vy's place.

"Do you want a cocktail?" Vy asked Alexia. Alexia was lying on the couch with her hand on her forehead. "Sure, why not?" Vy's cell phone started making a buzzing sound. "Your phone," Alexia called out from the living room.

"I hear it." Vy retrieved her cell phone from her purse. She had a text message from Shawn that read, 'Going into work at eight. Want to meet at Broody's at seven for a drink?'

"Alexia!" Vy called out. Alexia quickly got off the couch, and sprinted over to the kitchen.

"Are you okay?"

"Read." Vy handed Alexia the cell phone. Alexia took it upon herself to reply to the text.

"What are you doing, Lexi?" Vy yanked the cell phone from Alexia's hand. The screen read sent. "What the heck?"

"You have to meet with him, Vy. It's the only way to get answers. So, I simply replied with, *I'd love to*."

Suddenly, Vy's cell phone briefly buzzed again. Alexia read the text out loud, "Great, see you at seven." Vy downed her alcoholic beverage. "Vy, are you okay?"

"Get your listening device, Lexi. I'm going to get ready."

*****

Vy walked into Broody's feeling sexy and confident. Shawn walked up to Vy. "You look absolutely amazing." He kissed her cheek.

"Thank you."

"I saved us a seat at the bar," he whispered.

"Perfect." Shawn gently took hold of her hand and escorted Vy to her seat.

"So, you still have laryngitis?"

"Unfortunately, but I'm getting better. It's frustrating not being able to speak normally. I sound like Rachael Ray."

As Shawn's lips were moving, Vy was forming in her mind the questions she wanted to ask Shawn. "I took it upon myself to order you an Apple Martini."

Because that was the only sentence Vy had heard thus far, she simply replied with, "Perfect."

"Thanks for meeting me tonight. Our talk was cut short last night."

"I really wanted to see you," Vy said honestly. "How are you holding up?"

"Better each day," Shawn said. "Dave is still in the hospital, and James and I have been managing the bar, which I might add is very difficult. Everyone is relying on me for every little thing."

"Take it day by day. I'm sure that you'll be a pro by the time Dave returns." Vy smiled at Shawn and looked deeply into his eyes. He pulled Vy closer to him. He was about to kiss her, when Vy abruptly pulled away. Her heart was palpitating. "I'm sorry, it's that—" she stammered.

"You're seeing that detective." Shawn pulled away and graced her cheek with his hand. He smiled. "Our drinks are here."

Vy simply nodded. She was speechless. Vy slowly sipped her drink. "I hope this doesn't ruin our night," she finally said.

"Not a chance." Shawn winked at her.

Vy and Shawn talked about music, writing, the music industry, and what Vy's goals were. Time quickly passed, and she realized that she hadn't even come close to accomplishing tonight's mission. Shawn looked at his watch, "Damn, I have to go. Shall we?"

"Yes."

"Can you come by the Steel Horse tonight? I know the bartender personally. I'll make sure he gives you a really good discount if you keep him company for a while."

"Sure, but the discount better be worth it."

"Wow, that didn't take much."

"You had me at discount."

"I know the last place you want to be at right now is at the Steel Horse, considering that you have to sing there tomorrow night, so thanks for saying yes."

Shawn walked Vy to her car. She remembered the envelope. "Oh, Shawn, I almost forgot," Vy took the envelope out of her purse. "I was at the Steel Horse earlier this afternoon having lunch with my sister. A woman named Margarite asked for you, and James said you wouldn't be in until later tonight. She said that getting this envelope to you was very important. She didn't want to leave it with James, so I told her that I'd be more than happy to give it to you."

Vy felt horrible about lying. She didn't think it sounded very convincing. But it was convincing enough to pique Shawn's interest. He took the envelope from Vy's hand, and examined it. "So, she just gave it to you?"

"Yep." Vy didn't want to elaborate further than that, fearing that her voice would crack.

"Okay. Thanks, Vy, for hand-delivering it to me."

Vy couldn't tell if he was being facetious or not. She couldn't read his body language either. She was about to give herself up, but Shawn leaned close to her ear and softly said, “I’ll see you at the Steel Horse.” He nonchalantly turned and walked to his car.

Vy sat in her car for about one second retracing the evening she’d had with Shawn. “We Are Family,” blared from her cell phone. “Hi, Lexi.”

“How did it go?”

“I’ll tell you about it later. I’m headed to the Steel Horse now.”

“Okay, see you there.”

Vy felt safe knowing she had backup, a feeling she didn’t have a few minutes ago.

TESTING 16

The Triple Sensation band was playing at the Steel Horse Bar. Compared to the nights Vy played there, the bar was less than packed. Only two of the three pool tables were occupied, and there weren't too many people on the dance floor. A few people greeted Vy, asking her if she was going to join the band tonight. Vy saw Shawn behind the bar alongside James. She saw a small reserved sign on the bar. Vy assumed that sign was meant for her.

She made her way to the bar, and sat down at her designated area. "Twice in one day! And where's your second half?" James asked.

"Alexia is on her way."

"Are you bothering my special customer, James?" Shawn said playfully.

"Of course not, boss." James looked up. "And here she is." Vy turned around and Alexia was headed their way.

"Sir, do you mind letting this beautiful lady sit?" James asked the man seated next to Vy.

The man took one look at Alexia, and didn't hesitate to get up from his chair. "Here you are, little lady."

"Why, thank you. You are very kind, both of you," Alexia looked at the man then to James.

"It's nice to see you again. It seems as though you were just here," James said.

"You too, James," Alexia said flirtatiously. Vy smacked her knee, and Alexia gave her the 'I can't help it' shrug.

"What will it be, ladies?" Shawn leaned forward as he asked.

"Well, what should we start with?" Alexia asked.

"Can we have two Watermelon Jolly Ranchers?"

"Coming right up."

"You always know what I'm going to like. I don't have worry about getting some nasty drink. So, what happened tonight?" Alexia asked, keeping her voice low.

"Here you are, ladies; enjoy." James placed the shots on the bar, and tended to the next customer.

"I didn't get to ask him anything. I lost track of time. But I'll give you the recorder later, and you can decipher it for yourself. Maybe I missed something."

"Okay, don't fret. We'll ask him soon," Alexia said.

"Oh, and he tried to kiss me."

Alexia gulped quite loudly. "And you waited this long to tell me!"

Vy smiled, while taking a sip of her shot. "Only to see the reaction you're having now."

"Don't keep me waiting, elaborate."

"He moved forward, and slowly pulled me towards him. It was as though that moment was in slow motion. But then, I pulled away, and hinted that I was seeing Houston. Well, he actually figured it out before any words came out of my mouth."

"I knew you liked Houston." Alexia winked at Vy. "I don't want to say I told you so."

"Yeah, yeah." Vy and Alexia clinked their glasses, and made a toast.

"Oh, I did give him the letter," Vy whispered.

"And?"

"And he said thanks." As Vy observed Shawn mixing drinks, a strange feeling came over her.

"On the house. Enjoy." Shawn placed the drinks in front of Vy and Alexia, and went to the opposite end of the bar to take a blonde's order.

"Cheers!" Alexia raised her glass and placed her lips on the rim.

Vy grabbed her wrist and stopped her. "Wait."

"I said cheers," Alexia said.

"No, Lexi, just put your drink down."

"What? Why?"

"I don't know, but just trust me on this. Let's go to the restroom okay. And take your drink with you. Just follow my lead."

"Okay."

"Are you girls doing okay? I was told to give you the special treatment tonight," James said.

"We're great; thanks, James. We're just going to go the restroom. Mind keeping an eye on our seats?"

"No worries. I'll put the sign back up."

Vy and Alexia headed for the restroom. Luckily there was no one in there. The band playing was keeping all the ladies on the dance floor. Vy took Alexia's drink, and poured both drinks into the sink.

"What's going on, Vy?"

"I have a feeling."

"Oh no. Like one of mom's feelings?"

"Exactly."

When Vy and Alexia were younger, their mother would somehow know when they were being mischievous. She would be serving them dinner. Then out of nowhere, she would nonchalantly ask them about their day, but with an inquisitive look. 'We didn't do much today, mama,' was the response they had always agreed upon. That way if they were asked separately, they would be on the same page. But their mother would simply respond with, 'Really? Because, I had the strangest feeling that you girls were up to something.'

With that simple statement, Vy and Alexia would confess out of guilt.

Vy was experiencing that same strange feeling. She sensed that perhaps Shawn was up to something. Dave's words were continuously playing in her mind like a broken record. "Who can I trust? No distractions," Vy said to herself.

Do you think we should call Houston?" Alexia asked.

Vy remained silent for one second contemplating her question. "No. If he shows up that might ruin any chance we have to find out anything."

"Good point," Alexia said. "Okay, what's next?"

"I don't know yet. But whatever you do, avoid drinking anything that anyone serves you. And don't place any more drink orders from anyone either. It's better to be safe than sorry." Alexia nodded. "In the meantime, I'm going to walk around, ask some questions. So, I need you to keep James and Shawn entertained," Vy said.

"Alright. I'm ready to roll."

Vy looked at Alexia strangely. "You're ready to roll?"

"Isn't that the slang term that's being used nowadays?"

"Yeah, but it shouldn't be used by you."

"Fine. Gosh, I was just trying to sound cool," Alexia explained.

Vy chuckled. "You are cool, Lexi, in your own way."

Later, Vy and Alexia were sitting at the bar, empty glasses in hand. Shawn approached Vy. "You were gone a while."

"You know how it is—gossip in the girl's restroom."

Shawn smiled at Vy. "Another round of drinks, ladies?"

"My sister and I are driving, so we're going to hold off for a bit."

"Water then?"

"Yes, please," Vy and Alexia said in unison.

Shawn shook his head, laughing. "Coming right up."

"I'm sorry you feel like you can't trust him right now."

"I don't feel like I can trust anyone. Present company excluded, of course," Vy said smiling.

Vy pivoted towards Alexia. She placed her left elbow on the bar, and cocked her head to the side. "I like that Houston is an open book. He isn't musically inclined, and he and I don't seem to have anything in common. But I feel protected when I'm with him. I can be myself, and that's okay with him. He listens to me. And it doesn't hurt that he's an amazing kisser." Vy turned back around. "Maybe that's why I subconsciously backed off when Shawn attempted to kiss me. I know that there's something special between Houston and me."

"That's nice to hear you say," Alexia said. She held Vy's hand.

"Okay. Wish me luck," Vy said. She did a one sixty on the stool, and faced the dance floor. "I'm going to see what I can find out." She surveyed the bar and spotted one of the waitresses. "I'll be back. Do you remember our plan?"

"Yes." Alexia clapped her hands. "This is so exciting!" Alexia whispered.

"Lexi, you have to get out more often."

"Vy, honey, what are you doing here on your night off?" the waitress asked as she wiped down a table.

She had been a waitress employed by the Steel Horse Bar for over six years. More importantly, she was Dave's confidant. From what Dave had shared with

Vy, she had always been reliable, honest, and hard working.

"My sister Alexia is in town, so I'm showing her around. Shawn also invited us for drinks."

"Ah, Mr. Prince Charming. He's very popular with women. Be careful, Vy, you know how musicians are. No offense, sweetie."

"None taken, but my flirting keeps the bar busy and your tips high."

"Right; you're my friend," she said as she proceeded to clean the next table.

"How's Dave?"

"Unfortunately, I haven't been able to see him. I'm not on the visitor's list. And there's this nurse who doesn't give in, so I haven't even been able to see him for one second. Poor guy. We all miss him, especially me. He's the only one I feel comfortable talking to. But Shawn's doing okay at running the joint."

"Where's Cassandra? I haven't seen her tonight."

"Oh, well, Shawn told her to take a leave of absence so to speak."

"Why?" Vy asked.

"Apparently—"

"Miss, miss. Can we please order?" a lady yelled from behind Vy.

"Sorry, Vy. I have to tend to my tables. But we'll catch up tomorrow night. See you then!"

"Dang it," Vy said to herself.

Kyle wasn't working yet, and James and Shawn were being entertained by Alexia at the bar. So, Vy accidently made her way to the office. She casually turned the knob, and to her surprise it was unlocked. To be on the safe side, she called out as she entered the office, "Hello?" And luckily, no one was there. It was awkward not to see Dave sitting at the desk with his glass of red wine. Vy locked the door behind her.

"Maybe I shouldn't," she said to herself. Vy then unlocked it, and to make sure that the door was completely shut, she pushed it tightly closed.

"Okay." Vy heavily exhaled.

Vy sat in Dave's chair. She briefly glanced up at the monitors. Shawn and James were being kept busy by the customers slowly strolling in. Alexia had her back to the camera. Vy started to rummage through the desk but didn't find anything of importance to her. She quickly skimmed through the drawers, but she had no luck there either. "I'm getting nowhere," Vy said.

Vy spun the chair around, and reached for a Blow Pop from the candy bowl. She knocked off a jacket from the chair. When she picked it up, a note fell out from the inside pocket of the jacket. Vy slowly opened the note, and read it out loud, "We need to talk after work. Meet me in the alley. Kendra."

"Whose jacket is this?" Vy whispered. She instinctively glanced up at the monitors. James was in plain sight, but Shawn wasn't behind the bar.

"Crap!" She shoved the note back in the pocket, and placed the jacket back on the chair. She carefully exited the office, and quickly headed towards the dance floor. Shawn came up behind Vy, and slowly grabbed a hold of her hand, scaring the bejesus out of her, "I've been looking for you."

Vy turned and faced Shawn. "I was just saying hi to people. I was headed back your way."

"Good. You have a special drink waiting for you."

"Great."

"I'll see you there. I have to get more Vodka from the office."

Alexia was laughing at something James had said. Vy quickly sat down. "Don't worry, Vy; I was taking good care of her."

"I'm sure you were, James. Thanks." Vy smiled.

Alexia spoke from the side of her mouth like a ventriloquist, "I sent you a warning text."

"Didn't see it, now shush."

Shawn was back behind the bar. "Okay, ladies, this drink is on me. Enjoy."

Vy and Alexia briefly stared at each other. They raised their glasses, but this time it was Vy's turn to toast, "Here goes nothing." They each sipped their drinks and then set them down.

Later, Vy and Alexia were enjoying the band, and the people watching. Vy saw Kyle stroll into the bar and head to the restroom. "Alexia."

"You ready to go?"

"Almost. Kyle just walked in. I want to talk to him before his shift starts."

"Is this the guy that Tina had a date with?"

"Yeah, the bouncer. He just came out of the restroom. I'll only be a minute."

Alexia slightly turned towards Kyle's direction. "Do you want me to tag along? He seems intimidating."

"He's harmless. No worries."

"That's what you think. Remember, Vy, you can't trust anyone."

"It's cool, Lexi. I'll be back." Vy wanted to avoid Alexia's further paranoia, so she quickly got up and approached Kyle.

Kyle was tucking in his black Steel Horse t-shirt, and adjusting his belt. "Shouldn't you be doing that in the restroom?" Vy sweetly asked.

Kyle slowly turned around. Upon seeing her, his expression changed from grim to elated. "Vy!" He encircled her in a bear hug and slightly lifted her off the floor. "It's so great to see you," Kyle breathlessly said into her right ear.

"You too," Vy said.

Kyle gently placed Vy down and gradually let her go. "You aren't singing tonight, are you?"

Kyle had heavy bags under his pain-stricken eyes. "No. I came here to have a few drinks with my sister." Vy pointed to Alexia, and she waved back. Vy knew she was keeping an eye on her every move.

"Cool."

"Hey, you have a second to talk?"

"For you, always. Want to sit outside?"

"Yes. Lead the way." Vy quickly sent Alexia a text message telling her where she was going. She quickly looked at Alexia. She gave Vy a thumb up.

The summertime in Miami was finally setting in. It was humid and scorching outside. Vy didn't mind the heat. Her skin always welcomed it. Kyle's forehead, however, was showing signs of heat discomfort.

"If you're hot, we can go back inside," Vy said.

"No, I'm fine."

They sat on a decrepit, wooden bench. "You mind?" Kyle reached into his pocket, and pulled out a fattened cigarette.

"No, not at all. I didn't know that you smoked."

"I started up again. Too much going on to stay smoke-free. You hear me?" Kyle asked. Vy nodded.

As Kyle lit his cigarette, he squinted his eyes. He instantly inhaled the nicotine, and gradually released the smoke through his nostrils. Vy was analyzing his minor movements and various facial expressions. It was as though he was having a conversation with himself mentally.

"Kyle about the, well, the stuff that's going on, how are you holding up?" Vy knew it was a stupid question, but she had to start somewhere.

"When I found out about Kendra, I just—" Kyle became teary eyed. "Is it true?" He took a drag from his cigarette and looked off into the distance.

"Is what true?"

"That you found her?" He turned and faced Vy.

"It's true," Vy simply said.

Vy was now looking off into the distance. Unfortunately, she had a flashback of Kendra lying in a puddle of blood.

"It's just that you never know when to believe the rumors in this place."

"Kyle, do you know who would want to hurt Kendra?"

"So that's true as well?" Kyle let out a slight chuckle.

"What is?"

"That you're snooping around. That you're running your own investigation."

"Who are these rumors coming from?" Vy asked exasperated.

Kyle flicked his cigarette on to the sidewalk. "Listen, Vy, I want you to find out who did this to Kendra. These cops have no idea what they're doing. They don't even have a suspect in custody."

Vy was relieved that the rumor of her being a person of interest in Kendra's murder had not been made public. The sincerity in his eyes proved Kyle's innocence to Vy.

"There's Ricky's death to consider as well."

"Screw Ricky. That bastard got what he deserved." Kyle's tone and the gleam in his eyes shifted to a vicious one. Vy was taken aback by his reaction and response.

"But, Kyle, I think that," Vy started to say.

Kyle looked at his watch, and then focused on her. "Vy, be careful."

"Why does everyone keep saying that?" Vy said.

"Because there are a lot of eyes keeping track of you."

"Who?"

"I can't tell you that. I have my own reasons. But there's only so much I can do to protect you."

"You not telling me who to look out for is not protecting me."

"Vy, you'll soon understand. Open your eyes."

"But—"

Kyle kissed her cheek. "I have to go inside, my shift started."

"But Kyle."

"Just remember what I told you."

Just like that, Kyle went inside. Vy remained on the bench shivering, although it felt like it was a hundred degrees outside. "No one can tell me anything!" Vy yelled to herself. Vy headed back inside. She was so upset that she didn't even acknowledge Kyle. She joined Alexia at the bar.

"That was more than a few minutes, you know. I almost came out there."

"You won't even believe the conversation that I just had." She slammed her hands on the bar.

"Another drink, beautiful?" Shawn asked.

"Why not."

"Coming right up."

"What's up with you?" Alexia asked.

"Evidently, I have to keep my eyes open." Vy explained in detail what Kyle had shared with Vy.

"So that's it? He'd rather keep you susceptible to danger than tell you who the culprit is? That's it." Alexia started to get up from the stool, but Vy grabbed her arm. "Sit. I have it all under control."

"Here you are, ladies." Shawn winked at Vy and walked away.

The remainder of the night was unproductive. Vy and Alexia were relieved that their special drinks were like any other drinks. They were awfully tired, so they decided to go home. Alexia was anxious to hear what Vy had recorded earlier that night.

"Thanks. We had a great evening," Alexia said.

"The pleasure was all mine," James said to Alexia.

Shawn came around the bar. He hugged Vy, and faintly spoke in her ear, "I'd walk you to your car, but we're slammed."

"I know. Don't worry." Vy kissed his cheek.

"I know that you're dating the cop guy, but I was wondering if I could take you out to dinner on Saturday night."

Vy was bewildered by his persistence. "I'll call you. Have a good night."

*****

After the drive home, they parked the car and went into Vy's apartment. "This investigating thing is difficult," Alexia said.

"Tell me about it," Vy agreed.

Vy and Alexia plopped down on the couch. "Although I'm anxious to hear all the juicy details, can we take a break from all this for a minute?" Alexia asked.

"Music to my ears," Vy said.

"Can you play 'Nothing Compares to You'? I love when you sing it."

"I would love to. It's been a while since I've played that song."

Alexia fell asleep as Vy sang the chorus. For her own satisfaction, she finished playing the song, placed the guitar down, and leaned back on the couch and closed her eyes for what she thought was a second.

Vy and Alexia were awakened by someone banging on the door. "What the heck," Vy said irritated.

"Don't answer, Vy," Alexia said nervously. "I'm going to text Gunbar."

"I'm getting my stun gun," Vy said.

The banging persisted for about thirty seconds, and then it instantly stopped. Vy, Alexia, and Marilyn were standing three feet away from the door, staring at it. "Do you think that whoever it was is gone?" Alexia asked.

"I hope so. Did you get a hold of Gunbar?"

"Yeah, he's on his way. He said to stay put and to not open the door."

"You think?" Vy asked sarcastically.

Five minutes passed, and the banging commenced again. "Open the door, it's the police."

"How do we know that?" Vy yelled.

"See, and only because you wanted to save one hundred and fifty bucks on a door," Alexia whispered.

"I'll order the peephole door tomorrow," Vy whispered.

"Vy, open up! It's Gunbar."

TESTING 17

"Are you two okay?" Gunbar asked. He was scanning the apartment from where he stood. A significantly young officer proceeded inside with his gun drawn. "Sir?"

"Search the apartment," Gunbar ordered. The officer nodded and headed towards the bedroom.

"We're okay. We're just a bit startled. There's no need to search the apartment," Alexia said.

"Alexia, we have to cover all bases," Gunbar replied.

"Did you see anyone lurking around outside?" Vy asked.

"We're looking," Gunbar was interrupted.

"Sir, can I please have a word with you?" A younger version of Antonio Banderas addressed Gunbar.

Gunbar stepped outside with the officer. When Gunbar returned inside, he was holding a plastic baggy that contained a white piece of paper.

"Vy, Officer Ramirez found this note taped to the windshield of your car."

Vy took the bag and read the note out loud, "'I warned you once to stay out of it. This is your final warning.' This looks just like the first warning note," Vy whispered to herself. She shoved the bag back to Gunbar.

"Great, this is just great!" Vy said.

"Let's have a seat, okay?"

Gunbar led Vy to the couch. He sat down on the right-hand side of Vy with Alexia to her left. Vy was shivering. She wrapped the throw blanket around her upper body.

Gunbar seemed sincere. "I have a few men out there scoping out the area. Now, tell me exactly what happened tonight."

Vy and Alexia told Gunbar in detail the events of their night. When they finished, Gunbar closed his miniature-sized notebook, and gave them a tired look. "First of all, you two are exhausting to listen to. It's like watching a tennis match. But you were very thorough and that helps," Gunbar stated.

There was a knock on the door. "I'll get that," Gunbar said. Vy and Alexia followed behind him anyway.

"There was no one on the premises, sir," the officer told Gunbar.

"Thank you. You can head back to the station now. I still have a few more questions for the ladies."

"Have a good night, sir, ladies." He smiled at Vy and Alexia. He did an about face and left the apartment.

"Army?" Alexia asked.

"Navy." Gunbar laughed. "So, you ladies were snooping around again."

"Only because I'm a person of interest," Vy said defensively.

"Listen, Vy, I'm sorry. It's just," Gunbar stopped speaking. He was searching for the right words, "it's never taken me this long to close a case. Now, I have two murders and no suspect. This is not an excuse, it's an explanation."

Vy was now seated at the dining room table. "I understand," Vy moaned. "I want this to be over as much as you do. Somehow, this person thinks I know something, and now I'm caught in his or her sick scheme."

Alexia sat next to Vy, and put her arm around her. "Get the recording device. Let's listen to it with Gunbar."

"You recorded tonight's events?"

"Yes," Vy and Alexia said in unison.

"You two always have something up your sleeves. Come on, let's listen," Gunbar said.

After they listened to the recording, Gunbar stood up. "Do you mind if I take this with me. There might be something in the conversations you had with Shawn and Kyle that I might have missed."

"Did you question Kyle already?" Vy asked.

"Yes, hence his 'cops don't know what they're doing' comment. He was defensive and belligerent. Although the recording wouldn't be admissible in court, it gives me a better perspective on this guy. But now it's time to let the professionals handle it."

"I know what you're insinuating. Stay out of it," Alexia said.

"You got it."

"But—" Vy said.

"No buts, Vy. This person knows where you live, what you drive, and where you sing. You've been threatened. Good Lord, woman, what other signs do you want?"

"He's right, Vy. Let them do their job," Alexia said, visibly shaken.

"Okay. But Gunbar, do me a favor and catch this guy already."

There was a knock on the door. Gunbar answered it and Houston walked in. "Gunbar," Houston nodded, "everything under control?"

"Yes," Gunbar said. "Vy, I have a patrol car parked outside of your building. He'll be there until the morning."

Gunbar looked at Houston. “See you tomorrow, Houston. Ladies, stay safe.”

As Gunbar approached the door, Alexia ran to him and hugged him. Vy didn’t hear what Alexia said to Gunbar, but she heard him reply, “It’s what we do.” Gunbar’s arms hugged Alexia tighter, and then he let her go.

Houston seemed standoffish with Vy. “Hey,” Vy said.

“I’m staying here tonight.” Vy smiled, but Houston didn’t share her enthusiasm. “I’ll be on the couch. If you two need anything, let me know,” Houston said dryly.

“How about a long good night kiss?” That’s what Vy wanted to ask for, but all she said was, “Thanks. So, do you want anything to drink or eat?”

“No, I’m fine, thank you. You should go to bed. I heard you had a long, productive evening?”

“What?”

“Here you are.” Alexia handed Houston a blanket and a pillow.

“Thanks, Alexia. Good night, ladies.”

Houston situated himself on the couch. He had his back to Vy as he took off his shoes. “Good night,” Vy said as her last attempt to start a conversation. Houston hadn’t even bothered to look back at her. He just waved his hand in the air.

Vy tumbled into bed. “How do you manage to wrap yourself up in the comforter? You look like a human-size worm.”

Alexia giggled. “Sorry. Here you go.”

Vy managed to get comfortable, but mentally she was uneasy. She was contemplating if she should try to talk to Houston one more time.

“He knows,” Alexia said while staring up at Vy’s neon stars on the ceiling.

"You mean about Shawn?"

"Yep."

"But it's not what he thinks. I was just trying to get information."

"I know that, but he doesn't. Just let it go for now. He'll be fine in the morning."

"Tomorrow is going to be another exciting day," Vy said to herself as she closed her eyes.

*****

Vy drifted off into a dream. "Alexia, hurry, he's catching up to us!" Vy was short of breath, but she couldn't stop running. Alexia seemed to be getting farther and farther away from her. She tried to slow down, but her legs weren't allowing her to. The dark alley seemed never-ending. With every puddle Vy stepped in with her bloody, bare feet, she winced with pain. The rain drops shooting into Vy's eyes were piercing and blinding.

Vy glanced back to see if Alexia was any closer to her. Suddenly, Vy saw a tall shadowy figure catching up to Alexia.

"Alexia, he's right behind you!"

"Vy, I can't get to you!" Alexia held out her arm to Vy, but she was only grasping at thin air. There was now a combination of rain and tears running down Vy's face. She immediately made a one-eighty and started running towards Alexia. Her knees became weak, and she had painful cramps alongside her rib cage, but that wasn't going to slow Vy down. From a distance, she saw that Alexia had tripped and fallen onto the street. The shadowy figure now stood above Alexia. "Vy, please help me!"

"I'm almost there! Get away from her, you bastard!"

The figure raised his left arm ready to strike Alexia with an object. He let out a deafening, cynical laugh.

"No! Alexia, get up!" Vy said yelling and crying at the same time.

Vy abruptly awoke from her nightmare. She was in an upright position, and her forehead was drenched in sweat. She looked over to her right, but Alexia wasn't in bed. Marilyn, who was at the foot of the bed, slowly opened her eyes and stared at Vy. "Sorry, Marilyn. I didn't mean to wake you up. Bad dream." Vy patted her on the head. Marilyn stretched her lower half, and gradually maneuvered herself off the bed.

Vy walked past the guest restroom where Alexia was taking a shower. She was singing her own version of Taylor Swift's song, "You Belong with Me." After the nightmare she'd awakened from, she was happy to hear Alexia's cheerful, muffled voice.

"He's gone, Marilyn," Vy said as she carried her cat to the kitchen.

There was a post-it note on the coffeemaker that read, 'Thanks for the coffee. I'll call you later. H.' Houston left the bed sheets neatly folded on the couch. She picked up her guitar from the loveseat, strummed the C chord, and then placed it on the guitar stand.

Vy stood in front of her sliding glass door. The palm trees were at a standstill, and the sun rays were peeking through the leaves. It was a perfect, beautiful morning. Vy decided to take advantage of the cloudless sky, and go to the pool. She wanted to be relaxed for tonight's gig. She changed into her bikini, and banged on the restroom door, "I'm going to the pool!" She didn't want Alexia calling the police again. With all the commotion that had been happening at her apartment, the neighbors were going to start talking sooner or later.

"Okay! She wears short skirts, I wear t-shirts," Alexia continued singing.

Vy followed the sidewalk to the pool, coffee in one hand, mystery novel in the other. She saw a police vehicle parked at the entrance of her building. She waved at the officer, and changed her route towards the vehicle. "Good morning, officer?" Vy asked.

"Neely. Good morning, ma'am."

"I'm Vy. Thanks for keeping an eye out last night. My sister and I felt a lot safer knowing you were out here."

"My pleasure." He had Tom Cruise's adorable smile. Perfect white, straight teeth, and although he probably hadn't slept all night, his hair was perfectly slicked back. Vy wondered if all the officers at this station were this handsome.

"Would you like me to bring you some coffee?"

"No need, ma'am. I'm scheduled to leave in fifteen minutes. I'll be heading straight to Dunkin Donuts."

"Aw, my favorite. Well, thank you again, Officer Neely." The officer flashed Vy his movie star smile.

"I'm missing something," Vy said to herself. "Oh shoot." She'd forgotten her cell phone.

Vy went back to the apartment and made her way to the bedroom. Alexia came out of the restroom wearing her bikini. "I was just going to meet you at the pool."

"I forgot my cell phone."

She had a text message from Houston that read, 'How about lunch at the Green Tavern.'

Vy happily replied with, 'I'd love to.'

*****

Vy and Alexia got dressed for lunch.

"Does this look okay?" Vy asked Alexia while she stared at herself in the mirror.

"You look fabulous," Alexia said.

"You don't think there's too much cleavage, do you?"

"Mom is the one who taught us that if you have it and it looks good, then flaunt it. You look great, Vy."

Vy slipped on her sandals and fixed her hair for the last time. “I’ll call you when I’m done,” Vy said as she hugged Alexia.

“I’ll be here. Have fun and don’t be nervous. I’m sure that once you explain everything to Houston, things will be fine between the two of you.”

“I sure hope so.”

The Green Tavern had a busy lunch crowd. Vy spotted Houston next to the hostess. She walked over to him and gently patted his noticeably muscular biceps. “Hi. I got us a booth. After you.” Houston gestured with his hand. He didn’t even let Vy say hello. She thought maybe this wasn’t such a great idea.

Vy and Houston placed their food and drink orders. Houston broke the silence, “Listen, I know that you and I aren’t official. And I’m fine with you wanting to date other men, but I don’t want you dating Shawn.”

Vy wasn’t sure if she was angry because Houston didn’t mind her seeing other men, or because he didn’t want her seeing Shawn. Vy inhaled and exhaled heavily, “Well, hello to you as well.”

“I just wanted to tell you, and get it over with.” Vy simply smiled and casually looked towards the entrance of the restaurant. “Say something,” Houston concluded.

“Bryan, you can’t tell me who I can or can’t date.”

“But,”

“Let me finish,” Vy cleared her throat and continued, “For your information, I went out with Shawn last night because I wanted to try to get information from him, anything that could get me off the person of interest list.”

“So, you didn’t go out with him because you’re interested?”

“Maybe at the beginning I was, but the more time I spent with you, my feelings started changing. Did Shawn and I almost kiss, yes, but we didn’t kiss because I didn't want to. Listen. Yes, Shawn is handsome, charming, funny, and a great musician, but I'm into you."

Houston remained silent. "My feelings for you are undeniably stronger than the physical attraction I had for Shawn," Vy explained. "I mean don't get me wrong. I find you extremely attractive and I'm physically drawn to you. But what I feel for you goes beyond that." By this point, Houston was completely focused on Vy.

Vy let out a short sigh, tossed her bangs aside, and crossed her arms waiting for Houston's reaction. She was astonished at herself, for the openness and honesty about her feelings for Houston, but he was unresponsive.

"Here you are." The waitress placed their food on the table. "If you need anything else, just holler." The waitress's ponytail swayed from side to side as she walked away.

Houston took a bite out of his French fry. "Oh no you don't," Vy protested. "You can't just sit there with a poker face on. Don't you have anything to say? Do you have any idea how difficult it was for me to tell you how I feel about you?"

"One of the first things they teach you in the academy is that when you're interrogating someone, you have to ask your questions one by one. You shouldn't ask multiple questions at a time. It throws the suspect's focus off, and it's a distraction. And, I wasn't just sitting here. I was eating my fries," Houston stated.

"Ah!" Vy slammed her hands on the table. The plates jumped a centimeter from the surface.

Houston's grin could not get any bigger, "So, what you're saying is that you really like me, huh?"

"Are you kidding me? You make me so," Vy stammered, then Houston leaned over the table and kissed her. He knew how to shut her up. His lips disconnected from hers, and he continued to eat his fries with a grin.

"I can't believe you said my first name," Houston said.

"Yeah, well, I was angry. But I'm over it now," Vy said smiling.

Their topics of conversation varied throughout lunch. "So, how many siblings do you have?" Houston asked.

"I'm the youngest of six."

"But you're closest to Alexia?"

"Yes. I think it's because we grew up together. I never lived in the same household with any of my other brothers and sisters. I used to follow Alexia around because I wanted to be exactly like her." Vy looked down at herself, "but as you can see, that didn't happen."

"I think it's great that you had her to look up to. I don't have any brothers or sisters. But my grandmother, she was everything to me." Houston smiled. He was playing with his fork, and it seemed like he was reminiscing.

"Tell me about her," Vy said. She was intrigued to know about Houston's upbringing. She wanted to know what led him into becoming who he was today.

"When I was a little boy, I would constantly run into my Grandma Mildred's house crying because I had either scraped my knee or elbow. My Grandma would pat her knee, and she would sit me on her lap. She would look into my eyes and say, 'eye winker', and she would point to my eyes, 'nose smeller', and she would point to my nose, 'lip kisser', and she would point to my lips, 'chin chopper', and she would point to my chin, 'tickle, tickle, tickle', and she would tickle me under the chin. For some reason, I would laugh hysterically, jump off her knee and go back outside to play, completely forgetting what I was crying about in the first place. She was an amazing woman."

Houston was getting sentimental, so Vy quickly changed the subject. "Why did you become a detective?"

Houston pushed his plate to the side, and took a sip of his Sprite. "Do you want the long or short version?"

"I want the uncut, unedited version. I have plenty of time."

Houston straightened out his back, leaned forward, and clasped his hands. "Most of my scraped knee and elbow incidents were during my elementary school days. Most of my time was spent dressing up as an officer and upholding the law, especially on career day. My passion for the profession continued into my teenage years. My attention was captured by the authority figures on the street who wore the brown uniform, gleaming patent leather shoes, and accessories. The people who risked their lives without question had my utmost respect. It was in high school that I lost my grandmother to a fatal car accident. It was a car chase. A drug deal gone bad situation. They ran her off the highway into a ditch, and continued driving."

"Did they ever catch the people who did it?"

"Oh, they sure did. And that bastard is still paying for it."

"That must have been traumatic for you," Vy said.

"Actually, it was that singular event that led me to dedicate myself to law enforcement and create a better life for myself."

"Another round of drinks, folks?" the waitress asked.

Vy was so enamored with Houston's story that she completely forgot where she was. "Can I have a cup of coffee, please?"

"Make that two," Houston added.

As soon as the waitress walked away, Vy urged Houston to continue. "Please go on," Vy said.

Houston cleared his throat, "Well, I quickly found out that seeking your goals and aspirations came with a price. That included accepting that disappointments were a commonplace, and that desire wasn't enough. So, I kept at it and after five years of perseverance, I was accepted into the Metro Dade County Police Department and passed the academy. After working the road, midnights, and numerous positions within the department, I applied for Homicide. It wasn't an easy decision."

"So, would you say that becoming a detective stems from your grandmother?"

"You could say that. Joining the team made me question my decision to move from wearing shorts to work, driving basically anything I wanted, and free reign of the city, to dealing with death. However, after everything I've discovered in this career, it has become the greatest honor in my life. Murder is the ultimate crime, the big daddy of the little stuff. Changing someone's life, giving closure to families, and stopping someone from killing again, gives me the motivation to seek out those who have no respect for human life. To be a true dedicated cop, a protector of the normal man's reality," Houston air quoted normal. "It takes heart, dedication, and placing other people's wants and needs in front of yours."

Vy was pouring the creamer into her coffee without taking her eyes off Houston. "Don't you get tired of dealing with bad people, seeing dead bodies, and having the pressure of preventing awful things from happening?"

"It's in my heart ,Vy. It must be. If not, I wouldn't be doing it." Houston leaned back, but Vy leaned in closer to him. The table pressed against her stomach. "Vy, I live my life and act in accordance with three simple rules. One, there is no hunting like the hunting of an armed and dangerous man or woman. Two, no greater honor will ever be bestowed on an officer or a profound duty imposed on him, than when he is entrusted with the investigation of the death of a human being. And three, I have been where you fear to be, I have seen what you fear to see, and I have done what you fear to do, to protect—well—you."

"Wow, your story is incredible."

Houston was blushing. They were silent for just a moment, but then he quickly took the focus off himself. "Tell me about last night."

Vy spent the rest of their lunch time telling Houston about last night and her suspicions. "So, I now have two suspects on my list."

"On your list?" Houston chuckled.

"Do you want to hear my opinions or not?"

"By all means," Houston said.

"Okay, well after last night, obviously, Kyle's my number one suspect, but only for Ricky's murder."

"Hmm," Houston nodded.

"And I believe Cassandra's in on it somehow."

"Based on a photo, Vy?" Houston was right, but Vy had a hunch.

"How about Shawn?"

"No, because—"

"You like him as a person?"

"Here's the check. Please pay upfront. Thank you and have a great day." Saved by the waitress.

Houston escorted Vy to her car. "By the way, you look beautiful. The dress compliments your body very well."

Vy blushed. "Thank you. I didn't think you noticed."

"I noticed you the moment you stepped into the restaurant. For me, you were the only one in the place." Houston kissed her forehead. "I'll see you at your gig tonight."

"Screw it," Vy said to herself. She got on her tippy toes, grabbed the back of Houston's head, and pulled him in for a passionate kiss. Then she just as spontaneously pulled back, "Okay, see you tonight."

She got into her Mustang, revved the engine, and drove away. Vy started to laugh when she looked at her rearview mirror and noticed that Houston hadn't moved from where she'd left him standing.

TESTING 18

"I can tell by the look on your face, that your lunch date went very well," Alexia said as soon as Vy walked in through the door.

"You were right; once I laid all the cards on the table, everything fell into place. After the talk we had, I see everything in a different light."

"Sit down and tell me in detail," Alexia requested.

Vy gave Alexia a play-by-play of her date. She started from the moment she arrived at the Green Tavern, and ended with leaving Houston immobile with her kiss.

"I can't believe that you actually told Houston how you felt about him."

"I know! Can you believe that I didn't consult with you first? That's a big step for me," Vy said mockingly.

"Ah, my little sister's growing up," Alexia said.

"Very funny, Lexi. Anyway, I'm going to lay down for a bit. This sharing your emotions thing is tiring. I want to be energetic for tonight's gig."

"Okay, I'm running to the supermarket. Love you."

Vy made herself comfortable in bed and was about to close her eyes, when her cell phone buzzed twice in her purse. She knew by the two buzzes, that she'd received a text message. She contemplated getting up.

"Fine," Vy grunted. She kicked the down comforter off her and retrieved her cell phone from her purse. The text read, 'Have dinner tonight with me before your gig.' The text was from the one person that Houston refused Vy to see—Shawn.

Vy stared at her screen not knowing how to reply. If she said yes, she might be able to talk to Shawn about Cassandra, and their altercation. But if she said yes, Houston would be livid. Vy's argument to Houston would be that she was having dinner with Shawn for investigative purposes, although she did tell Gunbar and Alexia she would stay out of it. Vy couldn't postpone her response any longer. She replied, threw her cell phone back in her purse, jumped into bed, and resumed her comfortable position.

Vy dreamed she stepped inside her touring bus, and saw that it was ransacked. All her Matchbox Twenty posters were shredded to pieces, and her Ovation acoustic guitar was smashed in half. There was a post-it note on one half of the guitar that read, "This could be your face." Vy fell to her knees and started to cry. Suddenly, Rob Thomas was standing behind Vy, and he said repeatedly, "Vy, get up. Vy, get up."

"Vy, get up." She slowly opened her eyes to find it wasn't Rob Thomas, but Alexia shaking her, "Vy, come on; wake up already."

"I'm up. I'm up. Can you stop violently shaking me?"

"Shawn's here."

Vy quickly sat up. "What?"

"Yes, he comes bearing gifts."

"You've got to be kidding me."

"No. Go brush your teeth, fix your hair, and get your butt out there," Alexia demanded.

Marilyn was sleeping on the foot of the bed. She looked up at Vy with a good luck look and closed her eyes again.

Vy quickly cleaned herself up and went to the living room. Shawn was sitting on the couch holding a bouquet of lavender roses, Vy's favorite.

"Hi, Shawn, what are you doing here?"

Shawn stood up and walked over to Vy. "Your text said that you were too tired to go out to eat, so I brought dinner to you." Shawn looked over to Vy's dining room table. He'd brought her favorite Cuban dish—grilled chicken breast, white rice, black beans and plantain chips. She was speechless, "But how did you know?"

"I came here prior to your sister waking you up. I asked her what your favorite flowers were and what you liked to eat."

"You didn't have to go out of your way."

"I didn't go out of my way. I wanted to do this for you." Shawn was still holding the lavender roses.

"The roses are beautiful, Shawn, thank you." She took the roses from his hand, and gently brushed his skin.

Vy went to the kitchen to get a vase. She placed the roses in the center of the dining room table. "I hope the roses last," Vy said as she arranged them.

"If you water them in a couple of days, I'm sure they will last."

"Oh, that's not it. My cat Marilyn likes to bite on the rose pedals. It's this weird habit she has. That's why I rarely get myself flowers."

"You shouldn't be getting yourself flowers in the first place." Shawn lightly kissed her cheek. Her heart rate rapidly increased. Shawn was too sweet and thoughtful to be considered a suspect.

"Shall we eat?" Shawn asked Vy as he waited for her to sit down first.

Vy devoured her meal. "This was so good," she said with her mouth full. "I haven't eaten a Cuban dish in a while."

"I'm glad that you're happy. I personally know that it sucks to feel worn out and tired before a gig. I figured this would get your momentum going and your energy on overdrive."

"You figured right. Thank you."

Vy stood up to retrieve Shawn's plate from the table. He placed his hand on hers and stopped her. "Vy, can I tell you something?" *What now?* she thought to herself. She didn't think that she could handle another emotional moment. One was enough for the day.

"Sure, what's up?" Vy placed the plate down and sat.

"Vy, I like you a lot. You're an amazing woman. I wouldn't want anything to happen to you."

"What do you mean?" Vy's chest started to blotch. That signified that an uneasy feeling was creeping up.

"Sorry, that came out wrong. What I'm trying to say," Shawn paused. "What I was going to say was that—"

"Say it already!" Vy was getting impatient.

"Do you want to go on an official date with me?"

"Shawn!"

"You don't have to answer me right now. If you need to think about it, take your time."

"Listen, Shawn." Vy's thoughts were scattered. She didn't know how to respond without burning any bridges with Shawn. She did like him, but after her date with Houston, she had realized she wanted to give herself and Houston a shot. "I think we should just be friends for the time being."

"Is it because you're seeing that detective?"

"It's because I don't like to date musicians. I've learned my lesson several times." *That should stall Shawn until I figure out what's going on with the murders and my life,* she thought.

"Well, maybe I'll be able to change that in time. We'll just play it by ear then." Shawn smiled sweetly and kissed her hand.

After washing the dishes and cleaning up, Vy joined Shawn in the living room. Alexia was nowhere to be seen nor heard. Vy sat adjacent to Shawn. It was better to be safe than sorry.

"How's the bar running?"

"Busy as usual. Hopefully, Dave will get better sooner rather than later and take over." Shawn's eyes became saddened.

"I know it's been hard on you, but Dave will pull through."

"Vy, you have no idea how difficult it's been."

"Want to talk about it?"

Shawn hesitated. "No. It's cool."

"What happened with Cassandra? One of the waitresses mentioned that you sent her home for a while."

"News travels fast," Shawn said. "Cassandra took Kendra's death pretty badly. She was irritable and started taking out her frustrations on the customers. I can't have that. So, I had a talk with her and told her to take some time off. Take time for herself."

"That's sounds rational and logical," Vy said.

"Well, she didn't think so. She flipped out on me. Stormed out of the office, and I haven't heard or seen from her since. I tried calling her and texting her, but she doesn't respond to any of my messages. Kyle's going to check on her later."

"You tried to do what was best. Don't be so hard on yourself. James has been a big help, huh?"

"You have no idea." Shawn looked at his phone, "Listen, Vy, I have to get going. I have to run inventory before its gets busy tonight."

"Oh, okay." Vy followed Shawn to the door. "See you later?"

Shawn smiled. "See you later." He grabbed a hold of her hand, "Vy?"

"Yes?"

Shawn looked down and slowly made eye contact with Vy. He wasn't giving her a seductive look, it was more of a concerned look. "Nothing, I'll see you tonight."

Vy closed the door, and leaned on it. She felt as though there was a hidden message in Shawn's eyes.

Vy settled herself back in bed encompassed by her comforter and turned on the television. 'Tropical Storm Susie is strengthening, and will possibly become a Category Two hurricane by tomorrow, noon time.' Alexia knocked on the door and poked her head in, "Can I watch TV with you?"

"Of course!"

"Anything good on Lifetime?" Alexia asked.

"I haven't gotten to that channel yet. But it's probably the usual: love, deceit, and murder."

"I love it," Alexia said.

"The weather guy just informed me that the tropical storm is getting worse. It could possibly turn into a hurricane," Vy said.

"I heard. Dad just called to tell me. You know how worried he gets. He told me to be careful driving, and to avoid all flooded roads."

"You can't blame him; we're daddy's little girls," Vy jested.

"I don't rely on the weatherman anyway. One minute, a hurricane's coming, causing everyone to go frantic, and then it's only just a small tropical storm," Alexia said.

The rain drops banged against the bedroom window. Marilyn was nuzzled between Vy and Alexia's feet. "You mean, you killed her?" pronounced one of the actors on Lifetime. "Of course, she killed her, you idiot!. You had an affair with her, and then drugged her to go back to your crazy wife!" Alexia shouted at the television.

A Tide commercial came on just as the woman was going to stab the deceiving man. "I love these movies. They're so out there, but still addicting," Vy said.

"This takes me back to when we were kids. Remember when I used to call you into my room, and ask you to tell me stories so that you could put me to sleep?" Alexia said.

"Yeah, I remember. Mom and Dad would shush us when we would start laughing too loudly in the middle of the night."

"It seems like it was just yesterday." Alexia remained quiet then continued, "I don't feel comfortable leaving you alone."

"I've lived alone for years," Vy replied.

"There's a minor discrepancy now. There's a murderer out there who might be after you."

"Don't worry. I have Houston, Gunbar, Adrianna, and Tina who will be there in a flash if I'm in trouble," Vy stated.

"I know, it's just that I'm not here."

"You can't always protect me, Alexia. I know you want to be here twenty-four seven, but I have to learn how to take care of myself." Vy gave a comforting smile to Alexia. Normally it was the other way around. "Speaking of Gunbar, what are you two going to do once you return to Fort Lauderdale on Sunday?"

"Right now, we're at the dating stage. We agreed that on his nights off, he would come up and visit me, and sometimes I'd come down to Miami. Let's see how it works out. Long distance relationships aren't really my thing."

"Alexia, you're only forty-five minutes away from Miami. I don't think that constitutes a long-distance relationship."

"You have a point."

They returned to watching the movie on TV and Vy drifted off to sleep.

"Wake up, sleepy head. You have to start getting ready."

Vy slowly opened her eyes. "I actually fell asleep?"

"Yeah, and during the scene where the woman threw the other woman off the balcony. You missed it."

Vy smiled. "Thanks for waking me up."

Vy's preparation time for the show began. She took a long hot, soothing shower, and tried not think about Houston's well-defined chest. She then picked out an extremely sexy outfit, and tried not think about Houston's amazing eyes. She applied make-up, and tried not think about Houston's kiss. She styled her hair, and tried not think about Houston's smile. She fine-tuned herself, which consisted of adjusting her cleavage, wiping away any runny black eyeliner, and applied lip gloss one more time, while trying not to think about Houston in general. She took one last look at herself in the mirror, and grabbed her purse.

"Are you ready, Alexia?"

"In a minute," Alexia replied from the restroom.

Vy sat on the couch and started flipping through her *US Weekly* magazine. This week Britney Spears got a new tattoo, Beyoncé won "Best Video" award, and Denise Richards "Wore It Best." Vy couldn't wait until she was on the cover of *Rolling Stone*, which would read, nominated for "Best New Artist of the Year."

"I'm ready," Alexia announced.

"Like always, you look spectacular," Vy said.

"And you look like a true rock star. I'm ready to have fun tonight. It's my last official weekend with you, so I decided to loosen up a bit."

"So, you're going to have three drinks instead of two?" Vy asked.

There was a knock on the door. "I wonder who that could be?" Vy said.

"Don't open the door before asking who it is first." Although Alexia sounded like their mother, she had a point.

"Who is it?"

"Your knight-in-shining armor," said a muffled voice.

Vy instantly smiled and quickly opened the door. Houston stood there holding a bouquet of sunflowers. He was looking quite dapper. "I'm here as your date, slash bodyguard, slash undercover cop."

"Well, I like them all."

Vy hugged Houston and gave him a big smooch on the lips. She heard someone clearing their throat, and looked over Houston's shoulder. Gunbar was standing behind him with a dozen red roses and a wet, multicolored umbrella. Gunbar whispered to Vy, "Too corny?" She shook her head no, and smiled at Gunbar's romantic gesture. She didn't know he had it in him. Vy finally let go of Houston and let them in.

"Gunbar, they're beautiful!" Alexia kissed Gunbar, took her roses and Vy's sunflowers, and headed to the kitchen. Alexia's sashay had Gunbar mesmerized once again.

"I see you already have flowers," Houston said.

"A girl can never have enough flowers." Vy knew that response was corny, but she wanted to avoid telling Houston the truth just yet.

*****

They drove through the rain and arrived at the Steel Horse in half an hour. "This place is packed. It's a good thing you had Rob reserve a table for us," Alexia said when they arrived at the bar.

"It's also a good thing that we personally know the singer of the band," Houston sweetly added.

Vy went for Houston's hand hoping for a positive response. He reciprocated Vy's feelings and intertwined his fingers with hers. At this moment, everything seemed perfect.

"Vy, we have a problem," her bass player Rob said.

"I swear, if there's another dead body at this bar, I vote we never play here again."

"Vy, don't be ridiculous," Rob said.

"Go ahead; we'll be at the table." Houston kissed her forehead and gently let go of her hand.

"Thanks, Rob, for ruining my perfect moment."

Rob completely disregarded her statement. "As I was saying, there's a slight problem."

"Well, tell me already."

"Adrianna can't be here for another two hours. The roads in her area are flooded. And she hasn't been able to load her gear into her car due to the rain."

"But we start in one hour! What are we going to do without our drummer?"

"Acoustic set?"

"Look at this place, Rob. They're ready to dance. We can't kill the mood with a sappy acoustic set. Dang it," Vy replied in a frustrated tone.

"I told you we had a slight problem."

"I can play the drums for you. I pretty much know all the tunes you play. And the drum kit that we use for open mic night is here," Vy and Rob turned around to find Shawn standing behind them.

"You play the guitar and the drums as well?" Vy asked.

"And the bass guitar and keyboard."

"Great man. Meet me at the stage, and we'll go over the set list." Rob shook Shawn's hand and headed towards Carlos.

"Multitalented. Nice, but don't you have to work?"

"James can cover for me until your drummer arrives. You covered for me. It's time for me to pay you back. See you on stage, beautiful." Shawn slyly walked away.

Vy finally joined Alexia, Houston, and Gunbar. "Is everything okay?" Houston asked.

"Adrianna won't be here for the first set. But it turns out that Shawn can play the drums. They're going over the set list as we speak."

"He just wants an hour to stare at your behind. I should have him arrested for sexual harassment," Houston threatened.

"Do I hear the tone of jealousy?" Alexia mockingly asked.

"I'm a man. I know how men think. He just wants to stare at her butt."

"Can we please stop talking about my behind?" Vy said.

The hour went by quickly. Before Vy knew it, it was time to take the stage. "Break a leg, gorgeous," Houston said. "Well, not literally. Isn't that what musicians say?"

"I know what you meant, cowboy. Thanks." Vy kissed his cheek.

"How's everyone feeling tonight?" Hands went flying up. The crowd yelled different responses to Vy. The Steel Horse was crowded tonight. All the tables were occupied; there were no open stools at the bar, and people were standing by the entrance of the bar due to lack of standing room. It wasn't Madison Square Garden, but it was close enough for Vy.

For one second, Vy thought she saw Cassandra standing at the back corner of the bar. She wasn't one hundred percent sure. The cigarette haze, the stage lights, and the number of people made it difficult for Vy to see clearly.

"We're going to take a short break," Vy announced after finishing the last song of the first set. "We'll be right back!"

Rob walked over to Shawn. "Nice first set, man. It's always good to have a backup drummer for instances like these. Do you mind if we keep you on the roster?"

"Not at all. It would be my pleasure," Shawn said as he looked at Vy.

"Shall I carry you off the stage, gorgeous?" Vy looked down to see Houston waiting to sweep her off her feet, once again. She accepted his offer with pleasure. Houston's muscular arms engulfed her petite body.

"Can I talk to you outside?" Vy asked Houston. She led him out the back entrance of the bar. The gush of wind welcomed Vy.

"It's coming down hard," Houston said.

"It's a good thing I don't care about my hair."

It was eighty-five degrees and the humidity was intense. Vy and Houston stood behind the band's trailer, under an awning.

"Were you thinking about attacking me? I won't press charges," Houston smirked.

"No, silly. This is official business. I think I saw Cassandra tonight tucked in a dark corner of the bar."

"Okay. Is that a bad thing?"

"What I was told by another waitress was that Shawn banned Cassandra from coming into the bar. Then I confirmed it with Shawn. He told Cassandra she needed some R & R, but she didn't take it too well. She's been missing in action ever since."

Houston took a step back, and his scowl signified that he was now furious. "When did you speak to Shawn about this?"

"Does that really matter right now? The important thing is she could be in there, and you can ask her questions."

"Yes, it matters," Houston simply said.

Vy inhaled slowly, "I spoke to him about it late this afternoon. He brought me dinner. You see, he had sent me a text—"

Houston interrupted Vy, "After I specifically told you not to hang out with him."

"I know what you said, and I listened. But that doesn't mean that I should abide by your rules. He came over as a friend."

"A friend with probable cause."

"Don't you use your official tone on me, mister. I'm not going to have this discussion with you right now. You need to check out the bar and see if Cassandra is lingering around."

Houston remained silent for a few seconds, placed his hands in his pocket, and said, "I'll walk around and see if I spot her." He paused. "Let's go inside." He proceeded to the door.

"Houston, wait," Vy grabbed his arm, and stood directly in front of him. "You really don't have to worry about Shawn."

"Vy, I'm not worried about Shawn in a jealous way."

"Right, and I'm not secretly in love with Rob Thomas." Vy refrained from commenting.

"I don't know what it is about him that I don't like, and that's what worries me. I need you to understand that," Houston explained.

"I do understand that. But what I want you to understand is that I want this to be over already. I don't want to be looking over my shoulder and relying on you to be taking care of me twenty-four-seven. I mean, why me? I don't know anything."

"But the murderer thinks you know something, and that's why we have to keep an eye on you." Houston stepped closer to Vy, and took his hands out of his pocket. He wrapped his arms around her waist. "Have I told you that you look cute when you pout?"

Vy slapped Houston on his stomach. "On a serious note, we will get to the bottom of this. And," Houston lifted Vy's chin. "I want you to rely on me." Houston gently kissed her.

Vy heard the door open. "Vy, we're up." Another perfect moment ruined, this time by her guitarist Carlos. Vy and Houston parted ways. Shawn was adjusting the cymbals on the drum kit.

"Hey!" Vy said as she was connecting her ear piece.

"Hi there. By the way, I haven't been able to tell you that you look beautiful tonight. Those jeans really extenuate your—" Shawn said.

"Behind, I know!" Vy interrupted.

"I was going to say derriere. It turns out that Adrianna won't be making it tonight."

"I hope she's okay. Thanks for filling in on such short notice. We owe you one."

"You did it for me," Shawn replied.

"Well, you sound great. You're playing the actual timing of each song. Adrianna has the tendency to speed things up a bit."

"Thank you," Shawn said.

"So, James is fine with you doing the entire gig?"

"He has to be. I'm my own boss, remember?"

"Did you speak to Dave this evening?" Vy asked.

"I saw him before the visiting hours were up. He's doing okay."

"Can I go see him?"

"Sorry Vy; it's still family only. But he asks about you every time."

"He does?"

"Yeah, he seems really concerned about you for some reason. We talk a lot about you."

"About what?" Vy inquired.

"How much I like you."

"Ready, Vy?" Rob asked. This time, Vy was relieved that Rob had interrupted this soon-to-be-awkward conversation.

TESTING 19

Alexia and Gunbar were dancing to Vy's version of "Nothing Compares to You." Her head was nestled into Gunbar's neck. Vy knew Gunbar made Alexia happy. This was the last song of the set, and Vy wanted it to last longer for Alexia. She turned to Carlos and made a circular motion with her index finger. Carlos extended the instrumental ending of the song. The song came to an end and Vy saw Gunbar kissing Alexia's hand.

The band finally took a break. Vy joined Alexia, Houston, and Gunbar at their table. Alexia was devouring a chicken wing. "It's so good to eat fried food," Alexia said as she sucked the barbeque sauce from her fingers.

"That's because you're depriving yourself for that insane diet," Vy replied.

"Well, not tonight. I told you that I was going to loosen up tonight."

Houston answered a call, and quickly ended it. He looked at Gunbar. "We have to go, Vy," Houston said. "We have to go downtown. There's been a shooting," Houston concluded.

Alexia looked disappointed, but understood, "You boys be safe." Vy remained quiet. She didn't know how to respond to that. It's not like he said, "I have to go to Guitar Center to fix the neck of my guitar." Vy finally responded, "Yes, be safe."

He looked down at her and said, "Don't worry; nothing is going to happen to me."

"How did you know—" Vy started to say when Houston kissed her goodbye.

"If I'm not here by the time you're done, can you call Tina to pick you girls up?"

"Yes. Don't worry about us," Vy said.

"Keep in mind, the weather is extremely bad out there, so be careful driving home," Gunbar said.

"Yes, Dad," Alexia said with a smile.

Vy and Alexia followed them out with their eyes. "They both have extremely sexy backs."

"Alexia!" Vy smacked her arm.

"I only speak the truth. Anyway, that's a bummer," Alexia said. She then took out her cell phone, sent a text, waited, and then threw her cell phone back in her purse.

"You asked Tina to come to the bar?" Vy asked grinning.

"Of course. Tina was already on her way. But it's taking her a lot longer because a lot of the traffic lights are out. It's officially a girl's night out!"

"I have to go back on. Don't go too crazy," Vy said.

Vy went back on stage. Initially, the bass kick and the snare were the only sounds coming from the stage. That beat always got the crowd pumped up. They didn't know what song to expect and they were waiting anxiously, with a drink in hand. Vy took this opportunity to introduce the band. Shawn was the last one she introduced. "Everyone, give it up for our savior, Shawn, on the drums!" The women in the crowd started jumping up and down yelling out his name. Vy thought that was a little too much, but then again why would she care how the women reacted.

The lead and bass guitar kicked in and Vy started to sing, "How Far We've Come" by Matchbox Twenty. She noticed that Tina was sitting with Alexia. The two of them were holding up shot glasses. Alexia pointed down. Vy saw that there was a shot waiting for her by the base of her microphone stand. She picked up the shot glass, directed it towards the crowd, and said into the microphone while the guitar solo played, "Here's to you!"

At that instant, the lights went out. The emergency lights slowly flickered on. There was a combination of screams and laughter. Shawn's voice projected from behind the drum kit, "Everyone, stay calm. And please, remain at your tables." He stepped out from behind the drums and jumped off the stage.

Vy's eyes were still trying to adjust to the darkness. Shawn extended his hand to Vy. "Let me help you down." He helped Vy off stage, and walked her to the table where Alexia and Tina were seated.

"I'll be back," Shawn said.

By this point, Alexia seemed happily hydrated. There were about three shot glasses on the table. Alexia was sipping what seemed to be an Apple Martini. In the dark, Vy couldn't tell what Tina was drinking. "Don't worry, I'm drinking a Sprite. I'm the designated driver for tonight," Tina said to Vy.

"What happened?" Alexia asked giggling.

"The lights simply went out," Vy said.

"Oh." Alexia continued giggling.

"Oh my," Vy said.

Sitting in the semi darkness presented an uneasy feeling in the pit of Vy's stomach. She looked around the bar, and surprisingly enough, people remained at their tables.

Tina stood up. "I'm going to talk to Kyle and find out why the power went out."

"No, Tina, please stay here." Vy got up and followed Tina half way to the entrance of the bar.

"I'm just going over to where Kyle is."

"Tina, we were told to stay at our tables."

"Seriously, Vy, I'll only be gone a minute, okay?" Tina said.

"Okay." Vy walked back to the table. "Can you believe it?" Vy started to say to Alexia, but she was no longer sitting at the table.

Vy frantically yelled out Alexia's name. She started briskly walking around the bar like a mad woman running into tables and bumping into people. Someone grabbed Vy's arm. She turned around with the intention of punching him in the gut, but came to an immediate halt and she controlled herself. He was a regular, and quite drunk.

"Hey, Vy. There's a bad storm out there. It killed the power. Why don't you sing a Capella for us?"

"Have you seen my sister?"

"Oh, I've seen her alright. She's a hottie. What a nice girl."

"Have you seen her recently?" Vy asked.

"Oh, no doll. Besides, I can barely see with the lights on, let alone without."

Vy took in a deep breath, and ran her fingers through her hair, "Calm down, Vy," she said to herself. The next logical place she thought Alexia would be was the restroom. She briskly headed there and violently pushed the door open. "Lexi, are you in here? Alexia!"

She pushed open the first stall door and there was a woman peeing, "Do you mind!"

"Sorry."

The second stall was empty. Vy started to hyperventilate. She put her hand on her chest, bent forward and slowly walked out of the restroom.

"Vy, are you okay?" Shawn asked, his voice quivering.

"Where's Alexia?" she struggled to ask.

"I haven't seen her. I'm going to call 911. You need to go to the hospital."

"PAPER BAG!" Shawn left her panting, but returned with a paper bag. Vy took deep breaths until her breathing was steadied.

"Find my sister."

"I'm sure she's fine, no one has left the bar. The question is, how are you?"

"I said, find my sister!" she screamed.

Vy pushed Shawn out of the way, and continued surveying the bar anxiously. Neither Kyle nor Tina were at the entrance of the bar. Vy stepped outside where there was a hurricane-like storm occurring. She went back inside, and returned to their table.

"It's one hell of a storm. That's why the power's out," Carlos said. "Are you okay? You look terrible."

"I can't find Alexia. She was here one second and gone the next."

"Maybe she's in the restroom."

"She's not there," Vy said sternly.

"I'll help you look for her. I mean, this place isn't that big."

"No, stay here in case she comes back. She was buzzed. Maybe someone helped her up," Vy said under her breath. "Please stay here."

"Okay," Carlos said.

Vy jumped on stage, and pulled her cell phone out from her purse. She nervously dialed Houston's number. "Houston." He answered.

"Houston, the lights went out, Alexia disappeared, I'm hyperventilating, I still can't find her," Vy stammered.

"Take a breath, Vy. One sentence at a time." The connection was cutting in and out.

"Please come now! I can't find Alexia and I have a bad feeling that something's happened to her." Vy started to cry, "Houston, are you there? Bryan!" Vy's phone had lost signal. She placed her phone in her back pocket and ran to Carlos.

"Give me your phone."

"I don't have a signal. I think the storm wiped out the towers." Vy looked at Alexia's empty chair. Her purse was still hanging on it, which meant that Alexia had no way of letting Vy know if she was in danger.

"Dang it!"

"Don't worry, Vy, we'll find her."

Vy wasn't acknowledging any words of reason. She was determined to find Alexia. She ran to the office. She picked up the cordless phone, and pushed the talk button, but there wasn't a dial tone. "Our phones are out, Vy," James said.

"Jesus, you scared the crap out of me," Vy said, placing her hand on her chest.

"Well, I saw you run in here like a crazed maniac. I was wondering what you were doing."

"Obviously, I came in here to use the phone." James was standing firm with his arms crossed. "Have you seen my sister?"

"First of all, you shouldn't be walking in here without permission. And no, I haven't seen Alexia. Why?"

Vy dashed out of the office without responding to James. Vy pushed the heavy metal back door open. The heavy winds almost caused the door to reclose on her face.

"What are you doing? You shouldn't go out there," James said.

Vy ignored him and finally made her way outside. She yelled out Alexia's name, but the sound of the rain drops, and the thunder were her only response. She looked down the alley, but there was no sign of Alexia. "Alexia!" Vy called out once more.

The lighting strike illuminated a dumpster, and a bicycle that was leaning against it. Vy's dream was becoming reality. She pulled the back door open again with all her strength, and finally slid herself inside and stood there soaking wet.

"You're starting to freak me out, Vy. You're acting crazy." Vy again ignored James's crude remark and went back inside the bar and walked from table to table asking people if they'd seen Alexia.

"She's the pretty Latin woman, right?" asked a middle-aged woman.

"Yes, long brown hair. She's been hanging with me tonight. Did you see her?"

"Only for a second. I bumped into her and her friend. I think they were headed to the restroom."

"Do you know who the other person was?"

"Actually, I thought it was you. The lights had gone out already."

Vy heard Shawn's voice coming from the bar, "No one is to leave the bar until further notice. The power is out in this area extending North and South from here."

"I have to get to my kids!" A woman said. She pushed through the crowd and headed out the front door.

"Wait!" Vy said running after her. The woman looked terrified. "Who are your kids with?"

"The babysitter. I haven't been able to get a hold of her to find out how the kids are. I need to know if they are okay, Vy."

Vy didn't know this woman but apparently, she knew her. "Listen, sweetie, I'm sure your kids are okay. If you go out there, you might get hurt. You can't risk that. Why don't we go back inside?"

The woman hugged Vy. "You're right. Thank you, Vy." She let go of Vy and went back inside the bar.

Vy stayed outside. She looked towards the parking lot hoping that she'd get a glimpse of Alexia. She sat on the bench and started to cry. The wind was blowing the rain into her eyes. But she sat there frozen. She began retracing tonight's steps, while the tears ran down her face. "Why is this happening?" Vy engulfed her face with her dry palms, and tried to breathe normally.

TESTING 20

"Why are you out here crying?" Tina asked. Vy looked up and saw Tina and Kyle standing over her. Tina started to rub Vy's back, but she instantly pushed Tina's hand off.

"What's up? What is it with your attitude?" Tina asked annoyed.

"Where have you been?" Vy asked.

Tina's demeanor changed. She looked over to Kyle, then to Vy and said smiling, "We thought we'd escape for some alone time. But seriously, Vy, what's with the attitude?"

Vy took a deep breath, "While you were out there acting like high school kids, Alexia—you know, my sister—was kidnapped!" Deep down, she knew Tina shouldn't be blamed for Alexia's disappearance, but she was upset that her friend wasn't there for her.

"What? Kidnapped? That's not possible." Tina said.

"Oh, it's possible. I've spent the last hour trying to find her—and you, for that matter. The phones aren't working. I've scoped out every inch of this bar!"

"Calm down, Vy. I think you're overreacting."

Vy slowly stood up. "After all these years, you're telling me that I'm overreacting when it comes to the safety of my sister? Are you seriously telling me that?"

Tina remained silent. Vy turned and faced Kyle. "Is there a room in the bar that I may not know about, that I may have overlooked?"

"Besides the office, there's a supply room by the restrooms, but that's about it." Kyle's look of concern softened Vy up a little bit. Tina was teary-eyed.

"I'm sorry I lashed out at you, Tina, it's just that—oh my God! Did you say by the restroom?"

"Yes, it's—" Kyle started to respond, but Vy raced back into the bar. Tina and Kyle followed right after her.

Vy couldn't believe she'd bypassed this door. She went to open it, but it was locked. "Unlock it, Kyle, now!"

He pulled out a set of keys from his pocket, located the right one and unlocked the door. There was Alexia, sitting on the cement floor. Her hands were tied behind her back. Her knees were curled up to her chest. A black, thick sock was tied around her eyes. She had duct tape over her mouth. Mascara was running down her cheeks. There was a note pinned to her shirt.

Vy instantly dropped to the floor. "Alexia, I'm so sorry I wasn't keeping an eye on you." Vy slowly peeled the duct tape off, took the sock off, and untied her hands.

"It's not your fault. I don't even know what happened. I sobered up fast though. It's a good thing it wasn't you. You'd have had a claustrophobia attack."

Vy couldn't believe Alexia's sense of humor after what had just happened to her. Vy knew that she was being strong mainly for Vy. "This is not a laughing matter, Lexi."

Tina and Kyle were looking down at them. Vy sat there holding the note in her trembling hand. She was afraid to unfold it and what it might say. She didn't think she could handle another threat. Alexia took the note from her hand and opened it. Alexia read the note out loud in her sweet tone: "I told you to stay out of it. Next time, I won't be so nice."

"That bastard!" Vy snarled.

"Vy, Alexia, are you okay?" Shawn came rushing into the storage room, pushing Tina and Kyle aside.

"We're just dandy, Shawn," Alexia sarcastically replied. Vy helped Alexia up. Alexia was dusting herself off.

"I told you something happened to Alexia, but you disregarded it," Vy said, ticked off.

"Vy, listen."

"No, you listen. While I was untying my sister's hands, I came to a simple conclusion. Are you ready to hear it?" Not only did Shawn nod yes, but so did Alexia, Tina, and Kyle. "Here it goes," Vy said mockingly. "A Steel Horse employee kidnapped my sister, dragged her to this storage room, tied her up, and locked her in here. She could have suffocated!" Vy inhaled and exhaled slowly. She cleared her throat, "Kyle told me this door is always kept locked. Only employees who have the key can open this door, right?"

"Technically," Shawn started to say.

"Rhetorical question, buddy. But you can answer me this question, Shawn. Who am I sending to jail?" Vy shouted.

Vy had now lost all her composure and was yelling. She felt eyes staring at her, but she didn't care what anyone thought. The power was still off, so she felt better not knowing who was scrutinizing her. "I don't care how you do it, but you better have the cops here very soon. And," she looked past Shawn and yelled, "no one is to leave. Got it?"

"But, Vy," Shawn began.

"I don't want to hear it. Do it now!"

Shawn simply walked away. Vy exhaled the breath she'd been holding that entire time. Alexia patted Vy's shoulder and whispered in her ear, "Good job, sis."

Vy and Alexia stepped outside for a breath of fresh air. The wind continued to blow full force. The rain came down at a slant. There were people standing around the shopping center waiting to go home. One man sat on a bus bench and was reading the dripping wet *Miami New Times*.

"Do you think that Shawn will be able to get a hold of the cops?" Vy asked.

"I'm not too sure. You or I haven't been able to get a hold of Houston or Gunbar. I can only imagine how the streets are—no street lights, and flooding. But I think you scared Shawn enough that he'll do anything to get somebody here." They both smiled.

Vy took her cell phone out of her back pocket and checked her signal. Nothing. Vy wished she could telepathically send Houston a message. A negative impulse came over Vy. She ran to the middle of the parking lot and yelled at the top of her lungs, "Come out you coward and face me!"

Alexia grabbed Vy's hand, and pulled her back to the covered area. They sat down on a bench. Vy kept staring off into the oblivion trying to put the pieces of the puzzle together. Shawn was linked to Dave and Margarite. Kendra was linked to Ricky who was linked to Margarite. And then there was Cassandra who was not linked to anyone, but Vy sensed that she was involved somehow. This was a confusing six degrees of separation.

Alexia snapped her out of her trance. "Are you auditioning for *I Know What You Did Last Summer 3*?"

"This isn't funny, Lexi."

"I know, but you can't break down on me now," Alexia explained.

"How can you be so calm after what happened to you? I don't get it."

"You can't solve anything by acting irrational. And besides, I didn't mind being tied up," Alexia said with a smile.

"Okay, Lexi, too much information."

"At least it got a smile out of you." Alexia put her arm around Vy. "All kidding aside, yes, I was scared, but I was sure about two things. One, I knew that you were going to find me. And two, I had a feeling that this person who tied me up and stuck me in there, wasn't going to hurt me. This person, gently covered my eyes with the sock, gently tied my hands together, and gently sat me on the floor."

"Well, I guarantee you that when I find out who it is, I won't be so gentle on them."

Alexia laughed. "Okay, let's get you inside before you get sick. Mom would kill me if she found out I let you sit outside soaking wet."

*****

"I'm so glad the power is finally back on," Tina said to Vy, once the lights came back on in the bar.

Vy, Alexia, and Tina were seated at a high table away from the crowd of feisty people who wanted to go home. Houston and Gunbar had arrived and were keeping everyone in line. It was like the repeated chorus of a song; once again, questioning everyone, once again, no suspects, and once again, no witnesses, at least sober ones. The only lead they had was the lady who thought she saw Vy escorting Alexia to the restroom.

It was a little after three a.m. Little by little, the line of people dwindled down to only the staff, Alexia, and Vy. Tina had gone home with Kyle.

Shawn sat behind the bar. He was bending and unbending a skinny, red cocktail straw. Vy could only imagine how upset he was with her, but Vy was just as upset with him. Houston walked over to Vy. "I know you must be exhausted. Are you ready to go home?"

By the time Houston and Gunbar dropped off Vy and Alexia at home, it was close to five in the morning. "I'm beat," Alexia said as her body fell onto the couch.

"I'm so tired that I don't think I can fall asleep," Vy said as she got comfortable on the loveseat.

Alexia sighed and looked at Vy. "Do you want me to stay a few more days?"

"No, Lexi. I'll be fine. You should go back to your life, and to your job. And I, unfortunately, have to go back to work as well."

"It just doesn't feel right to leave you in this situation."

"I know. But listen, Houston's only a phone call away. And I have my stun gun and pepper spray. I think that whoever crosses me will get hurt one way or the other."

"Okay. I'm just too tired for a rebuttal. Let's go to bed. We'll go to lunch before I head back home," Alexia said.

It was well past noon before Vy and Alexia were up and running. Vy was standing in front of her sliding glass door. The day was gloomy, and the rain continued. The sky was a symphony of the sound of thunder and lighting strikes. The trees danced with the movement of the wind. Vy thought it was beautiful.

"Can you believe I had a nightmare?" Alexia said.

"About what happened to you last night?"

They sat on the couch. "Yeah, sort of. But it was a bit more graphic and convoluted. It turns out that I was kidnapped by a faceless person. I was trying to escape by beating him up with the heel of my shoe, but it would go through him, as if he were a ghost.

"Wow. What happened?" Vy asked.

“Well, I’m not sure exactly, but I finally nicked him somehow, and he started to bleed profusely. That’s where I woke up.”

“Sounds like one of my dreams,” Vy said.

“I know. Anyway, are you ready to go?”

*****

Chinese food was the lunch craving. They went to South Garden Chinese Restaurant and were sitting next to a lobster tank that contained three lobsters. “I wish I could free them,” Vy said as she watched the lobsters.

“Have you been researching PETA again?”

Vy smiled. “Maybe.”

The waitress took their order and scurried off like a frightened kitten.

“Finally, after all that driving around. I’m so happy this restaurant was open. It’s amazing how much damage the storm did,” Vy said.

“I know. But I was getting desperate. I was getting so hungry, that I would have settled for Rey’s Pizza.”

“Oh, that’s bad,” Vy said.

“Tell me about it,” Alexia said smiling.

“So, any plans to see Gunbar before you go home?”

“No. I told him that I wanted to hang out with you in a normal environment.”

“Right, one that doesn’t involve murder, kidnapping, questioning, and more questioning.”

“Exactly,” Alexia said.

The food arrived and there was silence for ten minutes. “I was so hungry,” Vy said as she sat back and took a break from eating.

“I can see that. You actually ate most of your food!”

“Ha-ha,” Vy responded.

“So, now what?”

“I’m just going to try to stay out of whatever mess I’m in and let the cops handle it.”

"I'm sorry you lost your steady gig at the Steel Horse."

"I'm not sorry. At least we still got paid for last night's gig. Maybe this was a sign to take a break from playing there. I just need to go see Dave at the hospital and explain to him what happened. I don't want him to think that I bailed out on him for no reason."

"I'm sure Shawn will tell him."

"I can just imagine what version he's going to tell Dave. 'Well, Dave, Vy went postal on the staff and customers. She kept everyone hostage at the bar until the police arrived.' I'm going to sound like a lunatic," Vy lamented.

"You did go postal, but for a good reason. Listen, I'm sure you'll work it out with Shawn and you guys can play there again."

"We'll see." They finished their lunch and headed back to Vy's apartment.

*****

Once they at the apartment they packed Alexia's things.

"That's the last of it." Alexia closed the trunk of her car.

"You sure had a lot of clothes to pack for a little getaway." Vy was holding a purple umbrella over their heads. She gave Alexia a big hug with one arm. "Call me when you get home. The weather is crappy."

"I will. Are you sure you're going to be okay?"

"Yes!" Vy stated empathically.

"Okay, okay, I'm just double-checking. That's what big sisters are for."

"I'll probably head your way next weekend. I need to get away from Miami."

"That's great! I can make you crab legs, and we can watch chick flicks," Alexia said with excitement.

Vy gave Alexia another hug. She stood in her parking lot watching Alexia's tail lights fade into the distance. Vy suddenly felt alone. She strolled back to her apartment. Marilyn greeted her with a purr and rubbed against Vy's leg. "It's just you and me now."

Vy picked up her beat-up classical guitar, sat on her balcony, and was going to do what she knew how to do best; she was going to compose a song. Vy propped up her feet on the adjacent chair. She looked out towards the flooded parking lot. Everything seemed desolate. There were no children playing outside. The neighbors below her weren't grilling and blasting Cuban tunes that would normally cause her floor to vibrate.

Vy placed her guitar upside down on her lap, and momentarily closed her eyes. There was a continuous drizzle. She could faintly hear the drops fall onto the palm trees. She immediately turned that into a beat for her new song. She slowly opened her eyes, and flipped her guitar over. She looked behind her only to find Marilyn's nose pushed up against the screen door. "No, Marilyn." Marilyn stared up at Vy, and gently laid herself on the tile floor.

"Okay, ready to write?" Vy asked Marilyn. Marilyn let out a soft meow, and quickly closed her eyes. "Well, this is a great audience."

Vy strummed the C chord once and stopped. She admired how easily the palm trees swayed. She started strumming again to the movement of the trees. Vy closed her eyes once again, and continued playing an unknown melody. A song gradually formed. "I think I'll get up today, maybe I can forget about you. Maybe today, it will be easy to do."

Vy's song was interrupted with a knock on her door. Marilyn's ears perked up, and she slowly stretched her body, and headed for the front door.

There was another knock. Vy went inside. "Who is it?" she yelled. She remembered that she really needed to go to the Home Depot for a door with a peephole.

"It's Houston." Vy's heart started pounding. It was like a techno song within her body. She opened the door and threw her arms around his neck.

"It's good to see you too," Houston said. "I'm glad that you're now asking who's at the door."

"I learn quickly."

"It was a test," Houston said.

"Did I pass, detective?" As corny as it sounded, she didn't care. She felt a sense of ease and happiness, now that Houston was in her presence.

"Come on in," Vy said with a southern twang.

"Where's your sidekick?"

"Alexia went back home today. Unfortunately, she has a life of her own."

"Don't worry, I'll keep you company."

Vy smiled and blushed. "Are you asking me out on a date?"

"Yes, I am. And this time, it will only be the two of us. But it's going to have to wait until tonight. I'll call you in a bit to confirm a time."

"Oh. Does that mean you have to go this very moment?"

"Yes. Remember that shooting I was called out to last night?" Vy simply nodded. "Well, Gunbar found the gun in a two-foot gap between a cement wall and a chain link fence near the area of the initial takedown. How insane is that!"

"Um, very insane," Vy said.

"Oh, sorry. Let me explain the situation. The good news was that we took the assailant down. The bad news was that we couldn't find the firearm he used during the shooting, and we eventually had to clear the scene. That really stirred up I.A., and a lot of questions were starting to arise as to whether the cops involved did the right thing."

"I.A.?" Vy asked.

"Internal Affairs," Houston explained.

"Oh."

"Exactly. There was going to be a lot of explaining to do. But, Gunbar decided to go back to the scene and was determined to find the gun. Well, the S.O.B. actually found it."

"It pays to be meticulous."

"That's why he's my partner," Houston said. "Oh, I wanted to let you know that tomorrow we're bringing in Cassandra for further questioning."

"Really, do you have something on her?"

"No, but I personally want to get her alibi for last night, and maybe get more out of her. People tend to crumble under pressure."

"That's if she knows anything. She just might be a strange girl. Nothing more to it."

"Maybe. But I don't take chances," Houston stated.

"You are so sexy when you talk cop stuff," Vy purred.

Houston chuckled. "Cop stuff, huh? And you are very sexy when you sing." Vy got on her tippy toes and gave him a light, lingering kiss on the lips. "Now that gets me motivated to finish up quickly tonight."

"I was trying to get you to stay, but I'll take finishing up quickly."

"I'll be back before you know it. I really came here to check up on you."

"I'm fine, thank you," Vy said.

Houston kissed Vy's forehead. "I'll see you later. Lock your door as soon as I leave. And if you do go out this afternoon, be careful driving. It's still raining, and your Mustang doesn't do well with slippery roads. I know, I probably sound like your dad, but I worry about you. You always manage to get yourself into trouble," Houston said, smiling. She back-slapped his stomach, but he didn't flinch.

"I hate driving in the rain anyway," Vy said as she pulled him in for a hug. Houston's cell phone started to buzz on his belt. "Do you need to answer that?" she whispered in his ear.

"Answer what?"

"Your phone, silly."

Houston placed his hand on his cell phone. "I have to figure out a way to not miss my phone calls. I don't feel it when I have it on vibrate, and I don't hear it when I have it on the ringer setting."

"Maybe it's not the phone, maybe it's your age," Vy said sarcastically.

"A singer and a comedian, quite a package." Houston said as he walked out the door.

Later, about six in the evening—Alexia had phoned Vy to let her know she arrived home safely. "The drive wasn't that bad considering the weather. So, what are you doing tonight?"

"Houston's coming over for dinner," Vy said giddily.

"You two finally get some alone time."

"It's not like that, Lexi. I'm taking my time with this one."

"Right."

There was a slight pause on the line, "I'll call you tomorrow, Lexi."

"You'd better. I want details. Love your face."

"Love you too," Vy said.

Vy looked at her cell phone and contemplated calling Houston. She didn't want to come off as needy and a stalker. "Just wait for his call," Vy said to herself.

As soon as she placed the phone in her pocket, it started to buzz. She answered it without taking note as to who was calling her. "It's about time. My stomach is growling."

"Vy?"

"Shawn?"

"Vy, please listen to what I have to say."

"I have nothing to say to you, and I don't have to listen to you." Vy hung up without giving him a chance to respond. He called three times in a row before he finally gave up.

Vy's refrigerator was stocked with food, but she had no cooking skills. "Pizza it is."

"Thanks for calling Treasure's Pizza. Can I place you on hold?" Vy didn't get to answer. As she was patiently holding, another call came in. Shawn's name appeared on the screen.

"My goodness, do you not take no for an answer?" She pushed the ignore button.

"Thanks for holding. Go ahead."

"Can I have a medium Hawaiian pizza, a half dozen garlic rolls, and a two-liter coke?"

The call ended after Vy gave the teenage-sounding girl her phone number and address, in return for the total. Vy had an hour to kill before the pizza arrived. Marilyn was rubbing up against her leg. "I'm feeding you now."

Vy popped in a Jack Johnson CD, got comfortable on her couch, and covered herself with her throw blanket. Marilyn nestled herself on Vy's stomach. Her eyes were slowly closing to the tune of "Bubble Toes," and the raindrops hitting the balcony's railing. She drifted off to sleep.

*****

"You go on in five," Vy heard a voice say.

"Wait. I thought I started in an hour."

"No. Don't you hear the sound check?"

Vy closed her eyes, and focused on the music that was playing on the other side of a black, solid door. "No way, I'm opening up for Matchbox Twenty?"

"It's your dream," said the unidentified man.

"What?" Vy said confused.

The song "Push" was getting louder and louder. Finally, Vy woke up to her cell phone playing the "Push" ringtone. Vy reluctantly answered the phone knowing by the ringtone that it was the Steel Horse Bar, "Hello?"

"Hey, Vy, its James."

"Hi." Vy was still offended by the fact that James had called her a maniac, but at the same time she was relieved that it wasn't Shawn.

"Were you sleeping? I didn't mean to wake you."

Vy looked at the clock; she'd only been napping for fifteen minutes. "No, it's fine. What's up?"

"I know I'm the last person you probably want to see right now, but one of your guys left a microphone and a stand here. I didn't know if whoever left it needed it anytime soon. Even though the bar's closed, you're more than welcome to come by and pick it up. I'll be here until midnight."

"How come the bar's closed?"

"Last night's storm screwed up something having to do with the electrical box. I didn't quite understand the technical aspect of it, but the electricians are fixing it as we speak."

"Okay, well, I'll give you a call when I'm on my way. Thanks for letting me know." Vy was about to hang up, when she thought about something, "Oh, James, wait."

"No, Shawn's not here," Vy thought she heard James smile.

"Thanks, J. See you in a bit."

Vy's cell phone rang again, singing, "We Are Family," "Hey, Lexi."

"Is Houston there yet?"

"Nope," Vy replied.

"Well, did you make dinner yet?"

"No. But I just ordered a pizza about twenty minutes ago."

"You didn't know what to do with half of the food in your fridge, huh?"

"Yes, but I just didn't feel like slaving over a stove," Vy explained.

"Of course," Alexia said giggling.

"I'm glad you called. Shawn has been calling me frantically."

"What's he calling you about?"

"I don't know. I haven't given him the chance to speak."

"You can't stay pissed off at him. He's probably trying to apologize," Alexia said.

"Well, I'm not ready to hear his apology yet."

"You're so hardheaded," Alexia said.

"Whatever. Anyway, I have to head out to the Steel Horse."

"Why?"

"One of the boys left a microphone and the stand there. I'm going to go pick it up."

"Can't Houston pick it up on the way to your place?"

"I don't know when Houston's coming over. I haven't heard from him since I saw him this afternoon. And besides, I have nothing better to do. I'm going crazy over here waiting for his call."

"I know. You're anxious and excited. It's natural," Alexia stated.

"Thank you, Dr. Phil," Vy responded sarcastically.

"I don't think you should be driving in this weather. I'll just call Gunbar and ask him to pick it up."

"Alexia, thank you for your concern, but Gunbar and Houston are working the case together. Besides, I'm a big girl. I can drive in this weather."

"I know, I know, 'I'm not five, blah, blah, blah, stop treating me like a kid, blah, blah, blah.'"

"Sometimes it's tiring to talk to you, you know that?" Vy said laughing.

"Vy, you shouldn't be hanging out by yourself. At least not until this case is solved."

Vy felt grateful, yet irritated at the same time. "Alexia, I know you're worried. But what if this case isn't solved until a year from now. I'm not going to change my lifestyle because of a crazed lunatic. Anyway, I promised I was going to stay out of it. That alone should keep me out of trouble."

"Fine. But call me when you get there, and call me on the way back home."

"Okay. I probably won't be long," Vy said.

"Do it anyway. Love you. Bye."

Vy had no intention of driving in this weather, but she didn't want to be cooped up in her apartment, and she didn't know if they were ever going to gig there again, so she might as well pick up the microphone and the stand. She let out a sigh knowing she was making excuses for herself. Vy didn't want Houston to think she was desperate.

By the time Vy got ready to leave, it was close to eight thirty in the evening. The pizza was in the oven. She didn't have any missed calls from Houston, so she made the decision to call him. It went straight to voice mail. "Hi, it's Vy. I'm headed over to the Steel Horse to pick up a microphone and a stand one of the boys left there. I left the key taped under the mat in case you get to my place before I do. Make yourself at home.

There's pizza in the oven if you're hungry. Um, okay then. See you soon, I hope. Bye."

"I probably sounded like a complete idiot," Vy said to herself in the mirror. "Hmm, not bad." Vy cocked her head to the side. Vy took her time to straighten out her hair to perfection. She was satisfied. "Sexy, but not desperate," Vy said to herself. She wanted Houston to gasp when he saw her. She grabbed her D & B purse, her keys, and headed to the Steel Horse Bar for one last good bye.

TESTING 21

Unfortunately, Vy was driving with the windows up due to the weather. She missed the feeling of the wind gently hitting her face. She was singing along to one of her favorite country songs, "Chicken Fried," by the Zac Brown Band.

The vehicle driving behind Vy kept flashing its high beams at her. Like that was going to prompt her into driving any faster than the thirty-mile-per-hour limit. For starters, Vy hated driving in the rain. So, she was not going to risk skidding down the street to satisfy a driver who wanted to speed.

Slowly but safely, Vy arrived at the Steel Horse Bar. The parking lot was deserted. The grocery store and Eat Em' Up' seemed closed as well. She called Alexia, and told her that she had arrived safe and sound. Vy placed the phone next to her leg, fixed her hair, and applied lip gloss. She got out of the car, straightened out her t-shirt, and walked towards the entrance.

When she reached the dilapidated, wooden double doors, Vy realized that she'd left her cell phone in her car. She figured she was only going to be inside for a few minutes, so she disregarded the thought of walking back to her car to get it.

Vy walked in and spotted James behind the bar. Only a few lights were turned on. She figured this was part of the electrical problem James had mentioned earlier. "Hi, James," Vy called out from the entrance.

"Come on over," James said and waved the bar towel at her. Vy hesitantly walked over to the bar. "Have a seat and have a drink, on the house."

"No thanks. I wasn't going to stay long. I just came for the mic and the stand. I'm surprised one of the guys left it." Vy looked around and saw a stand on the far back corner of the stage by the stairs.

"Oh, come on. One Malibu and pineapple won't hurt. Think of it as an 'I'm sorry' drink. I didn't mean to insinuate you were crazy."

"Apology accepted. How can I say no to an 'I'm sorry' drink? But I'll just have a Coke."

Vy made herself comfortable on the bar stool. James placed her soda in front of her, "Here you are, sweetie."

"Thanks, J."

"Listen, I didn't know Alexia's situation. All I saw was you going around the bar like a mad woman, no offense."

"Some offense taken, but it's fine," Vy said.

"No, Vy, it is not fine," James emphasized. "I completely felt like an idiot when I found out what the problem was. I should have been helping you look for Alexia, not insulting you."

"Seriously, James, don't worry about it. Last night is a night that I wish to forget. I don't want to talk about it anymore. It's over with. Thank goodness."

"Fair enough." James smiled. "Thanks for staying and keeping me company for a bit longer than you anticipated. It's been a lonely night for me."

"Where are the electricians?"

"They left already. Apparently, they were missing a part. They'll be back first thing in the morning, and evidently, so will I."

"Has Shawn been around tonight?"

"No. He decided to take a few days off from the bar. He said it was getting too much for him to handle."

"That's odd."

"What is?"

"Well, it's just—" Vy looked down at her soda. She stirred it a few times with the cocktail straw. "He's been calling me non-stop this evening."

"Oh yeah, what about?" James threw a towel over his shoulder, and began making himself a drink.

"That's just it. I didn't give him a chance to speak. I'm still upset about last night. I can't seem to get over the fact that he didn't want to believe me when I said Alexia was in trouble. He just brushed it aside."

"If I were you, I wouldn't let it get to you. This whole mess will blow over soon enough." James took a sip of his drink. "I think he's headed over to see Dave tonight. That should relax him a bit. Shawn's a big boy, Vy, he'll be fine."

"Drinking on the job? That's a first for you," Vy said.

"Technically, the bar is closed, so I'm not working."

"So, what happens now?" Vy asked while sipping her soda.

"I'll run the bar until Dave returns. Someone has to."

"How is Dave doing? I haven't been able to talk to him, or see him."

"He's slowly recovering. It'll be another week or so before he gets out of intensive care. My turn to ask you a question. Where's your beautiful sister?" James asked.

"She went back home this afternoon."

"Bummed out about that, huh?"

"Yes. I don't get to spend enough time with her as it is. Between my gigs every weekend, and her living an hour away, it doesn't us give enough bonding time."

"And what happened last night didn't help much either," James added.

"I definitely didn't want to spend my last night with Alexia searching for her, and finding her taped and tied up. But then again, we're not talking about that." Vy winked.

"Talking about what?" James smiled.

"Exactly. You know, I really don't know much about you. Do you have any siblings?"

"No, but I have a close friend that's like a brother to me. I'd do anything for him, just like you would for Alexia."

"It's good that you have a friend you can trust. Some people don't even have that. Cherish that person, because in the long run, that person is the one who's going to be there through thick and thin," Vy said.

"Listen, I know that you're avoiding last night's topic, but," James wholeheartedly looked at Vy, "how is Alexia doing after last night's events?"

"Surprisingly well." Vy stirred the ice cubes around with her straw. Vy had a flashback of last night. She couldn't get the image of finding Alexia tied up and gagged with a sock out of her head. Then Cassandra quickly came to her mind.

"What's going on in that head of yours?" James asked, interrupting her thoughts.

"Nothing, just irrelevant theories."

"Irrelevant to whom?" James asked.

"If I tell you my theory, you're going to think that I'm really crazy."

James smiled and simply said, "Try me," as he continued to dry off cocktail glasses.

Vy felt as if she was in one of those movies where the customer tells her whole life story to the bartender. In a way, she was relieved to share her speculations with someone other than Alexia, Houston, or Gunbar. "To make a very long theory short, I believe Alexia was kidnapped to scare me, or to send me a specific message.

"What kind of message?"

"I believe that someone is after me for some critical information. And they were trying to get it out of me."

"Someone is after you?" James said with a smirk.

"You see, I told you, you were going to think I was crazy."

"No, I don't. Continue please, from the beginning, so that I can fully comprehend."

"Okay, the night after Ricky's, well, demise, I ran into Kendra at a jazz bar. I sat with her for a few minutes. Well, it turns out that she knew how Ricky was murdered," Vy explained.

"That sounds interesting," James said after he refilled her glass.

"Thanks. I'm sorry to speak non-sense. I should get going. I have—I just have to go home soon."

"Time flies when you're having fun. But finish your theory. I'm interested in what you have to say."

Vy took a sip of her soda, not acknowledging the exchange of words they'd just had. "I can't seem to put the pieces together," Vy said mainly to herself in a low whisper.

Vy leaned forward, and rested her chin on the palm of her hand. She stared off in a stupor. The mirrors on the back wall were getting hazy to Vy's vision. "And then there's Cassandra," Vy blurted. She slightly leaned back.

"What about Cassandra?" James asked.

"She's the missing puzzle piece. But no one sees that but me." Vy dismissed her last outburst with a wave of her hand. "I really should go home."

"And Kendra?" James asked.

Vy had lost track of her story. "I'm sorry, what did you ask me?"

"Did Kendra tell you who murdered Ricky?"

Vy suddenly felt dizzy. She looked down at her glass, and pushed it aside. She was not used to drinking Coke. "James, I'm not feeling so hot. I'm going to head to the ladies' room," Vy said. She tried to stand up from the bar stool, but she quickly sat back down.

"Sorry, sweetie; restroom's out of order," James said dryly. He maliciously stared at Vy. No movement and no smile, he was somewhat statuesque.

"Why couldn't you just stay out of it?" said a female voice behind Vy. She gradually turned around to find Cassandra standing behind her. Her arms were crossed, and her body slightly slanted to the right. Cassandra's hair was in a ponytail. She had heavy bags under her eyes, and her skin was pale. She looked and smelled like she hadn't taken a shower in days. She was wearing all black. "No matter how many threats I sent your way," Cassandra continued, "you couldn't stay out of it. I thought that hiding your sister would knock some sense into you, but no, here we are."

Vy was trying to concentrate on every word she was saying. She was also trying to focus on one Cassandra as opposed to the three she was seeing. She tried to stand up again, but her body felt heavy.

Cassandra grabbed Vy's upper arm and squeezed it, "What did Kendra tell you?" Vy was too weak to yank her arm out of Cassandra's grasp. "Tell me!" Cassandra yelled.

"Enough!" James said to Cassandra. "She was going to spill it, but you got anxious and screwed it up."

Vy cupped her ears. The yelling was excruciating. Vy could barely keep her eyes open. She felt like she was experiencing the start of a migraine. But Vy had to disregard this immense discomfort, and had to start focusing on the conversation James and Cassandra were having. Vy placed her palm on her forehead, "Focus,"

Vy said under her breath. She deeply inhaled, and then turned her body to face Cassandra, "Kendra knew everything!"

Vy recalled Houston's comment about people tending to crumble under pressure. If Vy pushed Cassandra's buttons hard enough, maybe she'd give in and confess.

James slammed his hands on the varnished bar. "It doesn't matter now, does it, Cassandra? I took care of that minor problem." He quickly changed his focus to Vy, "and now I have to take care of another one, thanks to you!" James directed that last statement to Cassandra. "I specifically told you to stay away from here. But did you listen? Of course not!" Both Vy and Cassandra flinched at his tone of voice.

"But James," Cassandra started to say.

"Shut up, and let me think!" James was pacing back and forth.

Vy started to mentally absorb her surroundings. She quickly caught a glimpse of the microphone stand, which seemed miles away. She had to make her way over there somehow. One thing Vy knew how to do was handle a microphone stand.

Cassandra started to cry, "I'm sorry, James."

James stopped pacing and grabbed Vy's hand. He was cutting off her circulation. "I wasn't going to let Kendra ruin Shawn's life. And I'm definitely not going to let you ruin everything we have going for us."

"From what I was told, Shawn's life was already ruined," Vy said slowly.

"Who told you that, Kendra?" James threw his head back, let out a cynical laugh, and continued, "Well, she's not here to back you up, is she?"

Vy had to play the hand she was dealt. She took a leap of faith, "No, Margarite told Alexia and me."

"Margarite? Did Margarite also tell you that she pays Shawn five hundred dollars a week due to guilt?"

Vy pulled her hand from James's hold, but he immediately grabbed her arm and pulled her close to his face. Vy could smell the whisky he'd had earlier that night. "Listen, you don't know anything about losing someone you love. Margarite figured she could substitute Shawn's aunt's death with money. How shallow did she think Shawn was?"

"Did Margarite kill Shawn's aunt?" Vy asked.

"I'm done explaining myself to you. A nobody, a wanna be Britney Spears."

"Now you've crossed the line, buddy. I don't even like Britney Spears. Have you ever heard me sing any of her songs? I didn't think so. And, I don't lip sync," Vy said exasperated.

"You're not in any position to be sarcastic, Vy," James said scornfully.

Vy had to buy her life some time. "So, all this for Shawn?"

"I'm protecting him; I will always protect him."

"Like a brother," Vy said, more of a statement than a question. She was starting to put the pieces together.

Vy instantly heard banging on the back door of the bar. "I think he's here, James," Cassandra said.

"Well, don't let him in."

Cassandra scurried over to the door. James jumped over to the other side of the bar, and took a hold of Vy. "No, Shawn!" Cassandra yelled from a distance.

"Let her go, James. She doesn't know anything." Shawn looked at Vy sympathetically.

"After all I've done for you, you're going to defend her?"

Whatever drug James had put in her soda, began to severely affect Vy. Her weight was now shifted onto

James. He was the only thing keeping her from falling on her face.

"Don't you get it, brother? Ricky deserved it."

"Yes, he did, but she doesn't. She wasn't part of the plan," Shawn said.

"I didn't," Vy said breathing heavily.

"James, what's wrong with her?" Cassandra asked nervously.

"James, please let her go. She needs help," Shawn pleaded.

"Cassandra, watch her," James said. Cassandra quickly grabbed a hold of Vy. Vy vaguely saw James confront Shawn. They were in a yelling match, and James punched Shawn. Cassandra started sobbing, "Don't hurt him, James."

"I said, keep an eye on her. Shawn will be fine. This is temporary. He was just in the way." James threw Shawn over his shoulder, and headed to the storage room.

Cassandra moved in closer to Vy, invading her personal space. Cassandra seemed nervous and fidgety. Her eyes were irritated from crying. "You know, it wasn't supposed to turn out this way," Cassandra murmured.

This was Cassandra's moment of weakness, so Vy strung her along. "How was it suppose turn out?" Vy asked, short of breath. She wrapped her arms around her stomach and slightly leaned forward.

Cassandra said into Vy's ear, "James is right, you know, Ricky deserved to die. I mean, he did kill Shawn's aunt." Cassandra broke into a weary smile, "But Kendra—she wasn't part of the plan. She was part of my plan. I tried to stop her from eloping. I told her that I'd love her more than Ricky ever would. I would have taken care of her. But she looked at me like I was a freak."

That was the missing puzzle piece Vy had overlooked. “You loved Kendra, but, but she didn’t love you back?” This revelation surprised Vy, but she had to keep Cassandra talking. “You don’t kill someone you love,” Vy concluded.

Cassandra snapped her head back to Vy’s direction, “I didn’t kill her! James did, because of you!” Cassandra slapped Vy on the face.

“Did you really have to do that?” Vy placed her hand on her cheek. She was losing her patience and strength.

“Kendra had to go and tell you that Shawn poisoned Ricky. James had to get rid of her much to my despair.” Cassandra looked at her clenched hands, “If she would have kept her mouth shut, she’d be alive, and with me.”

Vy couldn’t control her anger much longer. “She didn’t want to be with you, Cassandra. She loved Ricky, not you. Get that into your crazy little head.”

Cassandra glared long and hard at Vy. She was preparing herself for another slap in the face. “Are you trying to manipulate me? You think that you’re so smart. Well, you’re not. I tried to warn you. But now you’re going to die,” Cassandra sang.

At this point, Vy really didn’t feel well. She started to hyperventilate. “I need a paper bag.” Vy looked at Cassandra. “Please,” she barely repeated.

“Oh great, James is going to freak out if I let something happen to you.” Cassandra angrily stepped onto a stool, and jumped to the other side of the bar to find Vy a paper bag. This was Vy’s opportunity to run. The adrenaline kicked in, and she headed to the stage area.

“Oh no, you don’t!” James said as he grabbed Vy’s hair and pulled her back. Vy fought him off for about one second, lost her balance, and fell to the ground hitting her head on the steps of the stage. She extended her arm to grab a hold of the microphone stand, but James turned her onto her back. He stood over her holding a plastic bag, "Since you're claustrophobic, what better way to die?"

"James, wait!" Vy faintly heard Cassandra yell, as she was losing consciousness. The last sound Vy heard was a gunshot.

TESTING 22

"Vy, can you hear me?" She heard that phrase three times in a row before she could respond. Vy quickly recognized the voice, and sluggishly opened her eyes. "We leave you alone for half a day and you end up banged up on the floor."

"Thanks for your sympathy, Gunbar," Vy said as she slowly sat up. There was a sense of relief and sympathy in Gunbar's smile. He was kneeling next to Vy, holding her up. "Houston's on his way."

"My head," Vy said as she rubbed her forehead.

"You hit your head pretty hard on those steps. The EMT bandaged you up. Don't worry, you don't have a concussion."

"I was drugged."

"Take it easy. We'll talk later," Gunbar whispered. He placed Vy's hair behind her ear. She was happy that Gunbar was around, which was a feeling she'd never experienced with him. Vy took his advice for once, and she didn't say anything further. She simply rested her head on his rapidly beating chest, closed her eyes, and waited for Houston's arrival.

*****

It was the following morning. Vy, Alexia, Houston, and Gunbar were eating breakfast at Ralph's Diner. "I can't believe you refused to stay in the hospital overnight," Houston sweetly said.

"It's a Cuban thing," Alexia answered for Vy. "See, our parents didn't believe in hospitals. There was no need to go to a hospital if we could recover in our own home." Vy nodded in agreement.

"Wow, you two are hardcore Cubans," Gunbar concluded.

"But, Vy, we could have brought you breakfast in bed," Alexia said.

"Right, and have four people sitting on my full-size bed, in my tiny bedroom? I don't think so." Vy smiled.

"No wonder you survived the blow to the head; you're very hard-headed," Gunbar said.

Houston moved closer to Vy. He had his hand placed on her thigh. "I'm sorry that I wasn't there for you."

"Don't be sorry." Vy caressed his cheek and gave him a peck. "You have a great partner. You said so yourself." She then looked at Gunbar, "How did you even know I was there?"

"Alexia called me saying that she hadn't heard from you in the timeframe that you'd given her. To be honest with you, I wanted to put off babysitting you, but she can be very persuasive."

"Well, I told you I had a feeling." Alexia shook her head in disapproval. "I called Houston first, but he didn't answer. So, I called Gunbar, and asked him to go check on you."

Vy became teary-eyed. Alexia motioned Houston to switch seats with her. As soon as Alexia embraced Vy, she started to cry. It wasn't the simple tears running down her face type of crying, but the sobbing, gasping for air crying. No one said a word. A few of the people at the surrounding tables were looking in Vy's direction.

"There's nothing to see. Continue eating," Houston said in his official voice. Vy couldn't help but giggle. She looked at Houston with her glassy, green eyes, "Thanks."

"You're going to be okay," Alexia said.

"I know. It just hit me now. I could have been killed."

"But you weren't," Alexia said.

"But, I could have been. Because I trust people too easily. Because I didn't keep my eyes open."

"Because you were at the wrong place at the wrong time, and because of that, you helped close this case," Houston said.

Vy reached over the table and held Houston's hand. She wiped her eyes. "Gunbar, finish telling me what happened."

"Well, luckily, James was stupid enough to leave the front entrance unlocked. I walked in on the bastard standing over you. You were completely passed out. I called out to him to get his attention. That only worked for a second. He instantly turned his focus back to you. He lifted up the microphone stand, and knowing what his intentions were, I had no other choice but to shoot him. The bullet caught him in the arm. That S.O.B. was forced to surrender."

Vy spaced out for a second; with the coffee mug in one hand and caressing Houston's hand with the other. She was gazing at a portrait of Marilyn Monroe. The actress was wearing a black negligee, sitting on a bed, leaning in towards the camera. Her smile was vibrant, but her eyes lacked happiness. "What happened to Shawn? I vaguely remember James knocking him out, and throwing him over his shoulder."

"Shawn was locked up in the supply room. You know, where you found your sister," Houston said.

"Yes. An image I wish to forget."

"We took him in for questioning as well," Gunbar added.

"You know, he did try to save me."

"I know, sweetheart, but that's not going to save him from getting what's coming to him," Houston replied.

Vy sighed, "What's his story?"

"You sure you want to hear it now?"

"I want to know what I got myself into, without knowing that I got myself into it."

Houston and Gunbar looked at each other. "What she's saying is to go ahead and tell us," Alexia said.

Vy pushed her coffee mug away from her. Houston leaned in towards Vy. "You're not going to like it."

"Just tell me."

By this time, the plates were cleared off the table. The peanut butter pie had been eaten to the last crumb, and they were on their second cups of coffee. Vy and Alexia were intensely focusing on Houston's explanation. He slicked his hair back, and proceeded, "Do you remember when I told you about Ricky's accident report?" Vy and Alexia nodded at the same time. "The unidentified woman who supposedly crashed into the tree, and died at the scene was Shawn's aunt—Dave's wife. After the crash, Ricky had placed her body on the driver's side to make it seem as if she was the one driving."

Vy placed her hand over her mouth. "But why would any human being do something like that?"

"Ricky had been drinking that night, and was heavily intoxicated. Shawn's aunt had offered to drive Ricky home, but he convinced her that he was fine to drive. But she wanted to make sure that he was going to get home safely, so she went with him. Unfortunately, they never made it to his home."

"How did he get away with it?" Vy asked bewildered.

"Let's just say that Ricky and the officer at the scene reached a mutual, financial understanding."

"He paid the officer to keep his mouth shut? That's, that's—" Vy stammered.

"Spiteful!" Alexia concluded.

"Exactly," Vy said.

"And that officer was none other than—" Houston started to say.

"Thomas Avery. No wonder he relocated," Vy said.

"Impressive. You pay attention to detail. You would be a good detective, Vy," Gunbar said.

"She would be good at anything." Alexia smiled at Vy. "The guilt that man must be living with," Alexia concluded.

"Not for very much longer. Avery will be arrested in a few hours and charged with racketeering," Houston said.

"Now you lost me." Vy was confused.

"In general terms, he's been charged with tampering with evidence and extortion, since he accepted money for it."

"Oh," Vy and Alexia said in unison.

"So, that's the reason why Margarite and Ricky got divorced. Margarite couldn't stand looking at a murderer, so to speak." Vy closed her eyes to keep herself from crying, and clasped her cold, dry hands. She deeply inhaled through her nose, and slowly released it. She opened her eyes. "I wonder why Margarite never turned Ricky in? And why pay Shawn five hundred dollars a week, and add to the turmoil?" Vy said.

"What a sick secret this family kept," added Alexia.

"That's just it. Shawn was kept from this dreadful secret until recently. The money never got to Shawn. It went straight to Ricky, but apparently Margarite didn't know that," Houston said.

"Poor Shawn," Vy said.

"Don't feel bad for him just yet, Vy. He's guilty of something," Gunbar replied.

"But for him, that 'something' had a logical, yet demented reasoning," Vy said.

"We don't back up logical, demented reasoning, Vy. We are trained to put the bad guys away no matter what their intentions are," Gunbar said.

"I know." Vy sensed that Gunbar was on the defensive, so she remained silent.

Gunbar continued, "Shawn stated that a few weeks previously, Dave called him, and told him about a job opening at the Steel Horse Bar. Shawn went to the bar and filled out the application. As he was about to turn in his application, he overheard a conversation that Ricky and Dave were having in the office. Apparently, Ricky was in one of his drunken episodes. Ricky had told Dave that the only reason he'd hire Shawn was because of Dave's wife's death. That's the very moment that Shawn found out the truth."

"What a crappy way to find out," Alexia said.

"Well, Shawn got the job. He kept his mouth shut for a few days, and then finally confronted Dave about what he'd overheard. Dave gave in, and told Shawn exactly what had happened that night."

"You mean, Dave never told Shawn that his aunt wasn't the one drinking and driving? He let Shawn think all this time that she was at fault?" Vy was distressed.

"Vy, I would protect you from any truth that might break your heart. I understand Dave's perspective." Alexia held Vy's hand.

"I understand, Lexi." Vy smiled at Alexia. "So, James didn't murder Ricky?"

"No, Shawn confessed to poisoning Ricky," Houston explained.

"But, by the way James was speaking last night, he made it seem like he murdered both Ricky and Kendra," Vy said.

"James did confess to Kendra's murder and he also confessed to helping Shawn murder Ricky."

"Goodness. Is this what you two have to experience every day on the job?" Alexia asked the two detectives. "I don't know how you do it. I would be mad at the world."

"This world is unjust, Alexia," Gunbar simply said.

"So, what happens to Shawn?" Vy asked.

"It doesn't look good for him. This was a premeditated murder. James and Shawn planned it for almost two weeks. They were just waiting for the right moment."

"Which was?"

"The moment you placed your martini down on the speaker. Evidently, Ricky decided he wanted to drink it, so he picked up your martini glass, but immediately placed it on the bar, and went to go speak to someone. That was the moment Shawn had been waiting for. He slipped the cyanide into the drink, and handed it to Ricky as he walked back to the office."

"Holy crap!" Vy exclaimed.

"So, you still think that Shawn had a demented, yet logical reasoning?" Gunbar asked.

"Now is not the time to be cynical, Gunbar," Houston said.

"Yes, sir," Gunbar said with a smile.

"He never wanted you to get involved. He really liked you, Vy," Houston said. "Shawn found out that Cassandra and James were trying to scare you off. He confronted James and told him you didn't know anything. Unfortunately, James didn't listen."

"What I don't understand is, what did Kendra have to do with Ricky's murder?"

"Kendra left Shawn a note stating that she knew the truth behind Ricky's murder. Shawn panicked, and told James he didn't know what to do. And the rest is history."

"But how did James even know that Kendra and I spoke?"

"James had followed Kendra to the jazz bar. Then he saw you two in deep conversation. He was convinced that Kendra had told you the truth about Ricky's death. He then took it upon himself to murder Kendra, and add you to the count, to protect Shawn."

"So, Kendra died because James assumed that I knew the truth?" Vy was flabbergasted. She didn't know what to think, or how to respond.

Alexia placed her hand on Vy's. "Don't go blaming yourself."

"It's just difficult to digest." Vy paused. "You know," she looked at the three of them, "Cassandra was in love with Kendra."

"We know. She shared that tidbit of information with us while she confessed to knowing who murdered Ricky and Kendra. It was a convoluted confession, but a solid one," Gunbar said.

"What happens to her?" Vy asked.

Gunbar leaned back. "Since she hindered the investigation, she will only be charged with a misdemeanor. But in my opinion, that girl needs psychological help."

"What about Shawn and James?" Vy asked.

Houston leaned forward. "Shawn and James are being charged with first degree murder."

"This might sound like an odd question, but what does first degree murder really entail?" Alexia asked.

"Have you heard of the terms first-degree, second-degree, and third-degree murder?" Gunbar asked.

"Only in movies. But I never really paid attention to the actual definition."

"Same here," Alexia said.

"Okay." Gunbar motioned with his thumb. "First-degree murder is when the murder is premeditated. You killed that person intentionally."

"Which is what Shawn and James did," Vy said sadly.

"Right. Second-degree murder," Gunbar now held up his index finger, "is when it's not premeditated. Let's say you get into a brawl with someone, you stab him, and he dies. And lastly," Gunbar's middle finger went up, "third-degree murder is when there is absolutely no prior malice or intent. It is committed when certain circumstances cause a reasonable person to become mentally or emotionally disturbed."

"So, first-degree is the worst out of the three," Vy said astounded.

"Yes, to the point that they can get the death penalty," Houston said.

Vy placed her hand over her mouth. Her skin had blotches of red. Tears streamed down her face. "Oh, my god, Dave will lose the only person he has left in this world."

"I don't want to sound like a jerk, Vy, but Shawn should have thought of that before he planned on murdering Ricky."

"You're right," Vy said as she wiped tears from her cheeks, "but you do sound like a jerk."

Gunbar continued, "As soon as James is released from the hospital, he'll be joining Shawn in jail. They will go to trial, and their fate will then be determined."

"And Dave?" Vy asked, more to herself.

Alexia gave Vy a comforting smile. "Dave will be okay."

"I'm not so sure," Vy said as she looked at Marilyn Monroe's empty eyes once again.

EPILOGUE

"So, are you having sister withdrawal yet?" Houston asked.

"It's only been a week and a half since I last saw Alexia," Vy said. "I'm fine."

Houston moved Vy's hair from her eyes. She inhaled slowly. "Okay, maybe I'm experiencing just a little withdrawal. But I'm heading to Fort Lauderdale next weekend."

Vy and Houston were nestled in Vy's full-size bed, listening to Jack Jackson. She had her leg intertwined with his, and her head was on his chest. "I'm sorry that I can't go with you. We're still finalizing all the paperwork on Ricky's case, and we haven't yet started on Kendra's file."

"I know; I understand. Now that I have more free time on the weekends, I figured getting away from Miami for a few days isn't such a bad idea. We have one more gig scheduled at the Steel Horse Bar before it completely closes. I think Dave did a smart thing by selling the place. It's time to move on, I guess."

Houston was now running his fingers up and down her back. Vy closed her eyes to soak in his touch. He said, "You know, if you think about it, we don't have much in common. You don't care for cops, I can't dance to save my life, and I don't know much about music."

Vy turned over and smiled at him. Houston was smiling, and continued caressing her back with his fingers. "You know," Vy softly said, "I'm sure I can think of creative ways to teach you about music. We can start now if you'd like."

"Shut the door, baby; don't say a word," Houston whispered.

"Did you just quote a Sugar Ray song?" Vy's lips got closer to Houston's lips.

"I have to start somewhere, right?"

THE END

ABOUT THE AUTHOR

This novel's main backdrop—the amazing city of Miami, Florida—is beloved and well-known to me. I was born and raised in Miami, and like the novel's main character, Vy, I am a singer/songwriter, as well as the lead singer to a self-proclaimed cover band. All things relating to music or literature are my passion. I keep a journal, and I am constantly writing poems, stories, and any thought that comes to mind. I have a fascination for black and white films that have elements of mystery. As I have been told by many, I have a very creative imagination.

Many years ago, I became an avid reader of cozy mysteries. The storylines were intriguing, engaging, and funny at the same time. I was so inspired by the authors that I then decided to take my musical experiences and put them on paper. I began writing this first novel in 2009. In between my full-time job, my weekend gigs, and my personal life, I finally completed the novel. The phobias, dream sequences, and the quirks of the main characters are all based on facts. I hope that I was able to bring the love I have for Miami, the Cuban culture, my family, and music to the readers of this book and to future books to come in the series.

www.ingramcontent.com/pod-product-compliance
Lightning Source LLC
Chambersburg PA
CBHW050404260626
47156CB00003B/868

* 9 7 8 1 9 4 6 0 6 3 4 8 9 *